THE

MASTER OF ST. BENEDICT'S

BY

ALAN St. AUBYN

COMPLETE

as much for them as lay in his power. He had educated the younger branches, and provided for the declining years of the elders. He had kept his two maiden sisters, one an invalid, in comfort and affluence. He had paid the mortgage off the farm and passed it over unembarrassed by debt to his elder brother. He had taken that brother's grandson and given him an education at his own University, and in due time had arranged for him to be presented with a college living. It was not a rich living: it was the only one that fell vacant when Richard Rae most wanted it, and he had accepted it gladly. He had married upon it, and brought up a family, six children, of whom one only was now living, a girl child, with whom this story has to do.

The old Master of St. Benedict's had aged perceptibly within the last few years. He was already in his second childhood. His strength had become enfeebled and his memory impaired. He could not walk down the long gallery of the lodge now or across the grass in the Fellows' garden without assistance; he could not remember the things of yesterday or of last week, but the crabbed characters of his old Semitic manuscripts were still as familiar to him as ever. He had lost a great deal since that stroke of paralysis five years ago, but he had not lost all. He remembered his old friends, and he could pore over his old books, but he was dependent upon his womankind for many things—for most things.

Mary Rae opened his letters and conducted his correspondence. She had conducted it so long that she knew more about the college than the Master. She transacted all the college business that had to be transacted in the lodge, and when any public function required the Master's presence in the Senate House Mary Rae took him up to the door on her arm and brought him back. It was also rumoured that she instructed him how to vote.

She was assisted in her responsible duties by the Senior Tutor of St. Benedict's, who would in the natural course of things succeed to the office of Master when it should fall vacant.

Mary Rae was a handsome woman well on in the thirties. She was a woman who could not help looking handsome at any age, and the few gray hairs that had put in an appearance in the smooth brown bands drawn back from her broad forehead only added a new dignity to her mature beauty. Perhaps the Senior Tutor thought that they supplied the only touch lacking to make Mary Rae a perfect and ideal mistress of a college lodge.

It was whispered in the combination room, where the old Fellows met after their Hall dinner, and discussed the affairs of the college over their walnuts and their wine, that when the Master received his last preferment she would not have to pack up her small belongings and leave the lodge.

It was one morning early in the Lent term that Mary Rae sat at breakfast in the cheerful bow-windowed room of the lodge. The Doctor's wife still presided over the breakfast table. She was younger than the Doctor, and had worn better. She was still active and cheerful—a bright, gentle, patient old soul, ever watchful and considerate for his comfort, and anticipating his every want.

While Mrs. Rae poured out the Master's tea, Mary Rae buttered the Master's toast and read his letters. There were not many letters this morning, but there was one with a black seal that lay uppermost. The writing was unfamiliar, and before opening it Mary glanced at the postmark.

'A letter from Dick, uncle,' she said across the table. She had to speak in rather a high key, as the Doctor was a little deaf, and some days he was deafer than usual.

'What does Dick say, my dear?' he said, smiling at her across the toast she had buttered for him. His voice was not very strong, but there was no North-country burr in it now—a kind, mellow old voice, courteous and gentle in tone, with a quaver in it now and then. 'I have not heard from your uncle Dick for a long time. I am very glad he has written now. I cannot remember when I last heard from him.'

'It is not from Uncle Dick,' said Mary, opening the letter; 'it is from his son—at least, his grandson—Cousin Dick, of Thorpe Regis. Don't you remember, uncle?'

'Ye—es, my dear; and what does Dick say?'

Mary read the letter in silence, and looked across the table with a shade of anxiety on her face.

'It is not Cousin Dick who writes; the letter is from his daughter; he had only one daughter—Lucy, little Lucy. You remember her, uncle?'

Mary Rae was evidently speaking to gain time, and the shade of anxiety deepened on her face as she spoke.

'Ye—es, I remember, my dear. Lucy was her mother's name; she was called after her mother. What has Lucy got to say about Dick?'

'She has not much to say, uncle; she is writing in great distress. Her father has died, almost suddenly. He was preaching a week ago, and now he is dead. The poor child is writing in great trouble.'

'Dick dead!' the old man repeated with a bewildered air, and putting down his cup with a shaking hand. 'Dick dead, did you say? He was not so many years older than I, and always hale and strong. I ought to have gone first. There were only three of us, and Dick was the eldest.'

'It isn't your brother, Anthony, that is dead; he died long ago, dear. It is his grandson, little Dick—Dickie you used to call him. You had him up here, and he took his degree, and you gave him a college living. You remember little Dickie, Anthony?'

His wife's voice recalled his wandering thoughts.

'Yes, yes, my dear; certainly, I remember little Dick very well. He took a second class; he ought to have done better. He disappointed me. I had no son of my own to come after me, and I should have liked my brother Dick's son—grandson, to be sure—to have done well. He did his best, no doubt; but he disappointed me. If he had done better, he might have got a Fellowship. So Dickie is dead, you say, my dear?'

'Yes, uncle; and he has left poor little Lucy unprovided for. She has written to ask you what she ought to do. She wants to go out as a governess—a nursery governess.'

'A nursery governess? Dick's little girl a nursery governess! No, my dear, that will never do. Tell her to come here; there's plenty of room in the lodge for Dick's little girl. Write to her at once, Mary, and tell her as soon—as soon as the funeral is over—her father's funeral—poor little girl!—to come to the lodge. What do you say, Rachel?'

'I wish we could spare Mary to go to her,' the Master's wife said, wiping her eyes. 'Someone ought to fetch her away at once, as soon—as soon as it is all over. I think Mary ought to go to her.'

The Senior Tutor met the Master's niece in the court as he was coming away from a lecture during the morning, and she told him all about the letter her uncle had received and the death of his nephew, or, rather, his grand-nephew.

'You remember my cousin Dick?' she said; 'he was my second cousin. I am a generation older than he,' and she smiled at the admission. She was not the least ashamed of her age.

The Senior Tutor smiled too; he was thinking how well she wore her years, how her age, or the signs of it, her gray hairs and the lines on her face, became her. She would grow handsomer with the years, he told himself as he stood talking to her in the spring sunshine, and her face would grow finer as time went by: it was a fine face already; it could never by any chance grow plain. He had watched a great many faces grow old in his time—old, and lined, and soured—but he had never seen any face grow finer with the years like this woman's face had grown.

'Yes,' he said, 'I remember your cousin, Richard Rae, very well; he was one of my pupils. He disappointed me, and he disappointed your uncle; he ought to have taken a first class. He went into the Church, and we gave him a college living, I remember—a very small living—and he married, I believe, directly after.'

'He married, and he had a large family and a sickly wife, and very small means. It must have been a hard struggle for him, poor Dick! He lost his wife, and his children died one after the other; there is only one left. And now he is dead, and the girl is left quite alone.'

'Oh, it is a girl,' said the Tutor in a tone of disappointment; 'if it had been a boy we could have done something with him here.'

'Yes,' said Mary, with a sigh; 'pity it's a girl; it would have been so much easier if it had been a boy. She must come here, of course; there is nowhere else for her to go.'

'What will you do with her when she comes?'

The Senior Tutor looked grave; the question had come into his head as he stood speaking to Mary, what should he do with this girl of Cousin Dick's when he occupied the Master's place? Of course Mary would stay, and Mrs. Rae—he could not separate the old woman from her niece during her few declining years; she would certainly remain an inmate of the lodge; but this girl? he could not make the college lodge an asylum for all the female members of the Rae family.

It was an idiotic question to arise; he was ashamed of it the next moment.

'I think you ought to go to Thorpe Regis,' he said, 'and be with your poor young cousin at this trying time. I will look after the Master while you are away, if that will make the going easier.'

'Ye—es,' said Mary slowly, 'it will make it easier. You really think I ought to go?'

There was a hesitation in her tone he could not but note; he put it down at once to her reluctance to leave the old Master.

'Most certainly you ought to go,' he said promptly. 'I will come over to the lodge every day. I will fill your place as far as I can. You are not afraid to leave the Master with me?'

'Oh, no, no! I am sure you will do all, more than all, that I do for him. I was not thinking about him. You are quite sure it is right to bring this girl back here? She is very young, not twenty, and—and she may be——'

'She may be attractive,' said the Senior Tutor with a laugh, 'and turn all our heads. I think, in spite of her attractions, her place is here with you and under her uncle's roof. We must protect ourselves against the wiles of this siren. We must not wear our hearts on our sleeves for Cousin Dick's little daughter to peck at.'

CHAPTER II.

DICK'S LITTLE DAUGHTER.

The Senior Tutor need have been under no apprehension for the men of St. Benedict's. They had no occasion to cover up their sleeves with their academical gowns. Cousin Dick's little daughter showed no inclination to peck at their too susceptible hearts, whether they wore them skewered on to their sleeves or out of sight in their accustomed places.

Lucy Rae was too full of her recent loss, the great sorrow that had fallen upon her and swept away all her household gods, to have a thought to spare for the undergraduates of St. Benedict's.

It had almost swept away all her moorings, too, but not quite; she still clung tenaciously to one idea—it was all she had left of the old life to cling to: she still desired to be a governess.

It was not a very ambitious idea. She wanted to be independent, and earn her own living in the only way that was open to her. She accepted the shelter of the Master's lodge thankfully, but she had no idea of settling down in the dependent position of a poor relation. When she had recovered from this shock, and the horizon cleared, she would find something to do, she told herself, and go away.

She was a soft, shy little thing to be so independent. She only looked like a girl to be kissed and petted and comforted; she didn't look at all fit to stand in the front of the battle.

She talked over her prospects—her little, humble prospects—with her cousin Mary a few days after her arrival at the lodge. Mary was sitting at the Master's writing-table in the library of the lodge—she was writing some letters on college business—and Lucy was sewing in the window.

It was a big gloomy room, and it was not at all a cheerful place for girls to sit in on a chilly spring afternoon. There was a fire burning in the old-fashioned grate behind the brass fire-guard—there were wire guards to all the fires at the lodge since that last seizure of the Master's—but it had burnt low; Mary, who was sitting near it, had been too occupied to notice it, and Lucy's mind was full of her prospects.

There had been no sound in the room for some time but the scratching of Mary's pen as it travelled over the paper, and Lucy sewed on in silence. She didn't like sewing, and she put down her work two or three times and yawned or looked out of the window. The window looked out into the Fellows' garden. The sun was shining on the lawn beneath, which was already green with the new green of the year, and the crocuses were aflame in the borders, and the primroses were in bloom.

An old Fellow was hobbling slowly and painfully round the garden—a bent, drooping figure in a particularly shabby coat and a tall silk hat of a bygone date. He was lame, Lucy remarked, and dragged one leg behind him. He had a long, lean, sallow face with deep eye-sockets, and his hair was long and gray—it didn't look as if it had been cut for years. Lucy wondered vaguely at seeing this shabby old cripple in the grounds of the lodge; if she had seen him anywhere else she would have taken him for a tramp. He had been a Senior Wrangler in his day, and had taken a double-first; perhaps he was paying the penalty.

'I am very dull company, child,' Mary said, as she blotted her last letter and pushed the writing materials aside. 'I have left you to your thoughts for a whole hour, and we have sat the fire out. What have you been thinking about, Lucy, all this time?'

'Oh, the old thing,' said Lucy, looking up from her work. 'I have been thinking what I can do.'

'Well, and what conclusion have you come to?'

''There is but one conclusion—that—that I can do nothing!'

The work dropped from the girl's fingers, and her eyes overflowed. She had wanted an excuse for weeping for the last hour, and now she had got it.

'Oh yes, you can,' Mary said cheerfully; 'the case is not quite so bad as that. You can sew, for one thing. See how nicely you are sewing that frill!'

'I hate sewing! And I shall never wear that frill when I have hemmed it! I can only do useless trumpery things!'

Lucy let the poor little bit of white frilling she had been hemming fall to the ground, and she got up and began to walk up and down the room.

Mary watched her in silence. It was not the first time her young cousin had shown impatience, but it was the first time she had shown temper—just a little bit of temper.

Mary had praised her in the wrong place: she was hurt and angry at this learned, superior cousin implying, with her misplaced praise, that she was only fit to do work—mere woman's work!

It was an unusual sound, that rapid pacing to and fro of impatient feet, in that scholarly room. The Master tottered feebly across the floor; the Master's wife moved with slow dignity; Mary walked quietly, with soft, firm footsteps that awoke no echoes. The floor creaked audibly beneath Lucy's rapid, impatient steps; the old boards that had echoed to the slow tread of scholars for so many, many years, shook and trembled—actually trembled—beneath the light impatient footsteps of Cousin Dick's little daughter.

The colour that that useless sewing had taken out of Lucy's cheek had come back, and her gray eyes were eager and shining beneath her tears.

Mary watched her pacing the room with a smile half of pity, half amused, as she sat at the Master's table. Perhaps she understood the mood. She may have been impatient herself years ago; she had nothing to be impatient for now. Everything was happening as it should do; and when a change came—well, her position would not be materially altered.

'I am sure you can do a great many useful things, dear,' she said presently, when Lucy's little bit of temper had had time to cool. 'You could not have kept your father's house so long, and done the work of the parish, without being able to do more useful things than most girls.'

'I don't mean that kind of usefulness; anyone can do housekeeping and potter about a parish. I hated parish work! I never took the least interest in it; no one could have done it worse than I did. I hated—oh, no one knows how I hated—those Bands of Hope, and Sunday-schools, and mothers' meetings, and visiting dreadful old men and women who would insist upon telling me all about their unpleasant complaints!'

Mary looked grave. She was accustomed to hear a great deal about old people's complaints, though she did not do any district visiting.

'Really,' she said gravely, 'most girls like these things! They are over now, and done with, and you will begin afresh. Tell me what you would like to do.'

'Like!' Lucy held her breath as she spoke, and her cheeks grew crimson. 'Oh, I should like to be a scholar, Cousin Mary!'

Mary looked at the girl with a kind of pity in her eyes. She had seen a good many scholars in her time, men and women; some of them were as eager once as this girl—eager and impatient with feverish haste to climb the hill of learning; they were hollow-eyed now, and narrow-chested, and their cheeks were sunken and sallow, and some limped like the old scholar in the Fellows' garden—that is, those who had lasted to the end; but some had turned back in time and regained their youth: most likely this girl would turn back.

'You would like to go to a woman's college?'

'I should love to go! I shouldn't mind whether it were Newnham or Girton, whichever uncle thought best. If I could only have three years at a woman's college, I should be provided for for life. I should want nothing further. I should be able to make my own way. Oh, Mary, do you think he will let me go?'

She was very much in earnest. She had stopped running up and down the room in that ridiculous manner. She was standing beside the table with both her hands pressed down upon it and her little lithe figure bending eagerly forward. Her eyes were shining, and her cheeks glowing, and her lips parted. She looked exactly as if she were making a speech.

The door opened as she was standing there, and the Senior Tutor came in. He shook hands with Mary, and he nodded across the table to Lucy. He thought he had interrupted a scene.

'I saw the Master as I came up,' he said, speaking to Mary; 'he had just finished his nap. He asked me to tell you that he was quite ready to take a turn in the garden, if you would put on your hat. I think you should go at once to catch the sunshine. You'll get it on the broad walk if you go now.'

Mary rose at once.

'It is lucky I have finished my work,' she said, glancing down at the little pile of letters, sealed and stamped ready for the post, that lay on the table. 'Poor little Lucy here was telling me about her plans. If you can spare time, Mr. Colville, sit down and talk them over with her, and advise her what she ought to do, while I am in the garden.'

The Senior Tutor could spare time; and after he had opened the door for Mary, he came back to the window that overlooked the garden and sat down.

He did not belong to the old school of Cambridge Dons. He belonged to that newer school that came in a quarter of a century ago with athletics. He was not lean and hollow-eyed, and wrinkled and yellow, like a musty old parchment, and he hadn't a stoop in his shoulders, and he didn't drag one of his legs behind him. He had rowed 'five' in his college boat, and his shoulders were as square now as ever. His shoulders were square, and his forehead was square, and his iron-gray hair was closely cut—it was only iron-gray still—and he had tremendous bushy eyebrows that, Lucy thought, made him look like an ogre, and that frightened the undergraduates dreadfully, and close-cut iron-gray whiskers, and a big red throat like a bull. His throat had not always been red; he had been mild-looking enough in his youth; but he was now a portly, pompous Don of middle age, with a florid countenance and fierce aspect.

'Well,' he said in his easy, patronizing way, as if he were speaking to a freshman who had just come up, 'and what do you propose to do, Miss Lucy?'

The colour went out of the girl's cheeks, and the long eyelashes drooped over her eager eyes, and her pretty little slender figure grew limp, and she didn't look the least like making a speech now.

'I am sure I don't know,' she said meekly, and she went back and sat on her old seat in the window on the opposite side to the Senior Tutor. It was a big bay-window, and there was a table between them littered with pamphlets and manuscripts in Semitic languages. The girl tossed them over as she sat there with a gesture of impatience. They were sealed books to her.

'What were you discussing with your cousin Ma—ry when I came in?'

He lingered over the name, and prolonged the last syllable. He seemed loath to let it go.

'I was telling her that I should like to go to a woman's college—to Newnham or Girton.'

'Exactly.'

The Tutor nodded his head. He was listening to the girl, but he was looking out of the window.

'No one is educated now—no woman—who does not go to Newnham, or Girton, or Oxford. No one has any chance of success in teaching who has not taken a place in a Tripos or done something in a University examination.'

The Senior Tutor was smiling, but he was only giving her half his attention.

'And what Tripos do you propose to take?' he asked in his bland, superior, lecture-room manner.

'I? Oh, I don't think I shall ever be clever enough to take a Tripos; but I might learn something—a little. I might learn enough to pass the—the—Little——'

'The Little-go?' suggested the Tutor; 'or, more properly speaking, the "Previous."'

'Yes; papa used to talk about the Little-go. He had dreadful difficulty in passing it. I should be quite satisfied if I could pass the Little-go.'

'I don't think you will find any difficulty in passing it,' he said. 'I do not remember that your father had any special difficulty; I was his tutor. He disappointed me in the Tripos. With his great gifts he ought to have done better.'

It was Lucy's turn to smile now, and to sigh.

'Poor papa!' she said; 'there was a reason for his failure. Perhaps you did not know.'

'No; I knew of no reason.'

'He had just met my mother, and—and he was in love. She got between him and his mathematics; he could think of nothing but my mother. Oh, if you had known her, you would not have wondered.'

The Senior Tutor looked across the table with a new interest in his eyes at the sweet downcast face. If her mother had been like her, he didn't wonder at poor Richard Rae getting only a second class in his Tripos.

'Are you quite sure that you will not fail from the same cause? are you sure that at the momentous time you will not do like your father—that you will not fall in love?'

'No—o,' said Lucy gravely; 'I don't think I shall fall in love. I don't think Girton girls do very often.'

'They do sometimes. They generally end by marrying their coaches.'

Lucy looked shocked.

'They can't all marry their coaches.'

'No, not all—only the weak ones. The superior minds never sink to the low level of matrimony.'

Lucy was quite sure he was laughing at her.

'I am not likely to need a coach,' she said stiffly; 'I shall never be clever enough to take a Tripos. I shall be content to pass the—the—the "Previous."'

She was going to say 'Little-go,' but she remembered he had called it the 'Previous,' and she checked herself in time.

'We shall see. You will have to begin with the "Previous" in any case. You need not take it all at once: there are three parts; you can take them at different times.'

'I should prefer to take them all at once.'

'But if you are going no farther, if you are going to stop at the "Previous," why should you be in such a hurry to get it over?'

'I don't know. It might be as well to get it over; but I have to get into Girton or Newnham first; I don't know that they will have me; and I have to get my uncle's consent.'

She hadn't fallen naturally into the custom of the lodge of calling Dr. Rae 'the Master' yet. It came easier to say 'uncle.'

'There will be an entrance examination,' the Tutor said, looking out of window and watching the Master walking in the garden below leaning on Mary's arm. 'I believe it is nearly as stiff as the "Previous" and takes in the same subjects. You will have to pass an examination before you can become a student at either college.'

'Do you know what the subjects are?' she asked eagerly; 'could you—could you get me the papers?'

He hardly heard her; his heart was out in that wet garden with Mary. How very indiscreet of the Master at his age to walk over the damp grass! He was actually sitting down on the bench under the walnut-tree. Lucy followed the direction of the Tutor's eyes, but she only saw the Master sitting in the sunshine. A tall, lean figure bent with age, with white, silvery hair falling over the velvet collar of his coat, and his rugged, worn old face turned up to the sun. The figure of the old scholar sitting on the old bench in the sunshine beneath the branches of the old, old tree, where he had sat in sunshine and in shade, oh, so many, many years, had no poetry for her. She only wondered, as she saw him sitting there, lifting his dim eyes to the sinking sun, whether he would let her go to Newnham.

The Senior Tutor didn't see any poetry in the situation, either. He was sure the old Master was catching a dreadful cold; and he was wondering whether Mary had changed her slippers.

'Could you get me a copy of the papers set at the last examination?' Lucy asked meekly.

'Yes, oh yes,' he said absently; 'I'll try to remember; but I think I must go down now and bring the Master in: I am sure he is taking cold.'

CHAPTER III.

ONLY A FRESHER.

It was rather hard work to persuade the old Master of St. Benedict's that Lucy ought to go to Newnham. He belonged to the old school—he was almost the last left of that school—that did not believe very much in women. He believed in a girl learning to sew, and to spell, and play a little air on the piano—he was very fond of 'Annie Laurie,' he could listen to it by the hour; he went so far, indeed, as the three R's in a woman's education—and he stopped there.

He had no sympathy whatever in the movement for the higher education of Women—spelt with a big W. He had voted consistently all his life against women being admitted to any of the privileges of the University, against their being allowed to take degrees; he had even voted against their being 'placed.' He regarded every concession made to the weaker sex as a step towards that dreadful time when a female Vice-Chancellor will confer degrees in the Senate House, and a lady D.D. will occupy the University pulpit.

With these views, and with his prejudices growing stronger rather than weaker with the years, it was no wonder that Mary Rae had great difficulty in reconciling the Master to the idea of Lucy becoming a student of Newnham.

He had to look at the question all round, from every point of view, and he had to talk it over a great many times. Sometimes he talked it over with himself after dinner, when he woke up from his nap, or didn't quite wake up; and sometimes he talked it over with his nieces.

'I don't think your father would approve of it, my dear,' he said one day when he was talking 'it' over with Lucy. 'He was a plain man, he hadn't the advantages of education that I had; but he had what served him just as well, he had common-sense. He knew what was wanted in a woman. A woman, he used to say, ought to be able to milk, and make butter, and bring up a family. Dick's wife could do all these, and her poultry was noted in all the country round.'

Lucy sighed. She had no ambition to make butter and bring up a family, and she had a distinct aversion to poultry. She hated cocks and hens and broods of yellow downy chickens. She remembered how they used always to be getting into the Vicarage garden and digging up her flower-seeds.

'I am afraid I couldn't get my living by making butter, uncle,' she said meekly, 'or milking cows.'

She never could remember to say 'Master,' like everybody else.

'No, my dear, no; I suppose not. Some girls have the knack of it, and some women, I've heard my mother say, may churn for hours and the butter will refuse to come. Dick's wife, your mother, my dear——'

'Great-grandmother,' murmured Lucy almost inaudibly. The Master hated to be contradicted, and he was always telling her that these far-off ancestors were her father and mother, this humble ploughman and his homely wife. There had been two generations of culture between, and Lucy had quite forgotten, until her uncle reminded her, that her great-grandmother used to carry her eggs and her butter to market. The worst of it was he used to tell everybody it was her mother.

'Yes, yes,' the Master repeated testily; 'my memory is not what it was. But it does not much matter which. She was a good woman; she did her duty here; she brought up a long family—nine children—and she has gone to her reward. She did not know a word of Greek or Latin, and she only knew enough mathematics to reckon up the price of eggs; but if she had gone to Girton or Newnham she could not have done more. She did her duty here; after all, that is the great thing, my dear. There is nothing else that will bring comfort at the last.'

It was a delightful reflection. It comforted the old scholar who had done his duty in this place for over sixty years, who had done it so well that by common consent men called him Master; but it didn't comfort Lucy at all. She was quite prepared to do her duty, only she wanted to do it in her own way.

There were other difficulties in the way of Lucy going to Newnham beside the Master's prejudices. There was a dreadful ordeal to be gone through before those sacred portals would be opened to admit her.

There was the entrance examination. The Senior Tutor was as good as his word; he brought Lucy over the very next day, not only the papers set at the last 'Previous' examination, but a copy of the last Newnham entrance papers. The next examination was to take place in March, and it was now the middle of February, and there were only a few weeks to prepare for it.

Lucy looked hurriedly through the papers while the Tutor stood by, and he saw her face fall and the pretty April colour, which was Lucy's especial charm, go out of her cheeks.

'They are stiffer than you thought,' he said.

He couldn't help putting a little feeling into his voice; he couldn't help being sorry for the girl. He could see she was dreadfully disappointed.

'I did not think they would be so hard,' she said, with something like a sob, and striving to keep back the tears; 'I had no idea that so much was required.'

Her voice was scarcely steady, and she finished up with a little wail—she couldn't keep it out of her voice—and she laid the papers down.

'You don't think you can do them?'

'No, I am sure I can't.'

'Not if you work hard—very hard?—you have three weeks before you—not if I help you?'

'You! Oh, Mr. Colville!'

The colour leaped back into her face, and her eyes brightened. She was quite trembling with eagerness.

'If you think with three weeks' hard work you can get through, I will help you,' he said.

It was something new to the Senior Tutor to have a pupil so eager and willing. The eyes of the undergraduates of St. Benedict's were not accustomed to brighten or their cheeks to flush when he proposed to give them a few hours' extra coaching.

'I am sure I can!' she said eagerly; 'and—and you are sure, Mr. Colville, you will not mind the trouble? I am a very slow learner, but I will do my best, my very best.'

'I am sure you will,' he said; and then he noticed that little helpless quivering about her lips that touched him with quite a new sensation. He had never seen Mary's lips quiver. 'It will be no trouble,' the Tutor said softly in quite a different voice; he even noticed the difference himself, with a strange sense of wonder. 'I shall be very glad to be of use to you.'

He had often been of use to Mary. She always consulted him about the college business; she made use of him every day; but his voice had never faltered nor his cheek grown warm when he had offered to help her with the Master's correspondence.

Lucy began her work the next day. She turned out from the little shabby box she had brought with her to the lodge some well-thumbed old school-books. Small as the box was, it contained all her personal belongings, and the books were at the bottom of the box.

Like Jacob, she had come into a strange land with very little personal impedimenta. It could all, everything, be stuffed into one small box, and the books were at the bottom. The books were shabby, like the box. They had belonged to her father, and she had read them with him.

There were his old Virgil and Xenophon, and a dilapidated Euclid with all the riders missing, and an old-fashioned Algebra. There had been newer editions since Richard Rae had used these in his college days more than twenty years ago. There had been delightful editions full of notes, and directing-posts along the royal road to a classical education; but Lucy had been plodding along the old, rough, dusty way.

The Senior Tutor smiled as he turned over these old books. They brought back to him the old days twenty years ago, the hopes and dreams of those early days, and the familiar faces. The dreams had been realized—at least, some of them—but the familiar faces had faded with the years, and the hopes—what could a man hope for beyond being Master of his college? Nevertheless, the Senior Tutor sighed. The sight of these old books had carried him a long way back.

'I think we can find some newer editions than these,' he said, smiling.

He not only found some newer, but he found the very newest. He found delightful books that smoothed away all the difficulties and made stony places plain. There will be a royal road to learning by-and-by. The road is getting smoother every day, and the way is getting shorter—a short, straight, macadamized road that one can travel over without any jolting or sudden pulls-up.

Old scholars who remember the dear old rough road, and the stony ways, and the hills of difficulty they had to climb, sigh when they look back. There is no time now, in these hurrying days, to toil over stones and climb unnecessary heights. The new ways are so much better than the old; but the old men, if they were to begin again, would go the old way, the dear old way, with all its difficulties. They will still tell you the old ways are best.

Lucy Rae was not a scholar yet, though the desire of her heart was to be one—a perfect Hypatia—and the new royal road was exactly what she wanted.

She made such rapid progress by means of these short-cuts and easy paths the Senior Tutor led her through that she was quite ready for that dreaded entrance examination when it came. She did as well in it as the girls who had been working for it for years.

There was nothing now to prevent her becoming a student of Newnham. Cousin Mary had talked the old Master over and smoothed away all the difficulties. She had wrung from him an unwilling consent. The Senior Tutor had done his part, too, in overcoming the Master's prejudices. He had backed Mary up in the most loyal manner; no girl could have had better advocates. When the Doctor had urged that there had been no precedent in his family of girls construing Latin and Greek when they ought to be making butter and carrying their eggs to market, the Tutor had reminded him that neither had there been a precedent in all the generations of the Raes of one of their number being the Master of a college.

He, on his part, had set up a precedent, and Dick's little daughter was going to set up another—perhaps a more astonishing precedent.

Lucy Rae went up to Newnham the next term. She ought to have waited until October, when the academical year commences, but she was much too anxious to begin at once. She couldn't wait till October.

She had taken a little draught of the divine nectar, and she was thirsting to drink deeply, ever so deeply—deeper than any woman had ever drunk yet. She was going to do very big things, and she couldn't afford to lose a minute. She would gain a whole term's work if she went up now, she would get in ten terms' work instead of nine, like the men, for her Tripos. She would get a whole term's start of them.

With this thirst upon her, and this emulation stirring in her heart, Lucy packed her little box and carried it up to Newnham. She did not exactly carry it in her arms like a housemaid going to a new place. It was not far to carry it, and for the weight of it she might have carried it easily, but girls do not generally go to Newnham carrying a bandbox, or a bundle tied up in a coloured pocket-handkerchief, and with two out-at-elbow little brothers lagging behind carrying a shabby box between them. Lucy, alas! had not two out-at-elbow little brothers, and she had respect for the feelings of Newnham, so she drove up to the door of Newe Hall in a hansom, with her modest little box on the roof.

She thought it was the happiest, the proudest day of her life, this first day at Newnham. She had been looking forward to it for weeks. She had lain awake all the night before picturing what it would be like, and it was not the least like anything she had pictured.

She had pictured sunshine and a blue sky, and the lilacs in the hedge budding, and the daffodils blowing beneath the windows. It was the middle of April, and she had a right to expect these things; it was very little to expect.

It had been raining cheerfully all the morning, and it was raining still when the hansom drew up at the gate of St. Benedict's; it couldn't draw up at the door of the lodge, because college lodges are cut off from the outside world by cloistered courts, and even royalty, when it visits the master of a college, has to leave its carriage at the gate and perform the rest of the journey on foot.

Lucy met Mr. Colville in the cloisters as she was hurrying through, and he put her into the hansom, and he told the man where to drive, and quite a crowd of undergraduates, who had come up early in the term, stood round the gate watching her drive away.

It was quite a new thing, a girl going from St. Benedict's to Newnham. It was the newest thing under the sun. No daughter, niece or granddaughter of any Master of St. Benedict's had ever driven from those gates before to Newnham.

Perhaps when there is a mixed University, and a female president at the lodge, they will not have to go so far; they may find rooms beneath the same roof.

Who shall say?

Lucy couldn't have driven away with more depressing surroundings. The sky couldn't have been grayer, and the trees were shivering overhead, and the hedges were dripping, and there was a nasty mist settling down over everything. She forgot all about the lilacs and the daffodils she had been picturing as she stood, a forlorn little black figure, in the big, cheerless vestibule of Newe Hall, paying the driver of the hansom. There was no one at Newnham to receive her, no one to show her to her room, only a housemaid, who went away directly she reached the door. She didn't even open the door of the room; she only pointed to it and went away in another direction.

It was a little bare room, it couldn't have been barer. There was a couch that served for a bed, a bureau with some drawers beneath, a table, a couple of chairs, and a thinly disguised washstand with imperfect crockery; and that was all. Unless, indeed, a chintz curtain drawn across a corner of the room for hanging gowns behind could be called a wardrobe.

There was no fire, and the barred windows were steaming and blurred with the mist outside, and the raw spring afternoon was closing in.

Lucy shivered and looked round the desolate room. She didn't know what she was expected to do next, or how she was to begin this new life. She was a member of the University now, she told herself with bated breath; she was really a female undergraduate, and she had got to begin as undergraduates began.

Should she begin with lighting the fire? While she was debating this point, and drawing off her gloves, a girl came in. She had left the door open so that anyone passing could look in and see her standing there, and the girl passing by looked in and saw her, and something in her attitude touched her, and she came in. Perhaps it was her black frock and her white face.

'Can I do anything for you?' she said. She didn't throw any sympathy into her voice; they never do at Newnham. 'I've got a kettle boiling if you'd like some water, or'—looking round the bare room and seeing that Lucy's things were not unpacked—'perhaps you'd rather have some tea.'

'Ye—es,' Lucy said quite thankfully; 'I would rather have some tea, please.'

'Then come into my room.'

Lucy followed the girl, a solid-looking girl with no profile to speak of, and a turned-up nose and violent red hair. She had not to follow her far, only across the passage.

There was a card slipped into a frame in the door of the room, and the name of the occupant was written on it—'Stubbs.'

'That's my name,' said the girl, pointing to it; 'Maria Stubbs—Capability Stubbs they call me. I suppose you are a fresher?'

'Yes,' said Lucy, 'I'm a fresher; I've only just come up. My name is Rae—Lucy Rae.'

'Not a bad name; but you won't have any use for it here. They'll call you Lucifer most likely; they don't call anybody by their right name here.'

Maria Stubbs' room was unlike most Newnham rooms. It was distinctly utilitarian. There was nothing æsthetic about it. The most prominent thing in it was a bookshelf full of books, and there was a cabinet in one corner with a lot of narrow drawers, which Lucy found out after were crammed with specimens. A bright fire was burning in the little tiled grate, and a cloth was spread, and some tea-things were laid on the flap of the bureau, which was let down for the purpose, and there were some cakes in one of the pigeon-holes.

'Take off your hat and sit down,' said Maria, drawing a low chair to the fire; 'there's nothing to hurry for, they won't bring in your things for a long time; they never hurry themselves at Newnham.'

'I don't think I ought to take off my things until I've seen someone,' said Lucy. 'There's Miss Wrayburne I certainly ought to see. Perhaps she doesn't know I'm here.'

The girl laughed—or cackled, rather; there wasn't the least fun in her laugh.

'Perhaps not,' she said, as she busied herself about making the tea; 'and I don't think it would make any difference if she did. You don't think the Dons are running about the college all day long shaking hands with the girls? You'll see Miss Wrayburne at the "High" at dinner, and she'll say "How d'ye do?" and smile—she always smiles—and that's all.'

'I didn't know,' Lucy said humbly. 'I'm only a fresher, you see; I shall know better soon. But it struck me as a very chilling reception.'

Miss Stubbs cackled in her unfeeling way.

'Chilling! that's lovely! You've come to the wrong place if you expect any warmth at Newnham, or sympathy either. It would be nothing better than a big girls' school if we were always "How-d'ye-doing" and shaking hands with each other—we should get to kissing soon! Thank goodness there is no spooning here! We are barely civil to each other; and we make a point of ignoring everybody if we meet 'em out-of-doors. I hope you won't, on the strength of this tea, nod to me if you happen to run against me in the street, because I shan't notice you.'

'No,' said Lucy, 'I certainly won't nod to you.' She didn't say it at all humbly, but she drank Miss Stubbs' tea. It was very good tea for Newnham.

CHAPTER IV.

PAMELA GWATKIN.

Lucy saw the Principal, as Miss Stubbs had said, at dinner. She came into the hall rather late, and took her seat at the High table.

It is necessary to spell it with a capital H, as it is distinctly a proper noun, and in Newnham parlance, like the tables in men's colleges where the Dons eat their dinners, it is known as the 'High.'

Miss Wrayburne came in rather late, after the rest were seated, and took her place at the head of the 'High,' and then followed a moment's interval for grace, and then the murmur of tongues began—a low, distinctly female murmur, and occasionally a laugh—a little low laugh. There was a good deal of talk to-day, as everybody had come up fresh, and the atmosphere of the vacation was still about them, and nobody had begun work yet. They would unpack their books by-and-by, and then everything would be changed.

Lucy did not know a soul in the place, except Maria Stubbs, and she sat at another table. She sat quite at the other end of the room, and never once looked Lucy's way, and brushed by her in the corridor as if she had never seen her before.

'She needn't be afraid I shall notice her, the horrid red-haired thing!' Lucy said to herself with quite unnecessary warmth, when Maria looked the other way. 'I wouldn't notice her for the world!'

There were quite half a dozen tables between her and Maria, long narrow tables, with some half-dozen girls at each—girls who ignored everybody else except their own set, and talked across a stranger as if she were a dummy.

They talked across Lucy, and she listened to their talk with a red spot burning on her cheeks and her heart beating. She had not much appetite for the dinner, and she got up from the table with a strange choking sensation that brought the tears smarting to her eyes. She took some comfort in the thought that some day she would talk across a fresher. Her turn would come some day; and while her mind was occupied with this agreeable reflection Miss Wrayburne smiled at her, and said:

'How do you do?'

'How do you do?' may mean a great deal, or it may mean nothing. It didn't mean very much from Miss Wrayburne's lips, and the smile that accompanied it meant less. If it had been a whole smile, or a smile meant entirely for Lucy, there might have been something in it; but it was only the fag-end of a smile that had already been distributed over half a dozen girls.

Lucy accepted it meekly; and with those red spots burning on her cheeks and a choky feeling in her throat she went back to her room—her little desolate, bare room. She felt so utterly miserable and lonely on this wretched first night that she sat down on the side of her bed and had a little weep. Everything was so different to what she had expected; all her castles had been so rudely thrown down.

And then, while she was weeping these foolish tears, she remembered a little curate—a weak-minded young man with red hair; perhaps Miss Stubbs had recalled him—who had once asked her to be his wife. She had refused him indignantly. What girl in her senses would accept a curate with red hair and one hundred and fifty pounds a year? She was not sure, if he had come to her now as she sat in that dismal room, feeling so utterly lonely and miserable, that she would have given him the same answer. She wanted a little love so much; and he loved her in spite of his red hair. She was not so certain, after all, that the higher education of women is quite the best thing—the thing most to be desired in the world. There are other things—she had not thought of them till now, as she sat weeping at the edge of the bed—that make up a woman's life: love, religion, duty, ministering to the wants of others; but love chiefly. She was not sure, after all, if this was not the summum bonum of a woman's life.

Lucy was so utterly miserable as she sat there weeping that, if the red-haired curate had come to her at that weak moment, she would have thrown over all her ambitions, she would have given up the higher education altogether, and she would have gone away with him to that poor little moorland cottage, and pinched, and pared, and slaved for him, as dear women before her have pinched and slaved for those they love ever since the world began.

While she was still thinking of the curate, and the tears were dropping into her lap, there was a knock at the door, and someone came in. Lucy started guiltily, and hurriedly wiped her eyes. It was not the red-headed curate. It was a girl—to be more correct, a woman. Everybody is a woman at Newnham. A second-year girl, who had called to see if she could help her to unpack her things and get her room in order.

It wasn't a formal 'call.' Calls at Newnham are usually made after ten p.m., when work is supposed to be over and one is yearning for bed. The second-year girl was a little bit of a thing—smaller than Lucy. A girl who looked as if she had shrunk—as if she had once been round, and plump, and bright-eyed, and soft-cheeked, and red-lipped as a girl ought to be at twenty. She was none of these things now. She was lean and angular; her eyes were dull, her lips were pale, and her cheeks had lost all their youthful roundness and rosiness, if they had ever had any. The roundness had gone into her figure, her back was quite round, her shoulders were bent and stooping, and her chest was narrow and flat like a board.

She had been at Newnham two years, and she was twenty now, and wore glasses, but, alas! not 'sweet and twenty.' She looked exactly like a girl who had used up all her brains.

'I think you have made a mistake,' she said, as she knelt upon the ground unpacking Lucy's books, 'in taking Classics. You should take the Natural Science Tripos. Classics are a thing of the past. They are quite worn out. They will be superseded altogether shortly. Soon—very soon—Latin and Greek will not be compulsory in the examinations; we shall have more useful subjects. Life is so short—so very short' (she was just twenty)—'that we have no time for learning things that will not help us in the rush. Life is getting more of a rush every day, and Science is the only thing that can help us forward. There is no knowing where Science will lead us!'

She clasped her hands, and gasped at the bare thought of it.

'No,' said Lucy, in a low-spirited way.

She hadn't the least interest where Science was going to lead the girl on the floor—it wasn't likely to lead her very far—but she did object to see her pet Classics turned out of the box in that scornful way.

'You will learn all this trash,' the girl continued, opening the pages of Lucy's Euripides and letting the leaves drop through her fingers as if they were not of very much account, 'and you will pore over these rubbishy stories of a quite barbarous age—stories and fables and metamorphoses that, if they were written at the present time, would lay the writer open to a prosecution for perverting the public morals. You will soak your mind with all this nonsense and impurity, and you will think that you have attained culture. Oh, to think how girls waste their lives!'

'I'm sure Classics are ever so much nicer than Natural Science,' Lucy said with some spirit. 'Look at the dreadful subjects you have to study! and to sit side by side with men in lecture-rooms, and listen to lectures on things most women would blush to speak of! Oh, I wouldn't be a Natural Science student for the world!'

The atmosphere of Newnham was beginning to tell. A few hours ago Lucy was as meek as a mouse, and if anyone had slapped her on one cheek she would have been quite ready to offer the other. Now she had plucked up sufficient spirit to defend her choice of a Tripos.

If Newnham doesn't do anything else for a girl, it teaches her to take her own part.

Lucy didn't learn the lesson all at once. It takes a long time to learn, when one has been brought up in the old-fashioned way, to consider other people first and to think of self last. It would never do to practise such a foolish doctrine at a college for women. There is only one person to consider—self, self, self!

Lucy had a great deal to unlearn when she came to Newnham, and a great deal to learn; and she did not learn it all at once. She had always had somebody else to consider first, and now it was ever Number One. Oh, that horrid Number One!

Everybody called upon her in Newe Hall the first week, and some of the girls from the other Halls called later on. The girls at Newe called generally after ten o'clock at night, when she was too sleepy to talk to them, and they went away and voted her 'stupid,' and took no further trouble about her.

Among the girls who called upon Lucy when she was nearly asleep, and went away and voted her stupid, was Pamela Gwatkin, a girl who was much looked up to and worshipped at Newnham. It was no wonder Pamela thought her stupid. She was the leader of the most advanced set in the college, and held opinions that would make one's hair stand on end.

There will be a good many Pamela Gwatkins by-and-by, when there are more Newnhams and the world is ripe for them. They will quite revolutionize society.

They will not be misunderstood like the Greek women of old. Nobody will question their morals because they seek to lead and teach men. Men will be quite willing to be taught by them. It will no longer be a shame for a woman to speak or preach in public. There will be nothing to debar them from taking orders.

Women have proved long ago that they can reach beyond such heights of scholarship as are demanded from a candidate for ordination. But women of Pamela Gwatkin's order will not go into the pulpit—their demands will be even more audacious.

Lucy hadn't any opinions in particular, she was only a fresher; but she was such a poor-spirited creature that she went with the herd and worshipped the very ground that Pamela Gwatkin walked upon.

She hadn't even the excuse of a nodding acquaintance with her after that unlucky call—she only caught glimpses of her at a distant table at Hall, or met her by chance in the library, or ran against her in the streets, coming and going from lectures, when Pamela looked over her head in her superior way and ignored her completely.

She could very well look over Lucy's head, for she stood six feet in her shoes—they had rather high heels. A tall, fair girl, not plump or round by any means, nor rosy-cheeked—she was not a milkmaid; she was an advanced thinker—but lithe, and elastic, and dignified—very dignified.

Lucy thought she had never seen anyone so dignified in her life as Pamela on the night of the first debate of the term at Newnham.

She opened the debate on this particular evening—it happened to be some question of woman's rights which she was always advocating—and she spoke for half an hour without a single pause or hitch.

Some people confess that they cannot bear to hear a woman speak; that when a woman stands up to speak in public it always gives them the sensation of cold water running down their backs. No one who listened to Pamela Gwatkin would have this uncomfortable sensation for a moment. It seemed as if she had been made to stand up in public; as if Nature had intended her for a female orator, and had given her the voice—the clear, penetrating, resonant voice—the quiet, assured manner, the full, free flow of words, without which no woman may attempt to stand on a public platform.

Pamela Gwatkin had all these rare gifts, and she had opinions—very advanced opinions—on every subject under the sun—religion, morals, science, philosophy—nothing came amiss to her. When women are admitted into Parliament she will probably represent an important constituency, perhaps the University.

Lucy, looking down from the gallery above, listened breathlessly, and when the debate was over watched her sailing down the hall in her pale violet gown, with the soft folds of her train gliding noiselessly after her. They didn't rustle and sweep like the frills and furbelows of the other girl, who came frou-frouing down the room, pencil in hand, counting the votes. She might have spared her pains; of course, every girl in her senses voted with Pamela.

There was a dance as usual after the debate, and the unique spectacle of fifty female couples spinning round untainted by the arm of man. Pamela Gwatkin danced as well as she spoke, but she didn't put any enthusiasm into it. She took it as the least troublesome way of taking exercise, but she didn't put any spirit into it. She didn't smile once all the evening, except in a weary, disdainful way when her partner broke down or fell out of the ring. She never broke down or fell out herself, and when she had tired out one girl she took up another. Lucy remarked that she always chose small girls—the smallest girls she could find—and that they were invariably 'gentlemen.' Lucy was wondering how ever they could drag her round, when, to her consternation, Pamela stopped in front of her.

She had worn out all the other small girls in the room, and she had to fall back upon Lucy. The silly little thing stood up in quite a flutter. If a Royal Highness had asked her to dance she could not have been more flattered. Of course, she would take 'gentleman'! She told the most outrageous fibs, and said she preferred being 'gentleman;' she always chose it when she had the chance.

After she had dragged Pamela round until she was fit to faint, and had ascertained how hard her whalebones were, and how regular her breathing, and that her favourite perfume was heliotrope, and that dancing with a goddess whose chin was on a level with the top of her head was not all pure bliss, she had her reward.

Annabel Crewe, the Natural Science girl, asked her to 'cocoa' after the dancing was over, and here she met Pamela. It was Lucy's first experience of a Newnham 'cocoa.' There was quite a spread on Annabel Crewe's little writing-table—sweets and cakes and fruit, and cups brimming over with the nectar of Newnham.

Pamela Gwatkin came in last; there was a crowd of girls in the room when she came in, filling it quite up, and occupying all the chairs and the ottoman and both sides of the bed. There was an art covering thrown over the bed embroidered with dragons, and a cushion with an impossible monster with a flaming tail; nobody but a Newnham girl would have dreamed it was a bed.

Lucy was occupying a low cushiony-chair—the nicest chair in the room—and she got up directly Pamela came in and gave it up to her. She accepted it in her superior way, and flopped down into it as if it were in the order of things for everyone to make place for her. Then that wretched little sycophant, Lucy, waited upon her in her servile way, as if she were nothing short of a Royal Princess. She brought her her cocoa, and sweets, and cakes, and fruit. She positively snatched them from the other girls to offer them to Pamela, and be snubbed for her pains. She hadn't the spirit of a mouse.

Everybody was talking at once, and there was such a clatter of tongues that Lucy couldn't have heard the goddess speak if she had deigned to speak to her. She did deign just before the party broke up.

Lucy hadn't anywhere to sit, and she was tired out with dragging Pamela round, and she had found an idiotic three-legged milking-stool, and she was trying to sit upon it. It was an objectionable stool; in the first place, it had been painted with yellow buttercups, and varnished before the paint was dry. It was not dry yet, and it stuck to Lucy's black gown and left a proof impression of the buttercups on the back. In the second place, the legs hadn't been stuck in firmly, and it wobbled under her weight and threatened to collapse every moment. Lucy sat in fear and trembling, trying to look as if she were quite comfortable and used to wobbling, and while she sat the goddess spoke:

'I have a brother at St. Benedict's,' she said; 'I dare say you know him; he is in his third year.'

Lucy murmured that she hadn't that pleasure; she didn't know any undergraduates.

'No, I suppose not,' Pamela said wearily—she generally spoke wearily, as if commonplace subjects were beneath her. "They are an uninteresting class; only Eric is so quixotic; he does such absurd things that I should not have thought he could have been anywhere long without being known and laughed at.'

'Really!' said Lucy, in rather a shocked voice; she didn't know what else to say.

'It was one of his absurdities to come up here as an undergraduate. He had qualified—fully qualified—for another profession. He was a doctor, and when he had passed all his examinations, after seven years' work, he threw it all up. He found out that he had missed his right vocation. He had some absurd notion that he was specially called for the Church—that the Church couldn't do without him—and so he has come up here.'

Pamela spoke scornfully, with her thin upper lip curling, and just a suspicion of pink in her face—her beautiful worn, weary face.

'Perhaps he has done right,' said Lucy. 'A man ought never to go into the Church unless he feels that he is called. Papa might have been Senior Wrangler, but he felt his vocation was the Church. He gave up everything for it, and——' 'And mamma' she was going to say, but she looked at Pamela and stopped short.

'It would be all very well if the Church were going to last,' she said wearily; 'but it isn't. Everybody knows that it isn't. Nobody but women and children believe in it now. Its methods are all exploded; its teaching is preposterous; it has had its day, like other beliefs, and now a new day is dawning. Oh, it was ridiculous of Eric to go into the Church just as it was falling to pieces!'

Lucy was past expressing an opinion. The milking-stool had collapsed. The three idiotic legs had all gone different ways; it had fallen quite to pieces, like the Church was going to, and Lucy was seated on the floor.

CHAPTER V.

AFTER CHAPEL.

The day succeeding the debate was Sunday, and Lucy went over to St. Benedict's to morning chapel.

She was so glad to go. It was quite a relief to get outside Newnham and shake from her skirts the atmosphere of so much learning. It was a distinct relief to take her place in the stalls of St. Benedict's and look down upon the men who took life so much more easily.

She was only just in time for the college chapel. The bell was going as she crossed the court, and the men were hurrying in in their white surplices. They were all smiling and debonair. There wasn't a single cloud on the brow of one of them, except the cloud of last night's tobacco. They were lusty and strong and fresh-coloured, and some of them had frames like giants; and they came across the court with a swinging stride, and health and life and vigour in every movement. Men take things so much more easily than women.

The choir and the Master came in directly after Lucy had taken her seat. The Master looked across his wife and Mary, who sat between them, and nodded to Lucy.

'Very glad to see you, my dear,' he said in quite an audible voice.

It was a longer service than usual at St. Benedict's on Sunday mornings. The Master read the Litany, and he took a long time in reading it, and Lucy had plenty of opportunity of looking among the men for Pamela Gwatkin's brother.

He was a twin brother, she had learned from Annabel Crewe, who knew all about Pamela, and therefore he ought to be exactly like her. Tall and fair and thin-lipped, with clear, steady eyes—blue ought to be the colour, or gray, she was not sure which; but she could not mistake the profile. There could be no doubt about that clear-cut face, without an ounce of superfluous flesh upon it.

Lucy looked at the men eagerly one after the other; she looked at every man in the chapel. The Senior Tutor from his stall on the other side saw her looking down at the men. She didn't look at him, and he wondered at the change in her. Her eyes were not wont to rove over the faces of the men sitting below in that eager way; they might have all been sticks and stones for the notice Lucy had hitherto vouchsafed them.

Was this the outcome of a week at Newnham? Had she seen so much—so very, very much—of women in her new developments that she was thirsting for the sight of man?

Cousin Mary saw her looking down at the undergraduates in the seat below, too, and sighed. She remembered the time when she used to look across the benches. She had seen so many generations of undergraduates come and go in fifteen years. She may have looked more than once in all that time to see if among them there was that one face that was to be her beacon through life; she had ceased to look for it now.

Lucy had decided before she left the chapel that the man in the third row near the top was Pamela's brother. A tall man with a thin, fair, fresh-coloured face and firm lips—a capable face, a face quite worthy of the brother of Pamela Gwatkin.

Lucy watched the men file out of chapel, and the man in the last seat of the last row naturally came out last. She refused to go into the lodge with Mary. She let the old Master and his wife toddle off down the cloisters together, and she stood holding Mary back and begging her to wait 'just a minute.'

The man in the back seat came out at last and took off his cap to the Master's nieces as he passed.

'There!' said Lucy breathlessly, 'this is the man I waited for. Is he Eric Gwatkin?'

'Eric Gwatkin!' Mary repeated impatiently; she objected to being kept standing in the court watching the men come out of chapel; she could see them every day—twice a day if she liked—and she had seen them for fifteen years. 'Eric Gwatkin?' she repeated. 'The man who has just come out is Wyatt Edgell, the best man of the year. He will take a very high place in the Tripos—perhaps the highest—and Eric Gwatkin is only a Poll man. He is taking the theological Special, I believe, and I dare say he will be plucked.'

'Oh, I am sure there is some mistake!' Lucy said hotly; 'Pamela's brother never could be plucked. She is awfully clever, and—and he is a twin.'

Cousin Mary didn't take the least interest in Pamela's brother; even the fact of his being a twin didn't move her. She went into the lodge and looked after the table that was spread for lunch. She altered the arrangement of the flowers, and put some finishing touches to it, and Lucy stood beside the window that overlooked the court watching her.

She couldn't help pitying Mary for being interested in such small things, for being taken up with such petty cares. She had lived in the midst of culture for fifteen years, and yet she could potter about that dinner-table and be absorbed in the arrangement of the flowers.

'I am very glad to see you, my dear,' the old Master said to Lucy when she had dutifully kissed him and whispered to her aunt how well he was looking—the sure key to that dear, kind, simple heart was to tell her how well the Master was looking. It would be a sad day when those welcome words could no longer be said.

'And how is the Greek getting on, my dear? Who would have thought of my brother Dick's daughter learning Greek? She didn't get the taste for it from her father, for he was no scholar. He was good only for his own work, none better. There was not a man in the parish who could drive a straighter furrow than my brother Dick, and his wife was famous for her poultry. I remember her carrying her butter and eggs to market. She had the corner stall in the old butter market, my dear. I mind the very spot.'

'It was my grandmother, or great-grandmother, rather,' said Lucy, feebly trying to set him right. 'Mamma never kept a stall in the butter market.'

'Never mind which it was,' said the Senior Tutor, who had just come in, and was shaking hands with Lucy; 'a generation or two doesn't matter.'

It didn't matter to him, who knew all the homely details of the Master's humble history; but suppose he were to go maundering about that stall in the butter market to Pamela Gwatkin, it would be all over Newnham that it was Lucy's mother, and that Lucy herself used to milk the cows. With such a pedigree there was no excuse for her tumbling off a milking-stool.

If Lucy hadn't been so full of her own concerns that she had no eyes for others, she would have seen the reason for Cousin Mary's anxiety about the dinner-table. The Senior Tutor was coming to dinner.

The lunch, or rather the dinner—for it was a real dinner; except on state occasions, the old Master dined in the middle of the day—was spread in the dining-room of the lodge—an old, old room panelled up to the ceiling with dark oak, with a delightful carved frieze running round the top, and a big oriel window with diamond panes and stained glass coats-of-arms of the old Masters who had occupied the lodge since it was first built, centuries ago.

There were portraits of some of them in their scarlet gowns on the walls, looking down upon them as they sat at meat. It was a ghostly company, so many old Masters, and soon there would be another to hang among them. He was painted already, and hanging in the gallery outside; he would come in here soon, and take his place, not at the table, but on the walls with the rest.

Perhaps the Senior Tutor was thinking of that not far-off time as he lay back in his chair glancing up at the dingy old walls that wanted beeswaxing dreadfully. There would be plenty for him to do when his time came. There had been nothing done here for years. He would have to go right through the house; he hardly knew where he should begin.

And then Lucy broke in upon his pleasant reverie, and asked him about Eric Gwatkin.

'Gwatkin?' said the Tutor absently. He was just considering whether he should have the oak varnished or beeswaxed. 'Ye—e—s; he's going in for his Special, but I don't think he'll get through.'

'Only his Special!' Lucy hadn't got through her Little-go yet, but she regarded the Special from the Newnham standpoint. No woman has ever yet descended so low as a Special. 'His sister is one of the cleverest girls at Newnham. She has already taken a first in one Tripos, and now she is working for another. She is sure to take a double-first. He is her twin brother, and I'm sure she expects great things of him.'

'Then I'm very sorry for Miss Gwatkin,' the Tutor said with a laugh. 'If he gets through it's as much as he will do.'

He declined to have anything more to say about Pamela's unpromising brother; and he talked to Lucy until the ladies left the table about her life at Newnham, and the progress she was making with her work.

The old Master did not sit long over his wine; it had come to one glass now after dinner—one glass of that old, old wine that had already lain a dozen years in the darkness of the college cellar when he had come up a raw scholar to St. Benedict's. It did him quite as much good as a dozen glasses of a less generous vintage. It brought a warm flush into his wrinkled cheeks, and a light into his dim eyes, and stirred the slow blood circling round his heart, and it sent him to sleep to dream again of the old time, and to win afresh the laurels of his youth. While the Master sat nodding in his big chair on one side of the wide fireplace, where a fire was still burning, and his faithful partner sat nodding on the other side, Lucy slipped out of the room.

She was only going to the old study to find some books, but she had to pass through the picture-gallery to reach it. The gallery of the lodge of St. Benedict's was very much like the galleries of most college lodges, only it was narrower—a long, low, narrow old room extending the length of one side of the cloistered court. It had been built when the cloisters beneath had been built, and it had suffered few changes since. The walls were panelled to the ceiling with oak, and it was lighted with deep, old-fashioned bay-windows; not particularly well lighted, as the diamond panes were darkened with painted arms of founders and benefactors, and old, dead and forgotten Fellows. The walls of the long gallery were hung with portraits from end to end. They began in the right-hand corner by the door in the fourteenth century—flat, angular, awful presentments of men and women whose names are household words in Cambridge, and they went on and on until it seemed that they would never cease. The walls were so full that it would be difficult to find room for another Fellow.

Lucy paused on her way to the study, and looked round with quite a new feeling on these old painted faces. They represented something to her to-day that they had not represented before.

She began dimly to understand what had made Cambridge the power it is in the land. It was these still faces looking down from the walls who had built up this great Cambridge. It was the men, after all, the patient men of old, whose toil had accomplished so much; and now the women were entering into their labours.

There were not many portraits at Newnham; it was only in its infancy. There would be plenty by-and-by. Lucy ran over in her mind the women whose portraits would hang upon those white walls between the windows. She could not in that brief retrospect think of any who were doing such great work that they would earn that distinction, only Pamela Gwatkin. She was sure Pamela would one day hang on the walls. She would be an old woman then, most likely, a lean, wrinkled, hard-visaged old woman, with gray hair and spectacles, and she would have a big book beside her—a book she had written or explained—and she would wear—what would she wear?

She would have gone quite bald by that time, like the old Fellows on the walls; her head would be bald and shining. She would wear it covered, of course, with—with a scholar's cap, with a long tassel depending over her nose, or a velvet Doctor's cap, which would be more becoming, and she would wear a scarlet Doctor's gown and hood. The picture would look lovely on the white walls of Newnham.

Lucy had just settled to her satisfaction how Pamela Gwatkin was to be handed down by a future Herkomer to another generation, when the Senior Tutor entered the gallery.

He, too, had been thinking. He hadn't been paying any attention to what Mary Rae had been talking about while the Master took his after-dinner nap; his thoughts were with Lucy in the gallery. He had watched her narrowly at dinner, and he had detected a change in her. He was used to watching men, and now he had begun to watch women. He remarked that her eyes were no longer soft; they were hard and eager, and had a hunted look in them. He knew the look; he had seen it in boys come up fresh from school—not brilliant boys from the sixth form of big public schools, but frank, fresh-faced fellows who had come up from country parsonages. He had seen the look on their faces when the work was new to them and the strain had begun to tell upon them. They lost it after a term or two when they bossed their lectures, and drifted away with the stream, or broke down, and went back to the country parsonages, and never came up again.

He had seen this hunted look on boys' faces, but he had never seen it on a girl's face before. He wasn't sure if it wouldn't be well to take Lucy away before she broke down. She would never want the mathematics she was getting up with such labour for the Little-go; she would be able to add up the butcher's book quite as well without. As the future mistress of the lodge—it had really come to that; he had ceased to think about Mary, and he had almost unconsciously put Lucy in her place—he would have liked her to have the prestige of Newnham, and, considering her humble antecedents, it was quite as well that she should win her spurs. She had pluck enough, if her strength would only hold out. She was a brave little thing; he had never seen a girl so brave. The Little-go examinations would soon be over, and then, if the result was satisfactory, he would speak. She would have quite culture enough after the Little-go—quite enough to condone even the stall in the butter market.

'I think you had better let me coach you for the exam.,' he said, as they talked about her mathematics; 'for the Additionals, at any rate, you'll find the dynamics and the statics rather stiff.'

'Ye—es,' Lucy said with a sigh; 'they are dreadfully stiff.'

'When will you come to me? Will you come here, or shall I come up to Newnham?'

'Oh no, no! It would never do to come to Newnham!'

Lucy turned quite pale at the suggestion.

'You have male lecturers,' said the college Don with a laugh. 'The difference would be that I should only be lecturing one girl instead of six.'

'I'm sure it wouldn't do; I'm sure Miss Wrayburne would object. I would rather, if you don't mind, come to you,' Lucy said meekly.

'Come, by all means. You had better come to my rooms; there will be less interruption than at the lodge. I can give you four hours a week, but it must be in the afternoon. When will you begin?'

Lucy was quite ready to begin at once. She settled to go to the Tutor's rooms the very next day. She didn't even think of consulting Cousin Mary about the arrangement, or the Master, or the Master's wife. She had already made a distinct advance; she had decided for herself; she had engaged a University coach, and arranged to spend four hours a week alone with him in his college rooms. The woman of the future could not do more.

CHAPTER VI.

BEHIND THE SCREEN.

Lucy went to her coach the next day. She ought to have known her way about a college staircase by this time, but she had never yet penetrated beyond the outer courts. She had never ventured up those mysterious stairways sacred to gyps, bed-makers and gownsmen.

A great many gownsmen must have climbed the stairs that led to Mr. Colville's rooms before her; they had left their marks here, if they had left them nowhere else in the annals of the University. Mr. Colville's rooms were in the oldest part of the college, and his staircase was as narrow and steep and dark as any lover of mediæval architecture could desire.

It was so dark that when Lucy reached the first landing she didn't see where to go; there was a passage in front of her and doors on either side. Instead of looking at the names painted over the doors, she went down the passage and knocked at the door at the end.

There are several ways of knocking at a door, but there is only one way of knocking at a college door if one expects to be heard. A timid rap with the knuckles is wasted effort; the knob of an umbrella, or the handle of a walking-stick, or any other form of bludgeon one happens to have at hand, is more effective; or a succession of well-delivered blows with a fist, or the body falling heavily against the door, have been known to attract the attention of persons within the room; but Lucy had recourse to none of these devices. She knocked feebly with her gloved hand on the door and waited. She was sure it was the right landing. She had read the directions painted on the door-post at the foot of the staircase:

First Floor—Mr. Colville.

She knocked again presently; and then, as nobody answered, she went in. The Senior Tutor was expecting her; it was surely right to go in. She thought she heard voices as she opened the door—at least a voice, a voice that had a familiar ring in it; she heard it clearer when she opened the first door; there was an outer oak, as usual to a college room. Lucy opened both doors and went in. She went quite into the room, and closed the door—there was a screen before the door—before she saw the occupants of the room.

What she saw didn't exactly make her hair stand on end, but she gave a little cry. She couldn't help crying out. On the couch behind the screen a man was lying, with the blood flowing from a wound in his throat, and on his knees beside him was a man praying.

The man who was praying stopped and looked up at the sound of that startled cry, and saw Lucy standing in the middle of the floor. He got up from his knees, and with a gesture of silence went behind the screen and fastened the two doors.

'I am glad you are come,' he said, going back to Lucy. 'I did not know the doors were open. You must be sure to keep them fastened. We don't want the authorities to know of this, and the Senior Tutor has the next rooms. You must be sure not to let him suspect anything. If you can do what is necessary for Edgell by day, I will sit up with him at night. It is not a bad wound; I don't think it is at all serious.'

Lucy stood frightened and speechless. What did the man mean? Did he take her for a nurse?

'I am afraid there is some mistake,' she said in a low voice; she couldn't keep from shaking. 'I—I thought this was Mr. Colville's room.'

Then a light seemed to break in upon the man, and he looked at Lucy with a quick, startled glance.

'Oh!' he said, 'I thought you were the nurse. I beg your pardon. There—there has been an accident here; our friend has not been quite himself—he has been overworking—and—and this has happened. Thank God it is no worse! It might have been fatal; a mere hair's breadth and it would have been fatal. We are anxious to keep it from the authorities. It would be very serious for him if it were known. It would ruin him for life. May we ask you to keep the chance knowledge of this most deplorable occurrence secret?'

What could Lucy say? Clearly it was her duty as the Master's niece to go straight to the lodge and acquaint him with the state of affairs. It was her duty to summon Mr. Colville without a moment's loss of time; he was only separated from the scene of this tragedy by a narrow passage.

Of course, the man lying bleeding there ought to have a doctor and a nurse, and his friends should be telegraphed for, and the whole college ought to be thrown into a commotion. Suppose the man were to die, what would her feelings be if she were particeps criminis in this dreadful secret?

All these things flashed through Lucy's mind as she stood there looking at the man on the couch. She knew him now; it was the man who had taken his hat off to her as he came out of chapel.

It was the man that Cousin Mary said was going to take a very high place in the Tripos, perhaps the highest. It was Wyatt Edgell.

She made up her mind in a moment.

'Yes,' she said, 'I will keep your secret. But I cannot go away from here and leave you like this. There is something I can do. I am used to nursing and sickness; tell me what I can do.'

She had torn off her gloves and thrown down her books, and was kneeling beside the couch where the man lay, wiping away the blood that was trickling beneath the bandage, and dropping down over his chest.

There was so much she could do that a woman could best do, and the man with his hand on the wrist of the patient stood by and watched her while she did it.

'You know something about medicine?' she said.

'I have been a doctor. I have spent seven years in acquiring a knowledge of surgery—seven years out of my life—but it has not been wasted if I have been the means of saving him;' and he nodded towards the bed.

'And you think you have saved him?'

Where had she heard this man's voice before, and where had she seen his eyes? She was asking herself this question as she was speaking to him.

'Yes, I think he is saved. He will do very well with careful nursing. One of the men has a sister at Addenbroke's, and he has gone to fetch her. I thought she had come when I saw you standing there. She will certainly be here presently. I don't think we need detain you.'

'I shall not go till she comes,' Lucy said with such decision that she quite frightened herself. 'I shall certainly stay here as long as I can be of any use.'

She had been of a good deal of use already. She had removed all traces of the dreadful deed; she had washed up every stain that could be washed away, and she had covered up the rest. She had fetched a pillow and some coverings from the adjoining room, and straightened the couch, and anyone coming into the room and seeing the man lying there with a white handkerchief over his throat, and the quilt drawn up over his chest, would not have dreamed of the ghastly sight beneath.

He looked as he lay there as if he had broken down in the middle of his work, and had thrown himself down there in a sudden attack of faintness. His face was dreadfully white, as white as the coverlet, and he was breathing hard, and there was a strange faint odour Lucy noticed as she bent over him. He was not sensible, but once he opened his eyes and looked at her with a strange, far-away look in them that haunted her for days.

They were beautiful eyes, tender and dreamy as a woman's, with a depth in them Lucy had never seen in any eyes before. But then she had not been accustomed to look into young men's eyes. She could not remember bending over a man before and seeing herself reflected in his eyes.

Perhaps it was the novelty of the situation that moved her. Having done all, everything she could do, she settled herself down in a chair by the head of the bed and began to weep.

The man was nothing to her, she had never heard his name till yesterday, and here she was sitting by his side weeping for him as if she had known him all her life.

The man who stood by let her tears fall unchecked.

'I don't think you will disturb him,' he said with a smile; 'I have given him an anodyne. Nobody could tell what he would do if he were left to himself, so I have made things sure by quieting him for a time. Pray have your cry out if it does you any good.'

He evidently knew something of girls. There is nothing like a little weep for soothing the nerves.

While Lucy was availing herself of her woman's privilege, he turned down the coverlet and examined the bandages; the blood was trickling down beneath them, thick and black where it had congealed, and a paler streak behind.

'It's broken out again,' he said quietly. 'I think there must be a stitch. Can you help me?'

If Lucy had been told an hour ago that she could have stood by and assisted as the man sewed up that gaping wound, and never by word or look betrayed faintness or alarm, she would not have believed it.

It was the little weep that did it.

'I think it will do now,' said the man, drawing up the coverlet over his work. "There is only one thing we can do more for the poor fellow, and that is commit him to God. Will you kneel down beside him while we ask His blessing on the means that we have used? Remember, when two or three are gathered together—we are two, and—and I am sure his mother is here with us.'

Lucy knelt down beside the couch while the man prayed aloud.

He talked to God as he knelt there as one who knew Him as a Friend of old. He made no preamble in entering this solemn Presence Chamber, but went straight up to the throne with his petition, and laid the poor, blind, suffering soul at the foot of the Cross.

Lucy had been brought up in the bosom of the Church; she had heard prayers read every morning and evening of her life, and she had never missed being in her place on Sundays. She had heard her father read the prayers hundreds of times, and she had heard, oh, so many sermons, but she had never heard a man pray like this.

It was heart speaking to heart; it was the spirit of man speaking to the Spirit of God.

While he was still speaking the door, or doors, rather, opened, and someone came in. He did not stop or get up from his knees, but went on wrestling for the blessing that he sought.

Lucy felt dreadfully guilty kneeling there. She heard the door open, and people—distinctly people—come in; and she had an awful overwhelming sense of guiltiness, as if she had been consenting to a murder. She was afraid to get up; she expected to see the Senior Tutor standing there and her cousin Mary. She didn't at all know why she expected Mary.

She was almost afraid to look up when she rose from her knees, and she felt herself shaking all over. But it was not Mary, and it was not the Tutor. It was a man that Lucy had often seen in the courts below, and he had a girl in a nurse's dress with him.

He looked over to Lucy in some alarm, and took off his cap.

'It's all right,' said the other. 'You didn't lock the door after you, old man, when you went out, and this lady found her way in—at least, God showed her the way in. If she hadn't come at the right moment it would have gone hard with our friend here. I am glad you have brought your sister. And now,' he said, turning to Lucy, 'we need not detain you any longer. This lady will stay with us, I hope, till late; and I shall sit up with him to-night. To-morrow, I hope, the worst will be over.'

'I hope so,' Lucy said with a sob she couldn't choke down—she hadn't the heart to say any more.

'I am sure you will respect our secret,' the man said, as Lucy was drawing on her gloves.

She didn't answer him; she only looked at him, and she saw the blood flush up under his skin. She remembered somebody else's cheeks she had seen flush in the same way—not a man's.

'I beg your pardon,' he said humbly.

Lucy was so angry with him for doubting her that she did not see his proffered hand; she drew her gloves on hurriedly, and picked up her books and went out into the passage, but she beckoned the nurse to follow her.

'I don't think the man's going to get better,' she said in a hurried whisper. 'It's like consenting to a murder to let him lie there and die; but I am not going to tell. I think his mother ought to know. I think someone ought to write and tell her that he is ill—dying!'

The nurse shook her head.

'It would kill her!' she said. 'She has such faith in her son—her beautiful son! He is such a noble, splendid fellow! Oh, it is a dreadful pity!'

'Why did he do it?'

'Why? Oh, don't you know?'

'No——'

The door of the room opened as they were speaking, and the nurse's brother beckoned her to come in.

'Come to me to-morrow morning at Addenbroke's,' she said. 'Ask for Nurse Brannan;' and then she went into the room and shut the door.

Lucy crept guiltily down the stairs. She quite shivered as she passed the Tutor's door: she would not have encountered him for the world. She didn't feel safe until she had got outside the college gate, and then she ran all the way back to Newnham.

CHAPTER VII.

LUCY'S SECRET.

Lucy felt dreadfully guilty all through that wretched evening. If she had assisted in a murder she couldn't have felt worse.

She had no appetite for dinner, and when she went back to her room, what was still more unusual, she had no appetite for her work. A Newnham girl is a gourmand where work is concerned; she may leave her meals untasted, but that terrible craving within creates an appetite that is akin to ravenous where work is concerned. When that craving ceases she goes down—or breaks down.

It had ceased quite suddenly with Lucy; she hated the very thought of work; she loathed with an unutterable loathing the sight of those mathematical books she had brought back from St. Benedict's. She shrank from them with a dreadful sense of faintness and sickness when she attempted to open them. They smelt of blood, or else she fancied they did.

The air was full of fancies. It was a stormy night, and the wind was wailing round her corner of the building, and every now and then a sharp blast of driving rain would strike upon her window. She heard the rain distinctly dropping down the pane like tears, and she fancied—oh, it was a dreadful fancy!—that it was drops of blood.

She bore it in that lonely room as long as she could, and then she got up and went out into the passage. The lights were out, and the place was quite still; everybody had gone to bed. Dark and deserted as the corridor was, it was not so lonely as her own room. There were girls sleeping behind every one of those closed doors. She heard them—for the ventilators of most were open—breathing audibly, and some were moaning in their sleep.

Lucy walked up and down the long corridor; her feet were bare, and she had thrown nothing over her shoulders. Cousin Mary would have scolded her dreadfully if she had seen her, with her white garments trailing on the stone floor.

She never thought of the draughts or the cold stones; she only thought of getting away from that everlasting drip, drip of the window-pane, that brought the scene of the afternoon so vividly before her. She was nervous and overwrought, and she was burdened with a secret she ought never to have bound herself to keep.

Wild horses shouldn't tear it from her, she told herself, as she paced up and down that draughty passage. Whatever happened, she would be true to her word. It would be hard if a girl couldn't be trusted as well as a man. What was the use of coming to Newnham if gossip and emptiness—the habits of the slave—still had dominion over her?

It was all very fine and high-sounding; but she would have given the world to have told somebody, to have eased her overburdened mind and poured out the dreadful story on some soft feminine, sympathetic bosom.

And then, while she was telling herself all these fine things, and repeating Lord Tennyson's nice verses about that open fountain that was to wash away all those silly human things and make woman perfect—quite perfect—a strange thing happened.

She heard the voice of the man praying. He was praying now; she heard him quite distinctly, but she could not catch the words. She was quite sure it was the voice; it had sunk down so deep into her ears that she could never forget it. Lucy paused in the darkness and listened. The voice came from a room at the door of which she was standing. She had no idea, in the darkness, whose room it was; she was only sure—quite sure—of the voice.

An overpowering desire to see the speaker—perhaps to get her release—seized her, and she opened the door of the room.

There was no man there praying; there was only a girl sitting reading by the light of a shaded lamp, and she was reading aloud. It was Pamela Gwatkin, and she was reading a Greek play.

Lucy went a few paces into the room and stood there as if spellbound, listening to the girlish voice, in low solemn accents, mouthing the rhythmic Greek. She didn't read it as if it were Wordsworth, or Cowper, or Keats, or even Tennyson; she mouthed it; and the noble words, falling in noble cadence, brought back the voice of the man wrestling with God for his friend.

Pamela heard the door open, and she looked up. She didn't divide the shuddering night with a shrill-edged shriek, and bring all Newnham about her, as she might have done at the sight of the white-robed figure standing in the doorway. She thought it was a girl walking in her sleep, and she got up softly and went towards her.

For a moment, as she came forward, she saw the figure swaying in the doorway, and as she came nearer Lucy tottered forward with her arms out-stretched like one walking in a dream, and fell upon her bosom—literally fell, with her clinging arms around her, and her head pillowed on Pamela's bosom.

'Oh, it is Eric Gwatkin!' she sobbed, 'it is Eric Gwatkin!'

Pamela got her over to the couch—it was a bed now, not a couch; the serge rug had been removed, and a snowy coverlet was in its place, and a real pillow, not a sham roundabout bolster covered with an embroidered dragon.

Pamela Gwatkin laid the girl down on her own bed and covered her up. She was shaking dreadfully, and her hands and feet were like ice, and she was sobbing hysterically.

When Pamela had covered her up, she shut the door of the room; it was no good making a scene and arousing everybody, because a girl—a little weak-minded fresher—had broken down under the strain and got hysterical. All girls get hysterical at times, only the stronger ones lock the door and wrestle with the enemy in secret.

'Oh, Eric Gwatkin!' moaned the girl on the bed. 'I can't keep it any longer; I must tell!'

'What have you got to do with Eric Gwatkin?' Pamela asked severely. 'I am sure he is nothing to you; he is never likely to be anything to anybody.'

'Oh yes, he is! He is everything to—to Wyatt Edgell. He has saved his life. Oh, you don't know what he is to him!'

'Saved his life? What are you talking about? What has Wyatt Edgell got to do with you, and with Eric?'

'He sewed it up—the wound—the dreadful gaping wound!'

Lucy covered her eyes with her hands to shut out the dreadful sight, and she was trembling so dreadfully that the bed shook with her. Clearly the girl was in a fever, and her mind was wandering. The name of Wyatt Edgell was familiar to Pamela; it was familiar to everybody in Cambridge. He was the coming Senior Wrangler. What could Eric have to do with him—poor Eric, who was grinding for his 'Special'?

'What wound?' said Pamela impatiently; 'and who sewed it up?'

'Eric sewed it up, and I helped him. I drew the edges together, while he put the needle in the quivering flesh. Oh, it was horrible!'

Lucy sank back on the couch, and her lips grew pale, and her cheeks gray, and Pamela thought she was going to faint. She hadn't got anything but eau-de-Cologne to give her—not a nip of brandy for the world; not even a pocket flask is allowed at Newnham. She went to the water-jug and poured out some water in a basin, and dabbed it over the girl's face and hands, and made her own bed streaming. Perhaps there was something in the girl's story, after all! She couldn't have dreamed these hideous details.

'Where was the wound? how had he hurt himself?' she asked presently.

'He had cut his throat.'

Pamela let the basin of water she was holding fall on the floor. She didn't scream as any less well-regulated mind would have done, but she let the basin slip out of her hands, and the water made a dreadful mess on the floor.

'Cut his throat?' she repeated faintly—she was nearly as white as Lucy—'and Eric——'

'Eric sewed it up.'

'Is—is he dead?'

She asked the question hoarsely, in a voice Lucy couldn't have recognised for Pamela's, but she was past noticing voices.

'No—o; Eric has asked God to give him back his life, that he may begin it afresh.'

'What use is that?' said Pamela bitterly.

'I am sure God heard him—we were praying for him when the nurse came in. He was asking that the nurse might be sent quickly, and she came while the words were on his lips.'

'Of course the nurse would be sent; you can get a nurse at any moment from Addenbroke's without praying for one.'

'Oh, you don't understand!' Lucy moaned; 'you don't know the worst. It had to be done secretly: no one must know. It would ruin him for life if it were known.'

'You don't mean that they haven't told anyone? that they are trying to hush it up, and not let the tutors know?'

Lucy moaned.

'Oh, what folly is this! I am sure Eric is at the bottom of it.'

'Yes; it was Eric made me promise I wouldn't tell, and I have told you,' Lucy murmured helplessly.

'Of course you have told me. Having told me so much, you must tell me all—you must keep nothing back.'

And so Lucy sat up in the bed with her arms round Pamela—she couldn't have told her without having something to cling to—and told her her wretched little story, and how she had pledged herself to keep this young man's secret.

'What do you think I ought to do?' she asked weakly, when the recital was finished.

'Do?' said Pamela, but she didn't answer the girl's question. She disengaged herself from her clinging arms, and she paced up and down the room, her feet dabbling in the water on the floor. She stopped presently in her walk, her chin up, and her face set with the light of a high resolve upon it towards the light that was breaking in at the east window; she might have been reciting that Greek play. 'Do?' she repeated, and her face was hard and cold and tired. The old weary look had come back to it—no wonder; it was three o'clock in the morning. 'Do? Why, go to bed, of course!'

She refused to say another word about Lucy's secret. She helped her back to her room, and put her to bed, and tucked her in, and drew back the curtains, that the light of the new day might drive away the ghosts of the night.

Pamela did all this without speaking a word; but when she got to the door of Lucy's room she stopped and looked back. She could see from the tremulous motion of the clothes that the girl was weeping, and she went over to the bed and put her cool lips to Lucy's forehead.

'Good-night, dear!' she said softly. 'I think you have behaved beautifully!'

CHAPTER VIII.

WATTLES.

As soon as she could get away from Newnham the next morning, Lucy went to Addenbroke's to see Nurse Brannan. She couldn't get away very early; there was a mathematical lecture at nine o'clock that wasn't over till eleven, and she had to plod, plod through those weary diagrams while her mind was far away. Oh, how she hated those problems and riders, and all the dreary, dreary round! She made one or two futile little diagrams on her paper, and then she rubbed them out again, and sat staring at the blackboard, and watching the perplexing white lines come and go while her mind was far away. She was calculating what would happen if the man had died in the night.

'What would they do with the body? Would Eric Gwatkin expect her to keep the secret, and assist, perhaps, at some mysterious obsequies?' It was with a distinct feeling of relief she saw the duster sweep over the blackboard and wipe all those cabalistic characters away. It was like wiping out the record of her guilt.

Lucy shook off the dust and gloom of the lecture-room and ran off to Addenbroke's. She really could run a good part of the way. She went across the Fens, as less frequented, and giving her space to breathe and think. It was such a blue day, and the fresh green of the year was over the low-lying fields, and the chestnut-tree by the bridge was budding, and the pollard willows that marked the winding course of the river were sallow-gray in the sunshine, and the daisies were in bloom. Lucy walked over quite a carpet of flowers; she crushed the little tender pink buds remorselessly under her feet in her hurry to get to Addenbroke's.

She had never been to the hospital before, and she was rather afraid to go in when she got there. There were a lot of people coming out with newly-bandaged limbs and white faces, and some children were carried in in their mothers' arms. There were people of all ages, men and women, and little children all with that sad patience on their faces which is born of suffering. Lucy was so sorry for the people. She had no idea her heart was still tender; she had rather prided herself on its growing cold and hard like Maria Stubbs and the rest of the Stoics of Newnham. There was a tired-looking woman coming up the path with a puny little creature in her arms, with, oh! such a white, white face. Its eyes were open, and it was smiling a wan little smile up into the mother's face, and she was crooning over it; she was a poor, weakly thing, and she carried it as if even its light weight were too much for her. Lucy turned to look after the sickly mother and the sickly child, and she noticed the child's arm—a lean, puny little arm—had escaped from the shawl in which it was wrapped, and was feebly embracing the mother's waist.

The sight of that small clinging hand brought a rush of tears to her eyes. There was compensation even here; there was something here between that sickly mother and child—there wasn't much to show for it, only a crooning voice and a wan smile and a little wasted clinging hand—that would last longer than the Stoics, that would last 'to and through the Doomsday fire.'

Strangely softened by this every-day sight, Lucy crept up the wide stone staircase to find Nurse Brannan. She looked so lost that a man going up, a medical student, asked her where she was going, and took her to the ward where Miss Brannan was nurse.

'I am afraid the doctors are going their rounds,' he said, as he looked in at the door, 'but I will take you into Miss Brannan's room, and you can wait there.'

He led Lucy through the ward—a large, delightful chamber, well lighted and cheerful, and with quite a bank of tall palms and ferns on a table near the door, an oasis of verdure for tired eyes to feast upon.

Lucy saw all this at a glance, and she saw also a group of men round a bed, and the nurses standing near, and she crept softly into Nurse Brannan's room.

She had time before the nurse came to her to see what a nurse's room was like. It was a tiny bit of a room partitioned off the ward, and it seemed all walls and ceiling. There was a little floor room, however, and a big window that went nearly up to the ceiling.

It was not unlike a room in a woman's college, only that there were texts on the walls, and there are no texts on the walls of the Stoics.

The occupant of the room must have understood Latin and Greek, for there were texts in both these languages. There was one text only in our common tongue, and that was over the mantelpiece. It was not an illuminated text, and it had no lovely floral border. It was written in plain, bold characters in black and white: 'Inasmuch as ye do it unto the least of these My brethren, ye do it unto Me.'

Lucy couldn't keep her eyes off those familiar words which she read now in a new light. There wasn't much else in the room to look at. There was a bed that was a couch by day; it was a bed still, though it was past eleven o'clock; Nurse Brannan had evidently not long risen from it. The room was in the disorder of the early morning, and the day arrangements did not yet prevail. It was as untidy as a nurse's room well could be: the breakfast things were still on the table, and the demure little bonnet and cloak looked as if they had hastily been taken off and thrown on the bed, and a pair of outdoor shoes were lying in the middle of the floor.

While Lucy was still noticing these details Nurse Brannan came in.

She was a little bit of a nurse, with pink cheeks and steady blue eyes and fluffy hair. She was not at all a formidable person.

Lucy ran up to her when she came in, and took both her hands. She couldn't ask the question that was on her lips, she was moved out of all sense and reason. The anxieties of the night and the mathematics of the morning, and the lean little encircling arm had moved her strangely, and now she was hardly master of herself.

Nurse Brannan shook her head.

'He is no better,' she said.

She didn't say it at all sadly. She was so used to such things—to sickness and suffering and death—it didn't move her in the least.

'I have just come back from St. Benedict's, and there is no improvement. He has had a dreadful night. They thought at one time of calling up the Tutor.'

'And they have not told him yet?' Lucy asked, pale to the lips. 'Are they going to let him die?'

'They have not told him; they have not told anyone in the college; but I don't know about letting him die.'

'You think he'll get over it? Oh, do you really think it possible with that—that dreadful wound he can get better?'

Only talking about the wound made Lucy sick and faint. She was made of very poor stuff. She would have been no good at Addenbroke's.

Nurse Brannan smiled.

'The wound is nothing,' she said: 'it is not at all serious. He will get better if he is well watched, and they protect him from himself. When the attack passes off he will not be much the worse—only it may occur again at any time.'

'The attack?' Lucy said feebly; she was quite at sea as to Nurse Brannan's meaning.

'Oh, you didn't know he did it in a fit of delirium tremens. This is the second time he has had an attack, and he has attempted his life both times. His friends ought to take him away and put him under restraint.'

Lucy didn't know what delirium tremens meant; happily she had been spared all her life from such miserable knowledge. She vaguely knew it was a 'possession' of some kind, an awful 'possession' like that which used to seize the men of old.

'You think the fit will pass?' she said.

'Oh yes; there is no reason why it shouldn't pass, and then the less they say to him about it the better. It would be well if he never knew; but the scar will remain, they cannot cover up that. There is no reason why he shouldn't be well enough to take his Tripos and go "down." The best thing that can happen to him will be to "go down."'

'Go down'—he looked very much more like going 'up,' Lucy thought, as she recalled the white face on the pillow; but she was immensely relieved by the nurse's assurance.

'And you have seen him this morning?' she said.

'Yes; I ran over for a minute directly I got up. I was not up till late. A woman was dying in the ward, and I stayed with her till she died. She did not die till daylight, and then I lay down for a few hours; and I had just time to snatch some breakfast and run over to St. Benedict's before the doctors came their rounds. I was only just back in time. I had to throw my things down and put on my slippers—I hadn't even time to put my cap straight. They were waiting for me in the ward when I came back. Oh dear! what a mess I left my room in!'

Her pretty plaited nurse's cap, that ought to be worn in the most demure fashion, that ought to be as straight as those lines of that detestable blackboard, was all awry, was positively jaunty, and her fluffy hair was quite outrageous. She didn't look the least like a real, staid nurse who is called upon to face death at any moment, and is always doing dreadful disagreeable things. She might have been playing at nursing, only her eyes were steady, and her lips had a great calm about them; they didn't quiver, and tremble, and curl, and ripple with laughter, like other girls.

Lucy was almost angry with her for the cool, not to say unfeeling, way in which she spoke of these dread realities—death and suffering. 'She has no heart!' she said to herself as she went back over the Fens to Newnham. 'Nurses are so used to pain that they have no sympathy. I wouldn't be a nurse for the world!' Then she remembered the words over the mantelpiece: 'Inasmuch——.' Was this the secret of that little fluffy, girlish nurse's hardness and endurance?

They don't do very much for other people at Newnham; and they do nothing for each other. They positively ignore each other. Perhaps this is owing to culture—the higher culture—and it hadn't reached Addenbroke's yet.

Lucy had written to the Tutor of St. Benedict's when she got back the previous day, excusing herself, in an incoherent fashion, for not keeping her appointment, and promising to come to his rooms at the same hour the next day.

She knew her way quite well this time, and she was five minutes before the hour she had appointed. The Senior Tutor's door was closed, and the way was quite clear. There was not a soul on the staircase; there was not a soul in the passage. Lucy could not resist the desire to knock at that closed door at the end of the passage, and find out for herself how the man was. She hadn't much faith in that thick-skinned little nurse; she would see for herself.

She knocked at the door at the end of the passage in her futile way, but of course nobody answered. If she had wasted all her strength upon it, it would have been the same thing, as the inmates of that mysterious room only gave admittance to privileged individuals upon preconcerted signals.

Lucy hadn't got the secret of that 'Open sesame,' and she was turning away. She hadn't got to the end of the passage, when the door really did open and someone came out. It was the bed-maker with a tray. Somebody had been having a meal, and she was carrying the débris away. Lucy stopped her at the end of the passage, and the two women stood looking at each other—the bed-maker suspiciously, and Lucy eagerly. There was no mistaking the anxious eagerness in Lucy's eyes.

'How is he?' she asked, more with her eyes than her lips, and she laid her detaining hand on the woman's arm. There must have been some Freemasonry in the touch, for the bed-maker softened, and the look of suspicion gave place to one of pity.

'He's quieter,' she said in a whisper, drawing Lucy back into the passage, out of sight of the Tutor's door; 'but he's been orful bad all the morning. As much as two of 'em could do to keep him in bed. It's a sad pity, miss, and such a nice gentleman—there isn't his fellow in the college!'

The bed-maker sniffed; she would have wept, no doubt, but she held a tray, and it would have been inconvenient, so she sniffed instead, and regarded Lucy with a watery eye. She evidently thought Lucy was his sweetheart.

Lucy took a coin from her slender purse and laid it on the tray. She didn't give it to anybody in particular, she only laid it on the tray, and the bed-maker curtsied.

'Will you ask Mr. Gwatkin if I may come in?' she said—'the lady who was with him yesterday.'

She didn't give her name, but the woman knew her quite well—every bed-maker in St. Benedict's knew her. She wasn't the least surprised at the Master's niece taking an interest in one of her gentlemen—the nicest gentleman in the college. She had a tender spot in her withered bosom, under that rusty old shawl, and she was quite flustered at an affaire de cœur on her staircase.

She toddled back, tray and all, and by a preconcerted signal the door was opened, and she said a few words to someone inside, and then Eric Gwatkin came out into the passage and led Lucy in and closed the doors behind her.

He was looking dreadfully tired, she thought, and there were quite deep lines on his face; he seemed to have aged since yesterday. Perhaps it was with want of sleep, but Lucy put it down at once to his guilty conscience. She was feeling old herself, years older than yesterday.

'He has had a very bad night,' Eric Gwatkin said, speaking in a low voice and with his lips twitching, 'such a night as I pray God I may never witness again. You were not praying for us last night. You did not pray for him—for me—when you went away.'

Lucy bowed her head; she remembered she had not prayed for these men. What were they to her that she should pray for them?

She had been walking about the passages and frightening Pamela out of her wits instead, when she ought to have been on her knees.

The screen had been moved since yesterday; it had been drawn nearer the bed, so that the middle of the room where they were standing was left clear.

'He does not like to see anyone whispering,' Eric explained; 'he is very suspicious, and the least thing excites him.'

'You were alone with him all night?' Lucy asked, with a perceptible quiver in her voice; 'you have been up two nights.'

'That doesn't matter,' he said, 'I shall have all the strength I need; but last night he was very violent, and—and I thought I should have to call Mr. Colville. It was a great temptation—I could hardly resist it.'

'Oh, why didn't you?' said Lucy. 'Why do you take all this responsibility upon yourself?'

Eric Gwatkin smiled. His smile was not the least like Pamela's. Lucy couldn't help thinking, as she stood there, how it would change Pamela's face and take the weariness out of it if she had that smile.

'I don't mind the responsibility,' he said, 'or the anxiety, if I can save him. It would be worse than death to him to have it known. Oh, I think you must go home and pray that he may be brought through this, and may be kept for the future. He will need all our prayers.'

'What on earth are you whispering about, Wattles? I wish you would speak so that a fellow can hear what you are saying.'

The voice came from behind the screen—an impatient voice, not weak by any means.

'All right, old man; Miss Rae has come to ask how you are. He saw you yesterday,' he said, turning to Lucy and speaking in a lower voice; 'he remembered you quite well.'

'It's awfully good of you,' Wyatt Edgell said as Lucy came from behind the screen; 'I'm afraid we don't look like receiving visitors. Old Wattles here insists upon making a mess.'

He was lying back on the pillow with a wet bandage round his head, and a basin of lotion and some rags on a chair beside the bed. His shirt was torn open as if in a struggle, and his chest was bare. There was a scarf round his throat, a large silk scarf striped with the colours of his college that concealed whatever was beneath. Lying there with his head thrown back and those wet bandages, and his chest open—his splendid manly chest with all the muscles exposed—he looked like a man stricken down with fever, or some head trouble; no one would have guessed what the scarf thrown so loosely around his neck concealed.

'I am so glad you are better,' said Lucy softly, coming over to the bed and bending over him; 'you ought to get well soon, you have got such a good nurse.'

'Old Wattles, yes; he's very well, only he persists in keeping me in such a mess.'

He took the bandages off his head as he spoke, and rolled them up into a ball, and flung them to the other end of the room, where they rolled under a heavy piece of furniture, and Wattles, or Gwatkin rather, had to go on his knees and fish them out.

'There!' he said, 'that will give Wattles an excuse for going on his knees. He has been going on his knees all night. He would be a good fellow if he weren't always preaching and praying.'

He rolled his head impatiently on one side, and flung the pillow after the bandages, and Lucy, looking down upon him, saw a dark light in his eyes she had never seen in any eyes before. It wasn't exactly terror, but it was disgust and loathing and impatience.

'I beg your pardon,' he said, 'but there was a creature on that—a toad. I hate toads!' He shuddered as he spoke, and his eyes followed the direction of the pillow. 'It's there now! I wish Wattles would put it outside. It's been here all night.'

Gwatkin took up the pillow and shook it, and appeared to take something off it, and opened the window and made a gesture as if he had thrown the thing into the court below.

'There, old man,' he said reassuringly, 'it's gone now. It can't trouble you any more.'

And then he brought back the pillow, and Lucy put it under the poor fellow's head while he supported it, and she arranged it and smoothed it as only a woman's hand can arrange a pillow.

When she had done this, she put on the wet bandages afresh and bathed his head, and as she bathed it the dark light seemed to fade out of his eyes.

'You are very good,' he said with a sigh; 'you have exorcised that hideous little beast. It is gone now'—and he looked round the room fearfully—'quite gone.'

'Thank God!' said Gwatkin. 'Your visit has done some good, Miss Rae, if it has dispelled that hideous nightmare that has been pursuing him all night. I think he will sleep now.'

'I'm sure you ought to sleep yourself,' Lucy said, as she suddenly remembered the time and began dragging on her gloves. 'It is quite gone,' she said to Edgell, bending down over the bed; 'I am going to pick it up as I go out and carry it away.'

Having told this little fib, she went out, and Gwatkin closed the two doors after her.

She had to tell another fib or two when she went into the Tutor's room. He had been waiting for her exactly fifteen minutes, and he had waited an hour the day before.

She was absent and distrait all through the lesson; she was thinking about the man in the next room, and the creature she had promised to pick up in the court.

The Senior Tutor had never coached such an unpromising pupil. She would never get through her Little-go, he told himself—never, never. She would get plucked to a certainty.

Oh, it would never do for the future Mistress of St. Benedict's to be plucked!

He debated with himself while he was bending over her, and remarking what a dainty little profile it was, and how the little rings of chestnut hair clustered on her forehead, and how clear, how deliciously transparent, was the carnation tint of her cheek, and the shapely curve of her throat—such a little throat he could clasp it with his hand—he debated with himself, as he remarked these quite every-day things that no man in his senses except an old bachelor Fellow of a college would have noticed, whether it would not be better to settle the thing at once, and stop all this unprofitable work.

If Lucy knew what was before her, she would have other opportunities of fitting herself for her high position besides poring over mathematics, for which she clearly had no vocation.

'I'm afraid you find the work rather hard,' he said with a preliminary 'H'm' and 'Ah' to clear his throat. He didn't know exactly how to begin. What comes by nature at thirty is uncommonly hard at sixty. It is like going in again for a hurdle-race, or taking the high jump. He could have done it easily years ago, but he couldn't do it now. He stopped with that preliminary 'Ah.'

'Yes,' said Lucy, 'it is not very easy, but I am going to work eight hours a day. It is more than a month to the exam.; if I work very hard eight hours every day, I think I may manage it.'

Eight hours a day for a whole month! She was so much in earnest; and when she lifted her little pale drooping face to his, with just a suspicion of a tear on her eyelashes, he was really sorry for her. He was very near taking her in his arms and kissing away that fugitive tear and settling the matter—he was never nearer in his life.

Perhaps it was the best thing he could have done, but he missed the chance, and Lucy picked up her books and began to talk about the work she was to prepare for the next lesson.

'I wouldn't work eight hours a day,' he said; 'you will get through easier than that. I would give an extra two hours to tennis.'

He had never given a man this advice—perhaps it was not needed. He watched her, out of his window, cross the court. She did not happen to pick up the thing by the way as she had promised. Her step was less elastic, he noticed, than it used to be, and her face was paler—paler and thinner. She would never, never be young again, and life would never open afresh. There is only one young life, one time of roses, one sweet blossoming time, and it was just a question in the Tutor's mind, as he watched Lucy cross the court, whether the loss of this were worth all the mathematics in the world.

CHAPTER IX.

A WOMAN'S PARLIAMENT.

Lucy saw Pamela Gwatkin once only during the day, and that was at dinner. She only caught a far-off glimpse of her at the High table. Pamela very often sat at the 'High' among the Dons. The younger Dons were very fond of her: her opinions kept pace with theirs—they were very advanced opinions—and sometimes they outran them. She would be a Don herself some day, and she would be a pioneer in quite a new school of thought.

Lucy watched her with a feeling of awe as she sat among those great minds eating gooseberry pie—Lucy wouldn't have sat there for the world. The presence of so much learning would have taken away her appetite. The presence of the Master of St. Benedict's at the dinner-table never took away her appetite, but the dear old thing never talked above her head. He was very fond of recalling those old days, as he sat at meat, when Dick—not Lucy's father, but her great-grandfather—used to drive a team afield, and his good wife kept the stall in the butter market.

But the President and the Dons of 'Newe' never discussed such commonplace topics. They talked of literature, philosophy, science, with a fine breadth of handling which is peculiar to a woman's college. Pamela Gwatkin was in her right place among them.

There was the weekly political meeting held after Hall—a little miniature House of Commons—where the affairs of the nation were discussed, a foretaste of what will be by-and-by, when things are rearranged.

When the House took its seat at nine o'clock, Lucy found herself in the Opposition, and a long way off from the benches occupied by the Government of the country.

Lucy only represented an insignificant little borough that nobody else would stoop to represent. She had a little freehold in it—her only freehold—six feet of earth beneath the east window of her father's church at Thorpe Regis. Most people have a freehold of this sort, but it does not always give them a voice in the affairs of the nation. Lucy was returned unopposed on the strength of her little freehold, and as her views, if she had any, were not at all advanced, she found herself in the minority.

Pamela Gwatkin, or, as the girls called her, Newnham Assurance, was the Leader of the House, and Annabel Crewe Secretary for the Colonies, and Capability Stubbs had been unanimously elected Chancellor of the Exchequer; every girl that was worth anything had a place in the Cabinet.

Lucy hadn't much interest in the business that was going on, and she took out her knitting and turned the heel of a sock while the great affairs of the State were being discussed.

It was quite clear from what she did gather from the speeches on the Ministerial side that the country had been misgoverned long enough by the feeble race of men. It was quite time there was a change. A great deal of time had been lost; ages had been lost in the history of the world. Men had been first in the field; women took a longer time to ripen. They had ripened now; they were quite, quite ripe; they were ready for the change.

Oh, it was beautiful to hear the girls speak! There is an idea among narrow-minded people that debating societies encourage volubility of speech. Perhaps they do among men, and the practice of public speaking is apt to make them too loquacious, too apt to air their elementary knowledge and crude information in senseless verbiage. But garrulity is not the sin of the students of colleges for women. They not only know a great deal more than men know, but they have the delightful gift of ready and accurate language. They do not haggle and hesitate, and 'H'm' and 'Ah,' and have that dreadful difficulty in finding words that even prevails in a real House of Commons.

It was remarkable to see with what ease the Newnham girls handled those topics which old-fashioned legislators have been puzzling over Session after Session. There was a certain fine breadth in their way of handling them that would have taken a Conservative Leader's (the Leader of a real House of Commons) breath away.

It didn't take anybody's breath away in the Ladies' Parliament. Everybody knitted and listened unmoved, and when eleven o'clock came two very important Bills that had been brought forward from last Session were advanced a stage.

There was an exciting division before the House separated, that resulted in an overwhelming majority for the motion, 'That the Legal Profession and the Church be thrown open to women.'

That foolish little Lucy voted in the minority; there were not a dozen girls in Newnham who showed such a poor spirit, and of these five, it was rumoured, were engaged to curates.

The girls ran off to their rooms when the sitting of the House was ended in the highest possible spirits. Some of them sang snatches of songs, and some caught each other round the waist and waltzed madly down corridors. The thing was practically settled. The Bar and the Church opened vistas, immense vistas, for every sort of talent, and especially for the kind of talent that Newnham produced.

There would have to be more colleges for women—Newnham and Girton could not turn out nearly enough—there would have to be a great many Newnhams. Some girls, no doubt, sat down at once and began to prepare a sermon, and others took down Blackstone and began seriously to study law.

Lucy went back to her room alone. The Chancellor of the Exchequer, though she 'kept' next door, wouldn't take the slightest notice of her. She had lighted her lamp, and was just thinking what she would give for a cup of tea, when someone knocked at her door. It wasn't a girl with a cup of tea, as she hoped it might be—the Chancellor of the Exchequer, with all her fine airs, generally brought her in a cup of tea before she went to bed, and sometimes she condescended to sit down for five minutes and discuss the burning questions of the day. It was not the Chancellor of the Exchequer—it was a far greater person—it was the Leader of the House.

'Well?' she said, when she came in and had shut the door after her—'well?'

She had come in so suddenly, and Lucy's mind was so full of the motion of the evening—this Parliamentary business was quite a new thing to her, and she had taken it au serieux—that she could not collect herself sufficiently to think what Pamela meant. Her mind was so full of the lady curates and the female barristers that she looked up at the Leader of the House in bewilderment.

'Well,' said Pamela impatiently, 'how is he? I saw by your face at Hall that he was not dead. Is he going to get well?'

Then Lucy remembered all about it.

'Oh dear!' she said, 'how could I have forgotten! Yes, he is going to get well, I think. He will owe his life if he does to Eric. Oh, Eric has been lovely!'

'Eric has done no more than anyone else would have done,' Pamela said coldly; 'no more than a woman would have done if a woman had been in his place.'

'I don't think a woman could have done what Eric has done,' Lucy said.

She was thinking of those stitches he had put in, and how he had struggled with the poor fellow all night, and how he had been watching and praying beside him for two whole nights and days.

Nurse Brannan would have done as much as most women, but she would not have done all this.

'Oh, you don't know what women can do!' Pamela said, with a little curl of her lip. Her lips were so thin and so hard—such crisp lips that they couldn't help curling. 'You are only a fresher; when you have been here three years you will have found out what a woman can do. He would never have cut his throat if a woman had been near him.'

'No,' said Lucy eagerly, 'I am sure he wouldn't—not if a woman he loved had been near. Oh dear! you should have seen the wistfulness in his poor eyes when I put the wet bandage on his head! It was enough to melt one's heart. Eric says he will be sure to do it again—at least, that we must never leave off praying for him. I am sure that there is only one thing that can save him from doing it again.'

'Only one thing?' Pamela repeated, with just an inflection of scorn in her voice. 'And what is this panacea for his wickedness and folly? What is this fine thing that is to save him from himself?'

'Don't speak of it so lightly; it is not a little thing!'

There were tears in Lucy's voice as she spoke, and in her eyes. She had the picture before her of the strong man, with his beautiful bare chest, and his splendid frame, and those wistful eyes, and the loathing and the dread with which he shrank from the creature on his pillow. The pity of it was strong upon her, and she was deeply moved.

'A great love would save him—the love of a good woman. He would do a great thing for a woman he loved; he would make any sacrifice. I don't think anything else would save him.'

The Leader of the House of Commons turned from white to pink. Lucy might have been talking about her. She wore a very pretty white gown of some soft silky stuff, and it was folded across the bosom, and the folds heaved up and down as Lucy spoke, as if she were breathing heavily.

'Perhaps he has done this for a woman's sake,' she said bitterly. 'Men are such fools! they will do anything for a woman's sake—not always a worthy woman.'

'I am sure he has not!' said Lucy hotly. 'He has been working too hard, and he has broken down. I heard at the lodge that he was working ten hours a day; that he was certain to come out first. Oh, you don't know how they are building upon him at St. Benedict's! It isn't a woman—it's overwork.'

Pamela smiled.

'You are a capital champion, my dear, only don't suffer yourself to get too much interested in this foolish young man; it will interfere with your work. You must not make a mistake and let pity drift into—love.'

She made a little pause before the word, and the colour came again into her cheeks. She looked ever so much prettier talking about pity—and love—than she did speaking on those troublesome Bills that had already occupied the time of two Sessions.

'Oh, he is never likely to love me!' said Lucy. 'He could only love his equal; no one else would have any influence over him. He would only love a queen among women.'

'Perhaps he has found his queen already. Most men have before they are twenty-three.'

The colour went out of the girl's face, and the cold light came back into her eyes, and her lips, that a moment before were tremulous and tender, were hard and firm.

'I wouldn't go too often to Mr. Edgell's rooms, if I were you, dear,' she said when she went away. 'The authorities would make a fuss if they heard of it. We are not supposed, you know, to visit a man's room without a chaperon. I don't think it would do to take a chaperon there. If you have any more interest in him, I will find out for you how he is going on from Eric.'

'Thank you,' said Lucy warmly; 'I can find out for myself. I can hear all about the St. Benedict's men at the lodge.'

She was quite frightened at herself for speaking in that way to the Prime Minister. She had got into the way now, since she had been at Newnham, of taking her own part; she was beginning to have no respect for dignities.

CHAPTER X.

'THAT CONFOUNDED CUCUMBER!'

Lucy didn't go to Wyatt Edgell's room again. She caught sight of the friendly bed-maker once or twice on the staircase when she went to Mr. Colville's room to be coached in mathematics, and she held a little whispered conference with her on the stairs.

Edgell was better: he was up again and at work—working very hard, the woman said (and bed-makers know something about work). He was 'going on as quiet and as steady as any gentleman on the staircase.' This verdict from such a quarter was as good as a college testimonial.

When there is a mixed University, and a lady President at the lodge, and a female Vice-Chancellor, and the affairs of the Senate are conducted by dowagers, bed-makers will no doubt be required to sign college testimonials.

The first time Lucy saw Wyatt Edgell after that day when she put the wet bandage round his head, and promised to pick up the dreadful thing Eric had thrown out of window, and carry it away with her, was at the college chapel.

It was a fortnight after the day when she had picked him out from among all the men of St. Benedict's as Pamela Gwatkin's brother. He was sitting in the same place, and he was very little changed; he was paler, Lucy thought, and he was muffled up round the throat for that warm May day. She couldn't help looking at him. Her eyes would wander over to the bench where he sat, do what she would to keep them fixed in quite an opposite direction.

The Master took such a long time over the Litany that morning. He had read it for so many years in that college chapel, Sunday after Sunday, but he had never read it so slowly as he was reading it to-day. The men yawned and fidgeted as he read, and the old fellows in the stalls opposite looked across with grave, questioning eyes—they would have to elect another Master shortly—and the women-folk kneeling by his side looked up anxiously; but Lucy's eyes had wandered again to the end seat on the last bench, while her lips were murmuring:

"'That it may please Thee to raise up them that fall, and finally to beat down Satan under our feet.'"

Wyatt Edgell looked up while she was praying for him—she was distinctly praying for him, she had prayed this very prayer for him every night and morning since Eric had told her how he needed her prayers—and their eyes met.

Lucy was covered with confusion. She was quite sure in that swift momentary glance that he had read her inmost thoughts. She was ashamed that he should know that she had been praying all this time that he should be strengthened and comforted and helped and picked up again when he fell, and that the enemy should be beaten down under his feet. She never looked at that end of the chapel again all the rest of the service.

It was over at last—the long, long Litany and the slow, faltering prayers: the men need not have been so restless, they would not hear them much longer. The old walls would echo another voice soon, and the feeble lips would be repeating another Litany elsewhere.

The old college chapel was full of echoes and shadows; there would be another shadow shortly, and the echo of a tremulous, quavering voice would join those other ancient echoes in the roof. It was a dark, gloomy old chapel; it had been built for hundreds of years, and it was full of old memories. Every bench and stall and desk had a memory of its own, stretching back, far back, into quite early ages—memories of old Masters and Fellows and scholars and undergraduates who had worshipped there through, oh! so many generations.

There was a musty smell of old Masters rising up from the vaults beneath and pervading the chapel, and in the ante-chapel beyond there were monuments on the walls, and brasses—quite lovely old brasses—on the pavement, and great hideous tombs of long dead and gone Masters and Fellows. It was touching to see how they were forgotten after a generation or two; how even their very tomb-stones were hidden away in a corner, and covered up with organ pipes. There was the marble effigy of an old, old Master, whose learning and virtues were recited in a long Latin epitaph on an elaborate tablet hidden away behind the organ.

Everyone had forgotten him years ago, and his old monument was in the way, and so they had covered it up. Music is so much more delightful than old memories. They will all be swept away soon, and a new chapel will be built. There will be no old memories and old ghosts and old storied windows, no decaying woodwork or musty odour of old Masters. It will all be fresh and bright and sweet-smelling and shiny as new paint and varnish can make it, and there will be a new organ with electric stops. It will be dark and shadowy no longer; the old echoes and the old ghosts will all be scared away—they will vanish quite away in the blaze of the new electric lamps with which the chapel will be lighted.

Lucy vanished out of the college chapel almost as rapidly as the ghosts will by-and-by. She did not linger in the cloisters to-day. She hurried back to the lodge, and left Cousin Mary and the Master's wife to toddle back beside the Master.

'How do you think your uncle looks to-day, my dear?' the old lady asked Lucy when they had got him safely back to the lodge, and had put him in his great armchair, and given him some wine.

There was a shade of anxiety in her voice as she asked the question. Lucy hadn't seen the Master for a week, so she might have been expected to notice any change in him.

'Oh, I think he looks lovely, aunt! He walked back from chapel quite strong.'

Mrs. Rae shook her head; she was not quite convinced.

'There were two of us supporting him, my dear, one on either side, and I thought he leant rather heavily.'

He had nearly crushed the poor little soul into the ground; she could not have supported his weight a dozen steps more.

'Perhaps you are not so strong yourself to-day, auntie dear; you are looking pale. Most likely the weakness is yours, and you are not so well able to bear his weight. He always leans heavily; I often wonder how you and Mary can keep him up!'

'Perhaps so, my dear. I hope it may be so!' But still the cloud on the dear old face did not quite vanish. 'I fancied that his reading in chapel was slower to-day than usual—that his voice was weak. Did you notice it?'

'Oh yes; I noticed that he read lovely! I never heard him read so well as he read to-day.'

'You really think so? I am very glad! The fault must be in me. I don't think I am quite so strong to-day—I can't expect to be at my age; but I am very glad there is nothing unusual the matter with the Master. You would have been quite sure to have noticed it, my dear, if there had been, as you haven't seen him for a week.'

She kissed that mendacious little Lucy and tottered out of the room. She was very feeble to-day—perhaps the Master's weight had been too much for her; but there was quite a glad smile on her patient face. She was so happy, the brave old soul, to feel that the weakness was hers, not his.

Wyatt Edgell went back straight from chapel to his own rooms. He met Eric coming out of chapel, and they went back together.

'Where have I seen that girl before?' he asked Eric when they got back to the room.

'Oh, you've often seen her in chapel. She's the Master's niece, or grand-niece, or something of the kind,' said Eric evasively.

But the other was not so easily put off.

'I have seen her somewhere else, besides in chapel,' he said thoughtfully. 'I've seen her in this room. I've seen her beside my bed. Good heavens! Wattles, you didn't let that girl in—when—when——'

'When you weren't quite yourself, old man,' said Eric cheerfully, filling up the gap. 'What on earth should the Master's niece come in here for? Be reasonable, and don't ask such foolish things!'

'Foolish or not, I'll be hanged if I didn't see her in this room, standing where you stand now! You may as well tell the truth, Wattles. You may as well say you called her in and showed her the spectacle!'

He was a very determined-looking young man, and he didn't look like one to be trifled with, as he stood with his back to the empty fireplace, leaning against the mantelpiece, and his great hands stuck down well in his pockets.

'Dear old man, you may take my word for it: I did not call her in; I should as soon have thought of calling the Master in!'

'I wish to Heaven you had called the Master in—I should have known the worst then; but for this girl to see me—in—in that state!'

He paused and groaned, and two upright lines came out on his forehead.

'You take too much for granted, old man,' said the other; but he couldn't put any heartiness into his voice. 'Haven't I told you that not a soul in the college but Brannan and myself came into the room—while—while you were ill?'

'Yes,' said the other moodily—'not a soul in the college; but this girl from Newnham came in. I'll swear it! I saw it in her eyes.'

It was no use Eric pretending. Edgell was not in a mood to be trifled with. He was a great big, determined fellow. He could have taken Eric up and flung him to the other end of the room with the same ease with which he had flung the pillow.

'Go on,' he said moodily; 'go on, and tell me all about it. Tell me why this girl came in, and the spectacle she saw. Let me know exactly the degradation to which I have sunk!'

There was no help for it. Eric had to tell him all about Lucy's visit—Lucy's second visit; he didn't say anything about the first. How could he tell the poor fellow that she had come in at that dreadful time; that it was her hands that had wiped up all the traces of his crime; that it was she who had helped him when he had put those stitches in that gaping wound in his throat!

Eric told him quite enough. His head had fallen forward on his breast, and he looked a picture of despondency. A despondent giant of six feet, with a great broad chest, and big muscular limbs, and a splendid head splendidly set on a splendid full white throat—it was muffled up now, but it was as white and shapely as a woman's beneath the crisp, close-cut whisker curling down below the cheek. His chin and his great square jaw were close-shaven, but there was a thin, slight, crisp moustache on his upper lip, and his short hair curled crisply at the edges. He wore it parted in the middle, not very neatly parted, and tossed back off his forehead. Everything about him denoted strength and courage—such a man could not be despondent long.

'Then she knows the worst,' he said—'the very worst. There is nothing else she has got to learn about me. There is only one thing to be done, Wattles, with a girl who knows so much about me: I must marry her. You must introduce me again, old man, and I shall make her an offer, and—and she will marry me.'

His gloom and depression had quite gone, and he was smiling again. He was a delightful fellow when he smiled. Not a man in the college could resist that delightful smile; it disarmed the wrath of all the Dons, and it won the hearts of bed-makers.

'Marry her!' said Eric, turning quite pale. 'Dear old man, don't be in such a hurry. Think it over. She isn't the sort of woman for you, Edgell.'

Wyatt Edgell laughed. His laugh was a full-blown edition of his smile; but Gwatkin looked serious.

'Perhaps you'll tell me, Wattles, what is the sort of woman for me.'

'Oh, I wouldn't pretend to say; only, old man, don't trifle with this poor little thing. She's the sort of girl to break her heart for a man. I wouldn't break her heart if I were you.'

'Perhaps she'll break mine,' said Edgell dryly; and then he sat down and ate his lunch which the bed-maker had already spread out on the table.

It was a very nice college lunch. It was not tinned beef, or brawn, or tongue, or any questionable dainty that had been soldered up a year or two in a metal case. It was a lovely head and shoulders of salmon, and it had been judiciously pickled, and there was cucumber cut up in a dish—little delicate flakes of cucumber which Edgell ate with the healthy returning appetite of a man who had long been denied this delicacy.

The salmon was followed by a chicken and a ham, to which he also applied himself with the same zest. The edge was quite taken off his appetite, when Eric pushed these things aside and set a jelly just freshly turned out of a mould before him.

'I don't want any of that stuff,' he said, and he pushed over his glass in the direction of the claret.

'I don't think I'd take any more, old man,' said Eric; 'you've already had four glasses. I wouldn't have any more. Have a soda?'

'I'll be hanged if I do!' said the other doggedly, 'unless you put some brandy in it. I must have a nip of brandy, Wattles. I'm sure that cucumber has disagreed with me. I haven't had any cucumber for an age, and it never did agree with me.'

Eric got up and unlocked a cupboard, and took out a liqueur-bottle more than half full of brandy, and poured a small—a very small—quantity into a glass, and filled it up with seltzer-water.

He had put the bottle back into the cupboard and the key into his pocket, and was putting on his gown to go out. He always took a service somewhere in the country, or did some open-air preaching on Sunday afternoons, and he was in a hurry to get away.

'I wish you'd leave that key behind you, Wattles,' Edgell called out when he got to the door. 'That confounded cucumber or the pickled salmon has disagreed with me. I may want the key before you come back.'

Eric took the key out of his pocket reluctantly and laid it on the mantelpiece.

'You'll be careful, old man,' he said; 'you'll be sure to be careful. Remember——'

'Shut up!' said the other angrily. 'Do you think I'm such a fool?'

Eric went out and shut the door. When he came back two hours later the liqueur-bottle was on the table empty, and Edgell was breathing heavily on the floor.

It was all that confounded pickled salmon and cucumber!

CHAPTER XI.

IN THE FELLOWS' GARDEN.

That mendacious little Lucy, in spite of all her assurances to the Master's wife, was a little anxious about the Master. He had not taken his dinner with his usual appetite; he had scarcely eaten a morsel, and he had not had his usual nap after.

He had left half the wine in his glass, and he had got up from the table earlier than usual; but he had not fallen asleep in his chair after, as was his wont. He had sat talking to Lucy all the afternoon about the old time. His memory was wonderfully clear about the things that had happened, oh! so long ago—more than half a century before she was born—and he talked to her about them as if they had happened yesterday.

He was always so glad to see Cousin Dick's little daughter; she brought back the past to him, and seemed a link between the old far-off time and the present. He recalled to-day his very earliest years, his first remembrances. He recalled the time when his brother Dick carried him on his shoulders to the fair.

'It was Midsummer Fair, my dear,' he explained, 'and your father left off work early; he was very fond of fairs, and junketings, and wrestling matches. He liked bull-baiting, too. I mind the bull-ring at the end of the village on a piece of waste ground; I dare say it is there now. I've seen many a bull baited there in my day. There was never a fair within ten miles but your father was there in his best, with a flower in his button-hole—he always wore a flower in the button-hole of his plum-coloured coat. I remember that coat well; it had gilt buttons, and he wore a waistcoat to match, with two rows of buttons on either side—it was the fashion then, my dear. He carried me on his shoulder all the way to the fair; it was held on the green; there was a large green in the middle of the village in those days, but it is built over now; things have altered since then.'

The old Master shook his head and sighed. He hated changes of any kind; he would have liked the world to go on in the same old grooves for ever. He was silent for some time, and his watchful women-folk thought he was going to sleep—that he would have his after-dinner nap, after all; but he was only thinking. Those old chambers of memory were unlocked, and the old faces of his youth were crowding around him.

'Yes,' he said presently, brightening up, 'your mother was there, too, my dear. Dick met her in a dancing-booth. She wouldn't look at Dick at first, she had so many sweethearts. She was a proud little thing, with a spirit of her own; she nearly broke Dick's heart before he married her, but she made him a good wife—a good wife and a good mother, and always in her place in church, and bringing her children up to work and to fear God. I don't know that women do more in these days when they learn so many things.'

Lucy couldn't help thinking of that motion in the House of Commons, which was carried with such an overwhelming majority, that was to admit women to practise at the Bar and in the Church, to say nothing of those other learned professions that were already practically open.

The old Master's views were very, very old-fashioned; the world had made rapid strides while he had been sitting in his armchair and reading his Sunday Litanies in that musty old college chapel.

'Your father had a spirit of his own, too, my dear,' the old man babbled on with quite surprising vigour—these old memories made him quite young again; 'he wouldn't stay there to be slighted, with all the neighbours looking on. He left your mother going round with a young spark who had come down from London, and with me on his shoulder he went through the fair. I mind the booths quite well, with the gilt gingerbread, and the toys, and the trumpets, and the drums, and the merry-go-rounds. There was a show with a fat woman—I have never forgotten that fat woman. I have never seen anything like her since. There was a dwarf there, too—the smallest dwarf that was ever seen. I remember him strutting about the stage with his little sword; he wore a sword, and a gold-laced coat, and a cocked hat. The fat lady took his arm when the performance was over—she had to stoop down to do it, and he had to stretch up. I shall never forget seeing them go off the stage, arm-in-arm—the funniest sight I have ever seen—or how the people in the show laughed and clapped their hands when the showman made a ridiculous speech as they went out. "That's the way they go to church every Sunday of their lives!" he said, pointing after them. I believed him, if the crowd didn't, and for years after I used to watch the church door to see them coming in; but I have never seen them since.'

Lucy was so anxious about the old Master that when she went for her lesson to the Tutor's rooms the next day she could do nothing but talk about him.

The Tutor was anxious too, perhaps, in another way. He had noticed a change in the Master, and he went over to the lodge with her as soon as the lesson was over.

The Master was very feeble to-day, but he was up, and downstairs, and he was talking about going out into the garden. He was very fond of the old Fellows' Garden, and the seat beneath the walnut-tree—a sunny seat in the winter, a shady seat in the summer. It was shady now, but the garden was full of sunshine; the lilacs were in bloom, and the laburnums were a blaze of gold, and the thorn-tree was white with may. It was the blossoming time of the year, and everything was at its prime.

The Tutor took him out on his arm and sat him down on his old seat. He noticed how heavily he leant upon him as he tottered feebly across the grass. He would have crushed a woman with his weight. The Master's wife came out too, and sat by his side, with his hand in hers, and Lucy walked with the Tutor in the shady, winding paths beneath the trees. The trees were all old and gnarled, and some had broken down with age, and were propped up. The borders were full of old-fashioned flowers—perennials that went down into the earth every winter, and came up again every spring. There was nothing new here.

The Senior Tutor, as he walked by Lucy's side, was thinking how he should change all this by-and-by. He would cut down those useless old trees, and he would have the turf rolled and laid out for tennis. Nothing could be better for Lucy than tennis, and she could invite her Newnham friends. Those old flower borders should be all dug up, and some standard rose-trees planted. He would have nothing but first-rate sorts, the very latest. He would do away with that vulgar cabbage rose in the corner, and that poor, shabby little pale blush that hung in clusters on the wall. It had hung there for so many years; it was quite time it should be cleared away. It seemed a pity to lose time. There were so many improvements to be made; it seemed a pity not to begin now.

Looking across the grass and the sunshine at the old stooping figure under the walnut-tree—it was bent more than usual to-day—he could not but feel that the time was not far off when it would be there no longer. There was nothing pathetic in the sight to him. He had waited for the place—the Master's place—so long. If he waited much longer he would be feeble and old and white-haired, too.

There is little pathos in the young. The sad realities of life touch only those who know something about them. One must have suffered one's self to have any sympathy with suffering.

Lucy, looking across the sunshine, was touched, in spite of herself, at the group under the walnut-tree. It didn't affect her as it affected the Tutor. It would be no gain to her if the old Master were to die; it would mean loss and change and being driven out again homeless into the wide world.

But it was not this consideration that moved her. She was touched by the tender picture of the two brave, patient old souls sitting hand-in-hand in that calm closing evening of their life.

Here was a love that Lucy knew nothing about—a love that had weathered all the storms of life, and was burning brightly at its close. Riches and honour and learning were nothing to it. They were the Master's still, but they were nothing beside love. He would leave these behind him, but love would cling to him out of time. He wouldn't shake that off when he shook off everything else.

Lucy didn't put the idea into words, but it touched her; and then, strangely enough, rose up before her the face of the man who had sat on the last seat in the chapel and had caught her looking at him. It was quite ridiculous to think of Wyatt Edgell at such a moment; there was nothing here to remind her of him.

There was an old disused greenhouse at the end of the Fellows' garden. Nothing had grown in it for years. A neglected vine was dropping down from the roof in one corner, and a great deal of the glass was broken, and the woodwork was decayed and rotting. The Tutor shook the door as he passed, and it opened, and he paused and looked in.

'I think we must have this place rebuilt,' he said, thinking aloud. 'You would like a greenhouse. We must get some ferns and palms and foliage plants. Do you like foliage plants?'

'Not much,' Lucy said. She could not think what he meant by appealing to her. 'I like flowers best. I don't care for leaves. I'm afraid my taste is very vulgar. I like geraniums, and mignonette, and camellias; I am very fond of camellias. We used to have some in our greenhouse at home.'

'You can keep as many as you like here,' he said. 'We will get all the varieties there are, and you can have geraniums in flower all the year round.'

He shut the door, and they walked down the path together, while Lucy wondered what he could mean. It would be scarcely worth while to do up the old greenhouse and fill it with flowers when it was not likely she would be there another spring to see it.

In the long path they met Cousin Mary coming towards them. She looked rather pale and worn in the sunshine, and she had on a most unbecoming garden-hat. It had been hanging up in the hall all the winter; it might have been hanging there for years, and it was battered out of all shape. There was not a bed-maker in the college that would have worn it.

The Tutor had never noticed before how gray her hair had grown, and that there were crow's-feet round her eyes, and that her cheeks were faded. She had not changed lately. She had looked like this for years, getting a little grayer every year, and adding a line or two beneath her eyes, but he had never noticed it before. He was very fond of her still; he had the highest opinion of Mary Rae, but he was very glad that Lucy had come in time—just in time—to save him from throwing himself away.

'Mr. Colville is going to have the old greenhouse done up, Mary,' Lucy shouted to her when she was quite a dozen paces away. 'He's going to have camellias and geraniums all the year round; but perhaps you don't like camellias.'

The Senior Tutor for once in his life blushed. It was not for Mary he was going to have those geraniums in perennial bloom.

'I don't think it's worth it,' said Mary bluntly—'at least, not for us. We shall soon be going away.' And she looked in the direction of the walnut-tree beneath which the old Master and his wife were still sitting.

'That should make no change,' the Tutor said awkwardly; 'the lodge would be still your home.'

He grew ridiculously red, and he did not dare to look Mary in the face.

'We need not talk about that yet,' she said with a smile; 'the dear Master is still with us. I came to ask you to help him in; he has sat there long enough. He is not so strong to-day; I can't manage him alone.'

'I should think not!' said the Tutor, and he hurried off across the grass and took the old Master back to the lodge.

Lucy did not go in; she slipped through the garden-door into the court, and hurried back to Newnham. She had promised to drink tea in a girl's room, and she was already half an hour late.

She went back by way of the Fens, and when she was near the bridge she saw some figures she thought she knew crossing it, and they stopped while she came up, and looked down into the water.

It was Pamela Gwatkin and her brother, and there was another man with him. She had never seen Pamela with her brother before, and she was struck as she came up to them with the points of difference between them.

Being twins, they ought to have been exactly alike. Eric was short, and Pamela was tall—tall and graceful and slender, as a girl ought to be, with a proud, self-reliant bearing that is peculiar to the students of a college for women. Eric was not only short, but he was stout, and not at all graceful, and he had no bearing to speak of. He was an awkward, well-meaning, commonplace fellow. There was nothing remarkable about him whatever, except that he was Pamela's twin brother. This in his case was a decided disadvantage—the ingredients hadn't been properly mixed. All the masculine characteristics had gone to Pamela, and the tender, endearing qualities to her brother. He saw Lucy come tearing along across the Fen, and he took off his hat as she came up to him.

'You have met Eric before,' said Pamela, by way of introduction.

She was looking very pink and white and cool as she stood there on the bridge looking down into the dark shady water, and Lucy had run herself into a fever, and was hot and flushed, and looking 'hideous,' as she told herself.

'Oh yes,' she panted—she was quite out of breath with running in the hot sun—'I have met Mr. Gwatkin before.'

She didn't see, until Pamela's brother introduced her, that the other man leaning over the bridge was Wyatt Edgell. She was so flustered with running, and so taken by surprise, that she blushed like a peony.

She felt she was blushing furiously, and that Pamela, cool and critical and self-possessed, was watching her. Oh, how she hated herself for not being cool and dignified and self-possessed like other people!

They walked back over the Fen and through the lane to Newnham in couples, Lucy and Wyatt Edgell in front, Pamela and her brother behind. Lucy would have given the world to have reversed the order, but the man took his place by her side, and he wouldn't go away until he left her at the gate of Newnham.

'You have met me before, Miss Rae, as well as Gwatkin,' he said, as he walked by Lucy's side. 'I believe he invited you in to see the spectacle.'

'He didn't invite me in at all,' Lucy said hotly; 'I came in. You were very ill when I saw you; I did not expect you would get well so soon.'

'No?' he said indifferently, 'I suppose not. It did not much matter either way.'

'It mattered a great deal!' she said sharply. She was very angry with him for speaking in that absurd way—absurd and ungrateful—considering what a trouble he had been to his friends. 'It mattered a great deal to Mr. Gwatkin. Oh, you don't know how anxious he was about you! He saved your life.'

'Yes,' he said in his slow, indifferent way, flicking with his cane at the nettles in the hedge; 'I believe he did. It was rather a pity he should have taken so much trouble, but I suppose he liked it. I believe he didn't get off his knees all one night. He's always glad of an excuse for getting on his knees.'

And then he laughed. It was such a delightful laugh that it ought to have been infectious, but Lucy looked grave.

'I suppose he was on his knees when you came in?' he said.

'Yes,' said Lucy shortly, but she didn't tell him that she had knelt down beside Eric and prayed that the life he valued so little might be spared. She was very angry with him; she could only trust herself to say 'Yes.'

'Oh, he is a good fellow is Wattles, but he has his little crazes.'

'He is a splendid fellow!' said Lucy warmly.

She was ashamed of her warmth the moment after she had said it, but they had reached the gate of Newnham by this time, and she was glad to say 'Good-bye' and run away. She left him standing at the gate waiting for the others to come up, while quite a dozen girls on the lawn were looking at him and admiring him, and making up all sorts of fine stories in their heads about him.

If they had only known what Lucy knew about him they would have made up a great deal more.

CHAPTER XII.

AN UGLY FALL.

There was a row royal when Pamela got back to Newnham. She told Lucy that her conduct was disgraceful, and that if it came to the ears of the Dons she would be 'hauled.'

There had been several girls 'hauled' lately for the same offence—walking with an undergraduate to the very gate of the college.

Lucy mildly suggested that she was not exactly alone, that Pamela and her brother were with her, and that she herself, when she came up to her on the bridge, was walking in the young man's society.

'You forget that Eric was with me,' Pamela replied sharply. 'It makes all the difference if you have a brother, or any male relative, with you; but to be walking alone, tearing along at the rate you were, and talking confidentially—anyone could see that you were talking confidentially—dozens of girls have been sent down for less than that!'

Lucy wasn't 'hauled,' and she wasn't 'sent down'; but Pamela behaved like a bear to her for the remainder of the term.

Lucy was so anxious about the Master that she went over to the lodge the next day directly after lunch. Cousin Mary was out; she had left him sitting in his chair taking his after-dinner nap as usual, and she had gone out. He woke up directly Lucy came in, and began to talk to her about her father and the old time. She was very glad that she had not brought Pamela in with her, or any of the Newnham girls, as she sometimes did. He would have told them that ridiculous story that was running in his mind, how his brother Dick had met her mother at a dancing-booth at the fair. He would have dwelt on all the homely details of their humble history. It would have been all over Newnham the next day that her father was a ploughman, and her mother kept a stall in the butter-market. Annabel Crewe, who had a fine taste for caricature, would have drawn delightful pictures of Lucy's progenitors—a lovely old man in a smock-frock with straw round his legs, and a milkmaid with her pail!

She couldn't divert the Master's attention from this ridiculous topic. He had forgotten all about the things that had happened in later years, and had gone back in memory to the old familiar scenes and faces of his youth. His eyes were brighter to-day, and he was more restless than usual; he wanted to go out into the garden and sit in his accustomed seat on the lawn. It was such a perfect May day that no wonder he wanted to get out of that dark, gloomy old room, with the stuffy moreen curtains over the windows, and the faded carpets, and the worm-eaten, old-fashioned furniture, and the musty old books, into the sweet summer sunshine, where everything was fresh and new.

There was nothing dark and gloomy and oppressive out there in that sweet leafy Fellows' garden. The lilacs were in their prime, pale puce and white and purple, every delightful indescribable hue, and the laburnum was dropping gold upon the grass. There was a cuckoo somewhere, calling, and the thrushes were singing, and the blackbird's note was still shrill and clear. It would soon be hoarse as a raven's, and the thrush would be silent, and the cuckoo would have altered his tune, and the lilac would have faded, and the gold of the gleaming, down-dropping laburnums would have turned to gray—and—and he might not be here to see it. If he wanted to enjoy the fleeting sunshine and the flying blossoms of the year, there was no time like the present.

The Master didn't exactly put it in this way, but he was impatient to be out in the garden, in his old seat, and he wouldn't wait a minute longer for anybody.

If Mary wasn't there he would go without her.

There are none so impatient as the old. The young have plenty of time to spare—they have their life before them; but the old have not a minute to lose. The Master went out as usual, leaning on the arm that had supported him so many years, that had never failed him yet. Mrs. Rae and Lucy took him out between them. He walked in his slow accustomed way, leaning rather heavily on these two frail props until he reached his seat beneath the walnut-tree, and here he ought to have sat down.

But he didn't sit down. He insisted on going farther; he insisted on going down the path to the greenhouse. Mary had been saying something about it, repeating what the Tutor had said yesterday about having it done up and turned to some account, and the Master would not be satisfied until he had seen it. He must be consulted about it; nothing should be done in the gardens without his consent. He had been worrying about it all night.

He had got half-way down the path, when Lucy fancied he was beginning to lean heavily, more heavily than she could bear, though she put out all her strength. There was not a seat near, but she stopped and begged the Master to rest awhile. He was so anxious to see the greenhouse that he would not listen to her. He never thought of the women who were being weighed down with his great weight. He was as eager and determined as a child.

'I am sure, aunt, you are not strong enough to keep him up,' Lucy said in despair; she was getting really frightened. 'We must get someone to help him back. Oh, if someone would only come in!'

There was not a gardener in sight, and it was not likely that anyone would come in. Nobody but the Fellows ever walked in that garden.

The Master tottered on, feebler at every step; but he would not be kept back, and the two frightened women held him up as well as they could. He seemed to want more support every step he took; he was as feeble and helpless as a child, but still he pressed on. Lucy was sure she couldn't bear the strain a minute longer, and the dear old mistress was straining with all her might to keep up with him. She was putting out all her strength. It wasn't much to put out at the best, but she didn't keep back a feather weight. Oh, if someone would only come!

They came in sight of that wretched greenhouse at last, and here the Master stopped. He didn't exactly stop, but he tottered forward, and Lucy with a supreme effort kept him up, and with all his weight upon her he swayed to and fro, and before she knew what was happening he had slipped through her arms to the ground. He lay on the path, as he fell, all of a heap. He had no power to help himself, and he lay panting and breathing heavily as he had fallen, and the women stood beside him wringing their hands.

Lucy didn't stand beside him long. There was a door in the wall beside the greenhouse that led out into one of the courts, and she flew over to it. Fortunately the door was unlocked. Lucy looked eagerly round the deserted court and raised her feeble cry for help. It was such a feeble, piteous cry; it was like a wail. A man sitting reading at an open window looked out at that strange sound, and Lucy called to him: 'Oh, come, come, do come!'

The man didn't stay to ask what had happened; he was at Lucy's side in another moment, and she took him in through the open door to where the Master lay. It was Wyatt Edgell. A gyp coming across the court had heard the cry for help, and between them they bore the Master back to the lodge.

When Mary Rae came in she found a little anxious group gathered round him, and Wyatt Edgell was trying to reassure the frightened women. Nothing very serious had happened. No bones were broken, but the Master was very much shaken, and he was not quite himself. Wyatt Edgell stayed with him until the doctor had come, and had ascertained that things were not very bad—not so bad as they might have been—and had calmed the fears of the women; and then Lucy was so shaken that he walked back with her to Newnham.

Lucy certainly would have been 'hauled' if the Dons had seen her walking back leaning heavily on an undergraduate's arm. She would have been invited to an interview with the authorities in the Principal's room, and she would have received a caution, perhaps a reprimand, and she would have been very lucky if nothing worse had happened. Lucy forgot all about the Dons and Pamela's warning. She only thought about that poor old man at the lodge.

'I don't think he will ever get over this,' she said, or rather sobbed. She was not herself at all. She was such a tearful, frightened little Lucy. She was not in the least like a Stoic.

'I am afraid not,' said Edgell. 'The Master has been failing for some time. The men all remarked that he would never read the Litany again in chapel.'

'You think he is so bad as that?' Lucy said tearfully.

'Yes, quite. Think of his age. His time must come some day, and he has lived longer than most men. You could not expect him, in any case, to live for many months longer.'

'No,' said Lucy sadly; and then he saw the tears dropping down her pale face. He could not believe she was weeping for that old, old man whose time had come, and who was a stranger to her till yesterday.

'What will you do when he is gone?' he asked abruptly.

'Do? I don't know—I have not thought. I shall stay at Newnham, I suppose, two years; I shall not be able to afford three; and then—and then I shall go out as a governess.'

'You shall never go out as a governess!' said Edgell with an oath.

Lucy looked at him, frightened and bewildered; she couldn't think what he meant, and then she broke down and began to cry.

'Dear Miss Rae—Lucy!' he said, and then he stopped and looked at the girl. He would have liked to take her in his arms, but there were several Newnham girls all hurrying down the road, and they looked at him, and they looked at Lucy. Some of them blushed, and some turned pale, and all were shocked. It was a dreadful precedent.

The atmosphere of Newnham revived Lucy, and she paused at the gate and looked up into his face with a little white smile.

'I am very stupid,' she said, 'but the Master frightened me so much, and I am not quite myself.'

He held her hand longer than he need have done, and he looked down into the small white face with a smile of ownership and protection that was quite new to Lucy. Nobody had ever looked in her eyes like that before, and, instead of drawing her hand away, Lucy hung her head and blushed like a poppy.

'Shall I bring you word how the Master is the first thing in the morning?' he said, still holding her hand; 'how early will you be out in the lane if I come?'

'Oh, as early as you like; seven o'clock!'

And so Lucy made her first appointment to meet Wyatt Edgell.

CHAPTER XIII.

SLIPPING AWAY.

When Lucy went out into the road outside the gates of the college, before seven o'clock the next morning, Wyatt Edgell was already there waiting for her. It is a short, narrow road, or lane, and it leads to nowhere, unless Selwyn College be considered anywhere. It has been the privilege of the students of Selwyn to use this road as a shortcut to their college, but it will not be their privilege much longer.

The road is now the private property of the authorities of Newnham, and a new wing connecting the old and the new halls will be built across the road, and the jealous walls that shut out the grounds from masculine eyes will be thrown down, and the old dusty lane will be covered with smooth, green turf, and it will be a thoroughfare no longer for the foot of man to pass over.

Perhaps they will restore again the old fortifications. There was a Roman camp here once, and a battle ditch running all the way to Grantchester. Every inch of ground here is classic, and strewn with remains of those old Romans who brought us all the gentler arts. Perhaps they brought the Muses with them and planted them at Newnham?

There was an old Roman dug up the other day, four feet beneath the surface, a noble skeleton, six feet six in length. The whole earth teems with ancient coins and pottery and Roman relics. They will have to build a museum in the new wing to preserve the 'finds' that are unearthed in digging its foundations.

Lucy was quite indifferent to the Romans. She would rather, if she had had the choice, have met one of their old ghosts in the lane than one of the Dons of Newnham taking her morning walk. She looked fearfully up and down the road when she got outside the gate, but there were only some Selwyn men going down to the bathing sheds; there was not a girl in sight.

Wyatt Edgell was walking up and down the path flicking at the sweetbriar hedge as he passed, and his eyes were looking down on the ground. He was so lost in thought that he did not see Lucy till he heard her little cry, and she ran to meet him.

'Oh!' she cried, a little pale and breathless, 'how is the Master? Is he worse this morning?'

She augured badly from Edgell's downcast look.

'Not worse,' he said; 'at least, I hope not worse, but I fear not better. When I inquired at the lodge when the gates were opened at six o'clock, they told me the Master had had a very disturbed night, that he had not slept at all, but that he did not appear to be in any pain. Your cousin has been up with him all night, and Mrs. Rae.'

'I was sure she would not leave him,' said the girl, the tears filling her eyes. She was thinking of the anguish in that kind old face when the Master slipped through her feeble arms. 'I think I ought to go over at once and relieve her; she must be worn out.'

Lucy didn't stay to think. She walked back to St. Benedict's with the undergraduate who had brought her the news; she didn't even stay to fetch her gloves. She walked down by his side in the morning sunshine, just as she had hurried out of her room, with a ridiculous little tennis-cap on her head and her ungloved hands. Two Newnham girls who were returning from an early—a very early—walk looked shocked, as well they might be, and some rude Selwyn men whistled as they passed. They were only jealous that she was not taking a morning walk with them.

Lucy found the watchers still up when they reached the lodge. Mrs. Rae would not be persuaded to lie down, and she was looking dreadfully tired and worn out. She looked ten years older, Lucy thought, this morning, and her poor face was as white as her hair. Mary looked pale, too. Perhaps it was the air of that close room that was still darkened; and there was a shade of anxiety under her eyes, but she would not own to being tired. She could stay up a week, if necessary.

The Master had fallen into a doze; but Lucy's light footstep or the whisper of their voices reached him, and he woke up when she came in. Lucy went over to him and laid her warm, moist hand on his, and the touch seemed to revive him.

'Is the milking over?' he asked, turning upon her his pale-blue eyes with that strange brightness in them that is peculiar to the very old. 'I have heard the cows lowing all night for the calves. You have taken the calves away?'

'It is Lucy, uncle,' she said, stroking his hand softly—'little Lucy, not Lucy's mother——' She was going to say 'grandmother,' but she thought 'mother' would humour his fancy best.

'Yes, yes: I know you, my dear. I have been watching for you all the night. You must not go away again for so long; they don't understand me here as you do. Where's Dick?'

'He is gone, uncle,' she said softly. She did not like to say that he was dead.

'Gone? Where is he gone? He was here just now. Is he in the field or in the barn? Send him to me when he comes in, my dear.'

Lucy turned away pale and trembling. She could not bear it; he did not recognise her in the least.

The Tutor came in while she was there, and went over to the bed; but the Master took him for Dick—the brother who had died fifty years ago.

His eyes lighted up when the Tutor came in, and with a strange, eager interest he asked him questions about the crops and the farm. All the later associations of his life had quite faded from his memory, and he had gone back to the scenes and faces of his youth.

The Tutor turned away from the bed with a sigh. He had waited for this half his life. He had looked forward so long as he could remember to being Master of St. Benedict's, and now, when it seemed within his grasp, he turned from it with a sigh. What was it, after all, this shadow he was grasping? Wealth, honour, position, it would all slip through his hands by-and-by, as it had slipped through the hands of the old scholar on the bed: all, everything, that had taken a lifetime—a long lifetime—to gain, would slip away, and there would be nothing left but old memories. Everything would fail; and he would go back to the old humble time, and the dear faces—if happily he had dear faces to go back to. There would be nothing left—nothing that he could carry away with him—but those old tender memories.

The Tutor turned away from the bed and went out of the room. On the landing outside he saw Lucy sitting in the window-seat weeping. The tears were in his own eyes, and he could not trust himself to speak. He went over, and took Lucy's hand, and drew her towards him.

'Oh,' she murmured through her tears, 'he does not know me the least bit. He thinks I am his brother Dick's wife.'

'And he takes me for Dick,' said the Tutor, with an involuntary smile, pressing the little warm hand he held. 'We shall all come to it, my dear, some day—to the vanishing-point, where everything slips away from us but the memories of our youth. Well for us at that time if we have nothing but innocent memories of kindly deeds and loving faces—if we have no regrets, no sorrow, no remorse! Perhaps it is the happiest lot to have the slate wiped clean of all the storms and passions of later years, and to go back at the last, and to take away with us only the memory of the old innocent early days.'

He was a good deal moved. He might have committed dreadful crimes since the days of his innocent youth, instead of being a grave, sober, reverend Tutor of a college.

'You don't think he will ever be better?' Lucy sobbed.

'I don't think, even if his life is prolonged, that his mind will ever be clear again. I fear it has gone, quite gone. Perhaps it is better so: he will pass away happier; he will have no regrets; he will leave nothing behind.'

Lucy sat sobbing in the window-seat. If she had been older she would not have wept so freely: the young have so many tears to spare.

'There is nothing to regret,' he said tenderly, bending over the hand he still held. 'The dear Master has lived his life—a good life, and, I think, a happy one—and he will exchange it for a better and a happier. We have only to concern ourselves about those who are left—Mrs. Rae and your cousin. They must stay with us, Lucy; they must make the lodge their home. You must let them understand, dear'—here the Senior Tutor really pressed Lucy's hand, that he had held all the time he had been talking to her, and she had never once thought of drawing it away: he would have taken her in his arms, but the servants were coming up and down stairs—'you must let them quite understand,' he went on, 'that their home is here with us. I am sure we shall do everything to make them happy.'

Lucy hadn't the least idea what he meant.

She would have stayed at the lodge and taken her share of the nursing night and day, but the Tutor would not hear of it.

'You have got your work to do, my dear,' he said. He called her 'my dear' now quite naturally. 'You have all your work cut out before you to be ready for the examinations in June. You can't afford to risk breaking down for the sake of doing work that any woman can do. A trained nurse from Addenbroke's will do all, and more than all, you three dear anxious women together.'

He sent in a nurse from Addenbroke's during the morning, and Cousin Mary and the Master's wife were turned out of the room. It was quite time the Master's wife was turned out of the room, or there would have been two to nurse instead of one.

The nurse who had been sent from Addenbroke's Hospital to nurse the Master was the little fluffy nurse that had been brought by her brother to Wyatt Edgell's rooms after that miserable folly, and had kept his secret.

If Lucy didn't like trusting a foolish young man she knew nothing about to this flighty nurse, she was much more unwilling to trust this valuable life in her hands. She watched with mistrust, and a certain dull glow of impatience, this little bit of a creature turn the Master's wife out of the room, and reverse everything that had been done under Cousin Mary's directions.

The nurse from Addenbroke's pulled up the blinds and threw open the windows, and let in the balmy air of the sweet May morning, that everybody had been so anxious to keep out; and she threw off the heavy quilts, and took away the pillows, and did everything according to the latest fashion in nursing. If people do not choose to get well when all this is done for them, it is their own fault, and not the fault of the system.

Before Lucy went back to Newnham she went into the little room—her own room till she had left it for Newnham—where the Master's wife had gone to lie down to rest. She had chosen this room because it was near the Master's, and she would be within call.

Lucy insisted on undressing her and putting her to bed, and perjuring herself with fibs of the deepest dye to set her mind at rest.

'I never thought he would go before me,' the dear old soul murmured, when Lucy was undressing her. 'I always thought I should go first; and it has been such a comfort to me to think that Mary could fill my place so well. And now to think that he should be called away first!'

'Who said he would go first?' Lucy said in her reassuring manner. 'He is not at all likely to go before you, you poor dear! If you had been yourself, he would not have fallen. You had no strength left, so he slipped through your poor arms. You hadn't the strength of a baby. Anyone can see how you have been failing lately, and you think it is the Master.'

'And you think it was my fault he fell—that the weakness was not in him?' the poor trembling old creature asked eagerly. She was so anxious to believe Lucy, and the faint colour flushed up under her white skin.

'Of course it was. The doctor will not tell you it was, because he doesn't want to frighten you. Anyone can see that you are much weaker than the Master.'

There really seemed some truth in what Lucy said. The Master's wife was trembling all over like a leaf—she couldn't have got into bed without Lucy's help; but she was trembling with joy.

'God bless you, my dear!' she said, when the girl went away. 'You have made me so happy!'

Lucy went back to Newnham with a heavy heart. It seemed as if everything were slipping away from her. It is so hard for the young to realize the great change. She felt dimly that it was not far off—that this was, indeed, the beginning of the end. Anyone could have seen that.

But it was not the personal sorrow of it that moved her; there was a deeper pathos than death in the fidelity of the dear woman who clung to the old Master with a love stronger than death itself. She could not but think of the look of relief on the old tired face as she walked back to Newnham.

The girls remarked that Lucy looked pale at Hall—that is, those who took any interest in her. Pamela Gwatkin never looked her way. She sat at the 'High,' among the Dons; she never condescended to look down the hall to the table where the freshers sat.

Capability Stubbs came into her room after Hall, as she sat trying to work, and brought her in a cup of tea. The tea was very grateful to Lucy's overwrought nerves: it was the only thing that was nice about Miss Stubbs. Pamela Gwatkin had given her a cup of tea once or twice, but it tasted of tooth-powder. She had packed the tea and the tooth-powder in a biscuit-tin when she came up, and the lid had got off the tooth-powder box, and it had got mixed up with the tea. It would not have been political economy to have thrown it away.

'Nice scandal you've been making in the college!' observed Miss Stubbs cheerfully, as she handed Lucy the teacup. She had only brought a teacup; she considered saucers superfluous, unless one happened to be a kitten.

'Scandal!' said Lucy, aghast. 'What scandal have I been making?'

'Oh! it was rumoured you had eloped with a Selwyn man. Somebody saw you going off.'

'With a Selwyn man!' said Lucy with fine scorn. 'As if I should elope with a Selwyn man! If it had been St. Benedict's it would have been different.'

'Or Hall?' suggested Miss Stubbs, who was rumoured to have a cousin at Trinity Hall, or to know a girl who had.

'Ye—es; even Hall would have been better. Who set the ball rolling—Newnham Assurance?'

Lucy was much too angry with Pamela to call her by her name.

'No, it wasn't Assurance. She took the other side. She said if you were going to run away with—with a man, you would have had the self-respect to stop and put your gloves on first.'

CHAPTER XIV.

WYATT EDGELL.

Late on the evening of the day when Lucy was supposed by the students of Newnham to have eloped, the man she was said to have eloped with sat working in his college-room.

It was not a Selwyn man. The crest on the pocket of the blazer he was wearing was the crest of St. Benedict's. It was nearly the eve of the Mathematical Tripos; there were only a few days more, and, having lost all the early part of the term, Wyatt Edgell was sitting down now at the last minute to recover by a tremendous effort the ground he had lost. He had always been sure of a first; he had never yet taken a second class in any examination at school or college, and his name had generally stood first in the lists. The authorities of St. Benedict's had predicted that it would stand first now in the coming Tripos.

There would have been no doubt about it but for that ugly 'accident'—he called it an 'accident'—in the beginning of the term. He had not been himself since he came up this May term. He had been moody and taciturn, and subject to fits of depression. He had given up his wine-parties, and his club suppers and breakfasts, and he had shut himself up in his rooms and sported his oak. Everybody, Tutors and all, said he was working hard, and they 'let him alone'; but his bed-maker knew better! Bed-makers know so much more about a man than anyone else.

She fetched Gwatkin to him one morning, when she had come in and found him lying on the floor in a fit of delirium tremens. They kept the matter quiet between them and put him to bed, and the bed-maker gave out to all the men on her staircase that 'he was a-readin' hisself to death.'

It was not a very bad attack—it was not the first, but Gwatkin didn't know that at the time—there were no violent ravings, only mutterings and depression—dreadful depression. Gwatkin and the bed-maker looked after him during the morning, and towards noon he fell into a deep sleep. It didn't seem at all likely that he would wake for hours. The bed-maker had had some experience of such cases, and she knew that the fever would take eight or ten hours' sleep to spend itself, and then he would awake with shaking hands and a splitting headache, and have a fine time of it for a week.

Leaving him as she thought sleeping soundly, she went about her work. She had to clear the tables of the other men on the staircase, but before she went she took the precaution to fasten his oak, and to take the key to Gwatkin's rooms.

Gwatkin ran over as fast as he could to Edgell's rooms. He had given such strict injunctions that he was not to be left alone on any pretence. Run as fast as he could, he was only just in time. Had he been a minute later he would have been too late. He took the razor from the poor fellow's hand, and he bound up the wound he had made with it as he best could without assistance. He had not the heart to call for help, to reveal his miserable secret to the whole college. He did for him as he would have wished others to have done for himself if he had been in his place. He kept his secret.

There was a man on his own staircase who had a sister a nurse at Addenbroke's, and when he had done all he could for Edgell, and fastened his arms down to the bed, Gwatkin ran across the court and brought Brannan over. He had to let him into the secret; there was no help for it. He saw exactly how matters stood. He was in his third year, and it was not the first time that he had helped to cover up an act of undergraduate folly. Brannan went away to fetch his sister. He could promise her silence. Phyllis Brannan was as true as steel; but in his haste and agitation he had left the outer oak open, and Lucy came in.

Wyatt Edgell's secret had been faithfully kept by these men and women. Only one of them had committed a breach of trust—Lucy had told Pamela. She couldn't help it, she explained, if she had had to die for it the next day; but Pamela had held her tongue. Not a soul in the college guessed his secret—his dreadful secret. Everybody looked up to him, and praised him, and expected great things of him—everybody but his bed-maker.

She knew something about that last orgie. She had helped to put him to bed, and she had cleared away the small sodas the next morning. She smiled when she saw him settling down to work on the evening of the day when he had brought Lucy to the lodge from Newnham. 'A lot of readin' 'e'll get through,' she said, shaking her head as she went down the stairs with her basket under her shawl. "E'll be under the table, I reckon, when I come in in the mornin'.'

Eric Gwatkin was doubtful about him, too. He was more anxious about Edgell's Tripos than he was about his own Special. He couldn't rest before he went to bed without coming over and seeing if he was all right. He found his oak sported, and he had to knock a good many times before Edgell would let him in.

'Confound it——' he began, and then he saw Eric and stopped. 'Oh, it's you, Wattles!'

He didn't say it very graciously, and Eric was sorry he had disturbed him. He really looked in working trim. He had thrown off his coat, and he was sitting in his shirt-sleeves. He wore a flannel shirt, and the collar was open and showed his white throat and chest, as it had showed it that day when Lucy leaned over the bed and put on the wet bandage. It showed, too, what it had not shown on that day, when a scarf was thrown over the throat—an ugly scar extending for some inches beneath the left ear. It was still purple and red and discoloured—a hideous livid mark on the beautiful white skin.

Eric shuddered when he saw it. The sight of it always made him shudder to think what a near thing it was—what might have been! He could not understand how Edgell could bear to see it in the glass, could bear to uncover it, that others coming in might see it.

'I am sorry to disturb you, old man,' he said, looking round at the work on the table, and the books lying open before Edgell. 'I only looked round to see—if—if you were all right.'

'To see if I had cut my throat again,' said Edgell calmly.

There was a shade of bitterness in his voice, and his lips curled slightly with amusement or scorn, or both. They were beautiful clear-cut lips, full and tender as a woman's, and they had a way of curving when he spoke. They never quivered, they curved; and his nostrils dilated. It was a strong face, with a massive square jaw, but it had these nervous tricks.

'Very kind of you, Wattles,' he went on with a laugh; 'but I'm not going to repeat that performance again—at least, not for the present. I'm going in for my Trip—and—and I'm going to marry Miss Lucy.'

Gwatkin's face fell.

'I don't think this is a time to talk of marrying,' he said, with a certain hesitation in his voice, and the cloud on his plain, homely face deepening. 'The poor old Master is dying.'

'So much the more reason to talk about it. Lucy will want a home. She won't be able to stay up at Newnham, she tells me; she will have no one but her cousin Mary when the Master is dead, and the old lady. I think I shall ask her to-morrow. I should like her to feel that she will not be left friendless when the end comes.'

'I should wait till after the exam., if I were you. I shouldn't let anything interfere with the exam. You will have all your life to marry in.'

Edgell lay back in his chair and laughed good-naturedly at his Mentor.

'Anyone would think, Wattles, that you wanted to marry her yourself.'

There was no occasion for that very common-place-looking young man to blush so dreadfully.

'I only meant to advise you for your good,' he said awkwardly, and then he went over to the door and said good-night; but when he reached the door, and he had the handle in his hand, he paused irresolutely, and looked across the room at the man with the scar in his throat leaning back in the chair. The scar was dreadfully visible in that light. It seemed to have a charm for Gwatkin. He couldn't keep his eyes off it.

'What's up?' said Edgell, seeing that he paused by the door.

Eric came back to the table where Edgell was seated, and laid his hand on his shoulder, a friendly, unmistakable grip.

'Dear old man,' he said in a broken voice, and the other could see that his foolish weak lips were quivering, 'you won't mind my speaking my mind to you; you will forgive what I say?'

'Fire away!' said Edgell; but he didn't look at Gwatkin, he looked at the opposite wall.

'Before you go any farther—before you ask Lucy Rae to marry you—pause and consider——'

'I've already considered,' Edgell interrupted impatiently, and with his face still averted.

'You have not considered everything. You have thought only of yourself. You have not thought of her.'

'I have thought of her!'

'No, no; you have not thought of her in the way I mean. Bear with me, dear fellow. God knows I am saying this for your sake and hers. You have not thought of her as orphaned and friendless, having no one but you in the world, being bound up in you, having all her happiness dependent upon you. A little, tender, delicate creature, with no spirit of her own, who would suffer, and break her heart, and never complain——'

'What would she have to complain of?' Edgell interrupted savagely.

'God only knows!'

'You—you think I shall go over the old thing again—that——'

'Hush! For heaven's sake don't let us even suppose it! You haven't got to consider yourself in this matter, you have to consider her. Do you think it fair to ask her—to—to—forgive me, dear fellow—to ask her to risk it?'

Wyatt Edgell bowed his head.

'You have no faith in me,' he said moodily, with his head upon his breast and his brows knitted.

'I have every faith in you, dear fellow; but I want you to think of her. It is the chivalrous thing to do. Forgive me for saying it. Unless you felt that you could make her happier than any other man in the world—and—and ensure her happiness, you have no right to ask her to marry you!'

Eric Gwatkin was quite astonished at his own temerity—astonished and frightened. He was a weak, nervous, emotional fellow; he couldn't trust himself to say another word. His voice broke, and his eyes were clouded, and he was afraid he had said too much, and with a grip of Edgell's great muscular shoulder he went away and left him sitting in his chair, with his head on his breast, and that ugly scar gleaming like the dark blade of a knife across his white throat.

END OF VOL. I.

CHAPTER XV.

IN THE LANE.

'The rain was raining cheerfully,
As if it had been May.'

Lucy was five minutes late the next morning in keeping her appointment—at least, her understood appointment—in the lane. There was a reasonable excuse for it. It was not a morning fit for a dog to go out in. It was a shivering, blowy, rainy morning. There are not many trees at Newnham, and what few there are tossed their arms wildly in the air, and sighed and moaned as the wind whistled through the leaves. They had not shed many tears as yet; they were fresh young leaves with the tender green of the year upon them, but they were shedding a great many to-day.

After this night of weeping they would never be the same leaves again; they would have grown darker and sadder; they would have begun to shiver by night and whisper by day. They were whispering overhead as Lucy stood beneath them, with her umbrella turning inside out, looking up and down the lane.

The man she was looking for was not there. His bed-maker, who was certainly a seer or a sibyl, had found him an hour before under the table of his room, with his lamp still burning, and the liqueur-case in his cellaret—at least, it was on the table—empty, quite empty.

She had fetched Eric, who was up betimes reading for his 'special,' and between them they had put him to bed, and Eric had come out in the wind and the rain to keep his appointment.

Lucy wasn't looking for Eric. She took no notice of the little fellow in a covert-coat who was sheltering behind the hedge. She was looking for a splendid manly form, clad in a big Inverness coat, perhaps, and indifferent to the wind and the rain.

Eric joined her directly she got outside the gate.

'I have just come from the lodge,' he said. 'The Master has passed a better night. He has had several hours' sleep.'

Lucy looked at him with a question in her eyes that had nothing to do with the Master.

'Why didn't Mr. Edgell come?' she said almost sharply. 'Why did he send you?'

Eric couldn't look into her eyes and tell her a fib. They were such clear, straightforward eyes, they seemed to look quite through him.

'Edgell is working for his Tripos,' he said evasively. 'He has only a few days longer before him.'

'He isn't working at this time in the morning?' said Lucy, looking straight at him.

He couldn't meet her eyes. He looked up admiringly at the red-brick front of Newnham as if he had never seen it before.

'No,' he said; 'he is not working now—he is——'

'I know what he is, without your trying to shield him,' Lucy interrupted with fine scorn. 'He is lying most likely drunk and incapable on the floor, or he is raving on his bed, and seeing hideous things. Oh, Mr. Gwatkin, what is the good of your friendship if you cannot keep him from this?'

Eric hung his head.

'He is beyond my keeping,' he said sadly. 'He is beyond the reach of my poor prayers. God knows I pray for him night and day!'

Lucy didn't say that she had been praying for him that very morning, that she had only just got off her knees, and come out in the rain to meet him.

'Will nothing save him?' she said, wringing her hands.

'Yes,' Eric said slowly, looking at her with troubled eyes; 'there is one thing that would save him.'

She looked up at him, and their eyes met, and her heart gave a great bound, and something seemed to surge up in her ears, and swim before her eyes, and choke in her throat. She wasn't quite sure for a minute if anything had happened to her; and when her heart beat again, and the wave went back, and the trees and the college ceased to go round, Eric was looking down at her with his troubled eyes, and his weak lips quivering as he spoke.

'The one thing that would save him would entail sacrifice—the sacrifice of a life—and only a noble woman could make it——'

'You mean,' she said, speaking hoarsely—that lump in her throat hadn't gone yet—'you mean that a woman could save him?'

'Yes,' he said, almost with a groan; 'but it would be at her own cost.'

'Not if she loved him?'

'Yes; all the more if she loved him.'

Lucy turned away, and the wind got under her umbrella and turned it inside out, and made a diversion.

'There is no other way?' she said, when Eric had brought it back into something like shape, and returned it to her.

'No,' he said, 'there is no other way.'

Lucy put down her umbrella—she would battle no more with the storm—and the rain came down in a sheet and wetted her through and through as she walked slowly back to the college.

There was a crowd of girls round the table in the hall when she came in. The postman had just been, and the letters were lying on the hall table, and the girls were crowding round. Among the girls standing by the table was Pamela Gwatkin. She looked up when Lucy came in wet and draggled, and a dull red flush crept up under her skin, and her lips tightened.

'Wherever has she been such a morning as this?' said one of the girls aloud as Lucy passed them.

She didn't pause at the table and look for her letters like the rest. She didn't expect letters by every post like other girls; the coming of the postman never stirred her pulse the least. She had no one to write to her.

Pamela didn't vouchsafe Lucy another look, but went back to her room with her head lifted high, and her letters—she had quite a sheaf of them, letters and papers—clutched to her bosom. She didn't attempt to open them when she got back to her room. She went straight to the window and looked out at the blinding rain.

'She has been to meet him again,' she murmured; 'and such a morning as this! She must be very far gone. Oh, it is outrageous! It is quite indecent!'

Another girl who had seen her come in followed Lucy back to her room, and just as she had reached it Lucy shut the door in her face.

Nothing daunted, Capability Stubbs tried the handle of the door, but Lucy had locked it on the inside; no doubt she was taking her wet things off. One doesn't take the occasion to hold a levee when one is wet to the skin.

Lucy did not appear at breakfast. Nobody missed her but Maria Stubbs; everybody else was too much occupied with her own affairs.

The very air of the place was full of examinations, and the loss, the total disappearance, of half a dozen girls, more or less—freshers—wouldn't have been noticed at this exciting moment.

Before she went to her morning's work Miss Stubbs tried Lucy's door again. It was open this time; the housemaid had just come out, and there was that silly little Lucy sitting at her table with her wet things still on. There was a strained look on her white face, as if she had been working at a problem all night, and it hadn't come out right yet.

'Oh, good gracious!' Miss Stubbs exclaimed, when she came over to the girl and put her hand on her wet shoulder. 'Whatever are you sitting here for?'

Lucy looked up with a faint look of wonder in her eyes, and then, finding she had forgotten to take off her wet things, she began slowly to peel them off one by one.

Maria Stubbs had no patience with her. She pulled and dragged at her clinging wet garments, and tore off her shoes, and wrapped her up in a warm dressing-gown of her own that she ran across the passage to fetch. When she had got her out of her wet rags, she fetched her a cup of hot tea from the hall, where the tea-urn was still steaming, and then she began to bully her.

'A fine cold you will catch,' she grumbled, 'and give no end of trouble. I dare say you'll expect us to stay up of nights to nurse you. I give you notice, it's no use to expect me to nurse you; I've got my own work to do.'

Lucy feebly protested that she didn't expect Miss Stubbs to make a martyr of herself, and that she had no intention of being ill, but Maria was not so easily appeased.

'It isn't as if it were an examination,' she said in an aggrieved tone; 'then we could understand it. There'd be an excuse for a girl making an idiot of herself if she had been ploughed in an exam. I've known a girl refuse to eat anything for a week, because she failed twice in her additionals; and another girl—but this was a more serious case; her mind gave way quite on the last day of the exam., and she had to be sent to an asylum. I shouldn't be at all surprised if they were to send you to——'

'Not to the asylum!' said Lucy, in a sudden fright.

She was so bewildered she felt very much like going there already.

'I didn't mean that, silly!' Miss Stubbs said scornfully. 'I was going to say the infirmary. If you will go and get influenza, you can't expect to stay among people who are going in for examinations. Suppose I were to catch it—or Assurance! I'm not sure that Assurance hasn't caught something already. She begins her Tripos on Monday, and she's about as amiable as a bear.'

Maria Stubbs went back to her work—she was going to be shut up four hours in a laboratory among delightful smells—but before she went she made Lucy promise that she would ask the housekeeper to give her some breakfast.

Later in the day Lucy went over to the lodge to see the Master. The wind had gone down, but a gray mist hung over everything, and the trees were no longer rustling their leaves overhead. The branches were drooping with their own weight, and the leaves were limp, and dropping slow tears upon her as she passed beneath.

The Master was better to-day, decidedly better. He had slept several hours during the night, and he looked quite himself, Lucy thought, when she went into the room and saw him propped up in his chair. He was up and dressed; he had insisted on being dressed; they could not keep him in bed; and his chair was wheeled over to the window, where he sat looking out on to the river, and the path beneath the trees where an old, old philosopher used to walk long ago.

He had always loved that path by the river-side. It had been his favourite walk once. Perhaps the old associations had something to do with it; they have with most of the things men value in Cambridge. A great past seems to meet one at every college gate. Every inch of ground has its own sacred memories, and the path beneath the trees had echoed to the tread of generations of poets, sages, and scholars since the old philosopher walked there.

But it was not of the philosopher that the Master dreamed, as he sat looking out on the gray path and the blurred river. It was no longer the Cam he saw; it was the babbling trout-stream that ran by his father's farm—the gray shallow river that skirted the meadows, and swept beneath the arches of the old bridge, and roared in a torrent over the weirs.

'You are better to-day, uncle,' Lucy said, as she stood beside his chair and looked down at the worn old face, and the white hair on the pillow.

'Better? I am quite well, my dear. I have just come in from fishing, and I am tired. I have caught quite a large basket, and I have walked a long way beside the river. Dick wouldn't wait for me. He went home early. Perhaps it was as well.'

Lucy looked anxiously at the nurse.

'He is better in himself,' Nurse Brannan said softly. 'He has had a good night, and has awoke much refreshed, but his memory is gone. I don't think it will ever be better.'

Nurse Brannan had made a great change in the sick-room; it didn't look like a sick-room. It was as light and bright as it well could be on such a dull day, and there was a small fire burning in the grate, and a big bowl of lilac on the table—the Master was very fond of lilac.

Lucy ran her fingers through the sweet pale-purple buds as she stood beside the table. She was not fond of picking things to pieces like the Science girls, who can never see a flower without tearing its heart out. She was content to bury her face in a posy and drink in its sweetness and beauty. She buried her face in the bunch of lilac as she stood beside the Master's chair, and the old man watched her with his dim eyes.

They suddenly brightened as he watched her; they were dim no longer; they were bright and shining. Something in her attitude, or in the smell of the flowers, had brought back to him the old time: the old lane that skirted the farm with the blossoming hawthorn-trees on either side, and the orchard with the smell of the apple-blossom, and the lilac hanging over the garden-wall.

'Ah,' he said, 'you picked this from the old tree by the gate. I noticed it was coming into bloom this morning when I passed, and the pink thorn is in bud, and the orchard is a sight to see.

The fragrance of the old days was about him, and its colours were unfaded. Lucy left him babbling to the nurse about the flowers that used to grow in the old garden of his childhood. His heart, like that of a little child, had gone back at the close of the journey to the place from which he had first set out.

Cousin Mary was with Mrs. Rae; she had been up with her all night. There was as much need for nursing here as in the Master's room. Lucy was quite shocked at the change that a few hours had wrought in the Master's wife. She looked years older to-day, and her face had changed. All the cheerful brightness that had given an air of youthfulness to it into extreme old age was gone now. It was placid and resigned, but it was youthful and bright no longer.

There was nothing the matter with her, Cousin Mary said, but the shock had been too much for her. A few days' rest and quiet, the doctor thought, might bring her round.

'You have seen the Master?' she asked Lucy eagerly when she came into the room.

Lucy noticed that the voice, like the face, had changed, and grown feeble and old.

'Yes; I have seen the Master. He is so much better to-day. He is sitting up by the window. He is quite himself.'

She didn't say anything about that fishing excursion of his, nor how tired he felt now the day's work was done.

'He is really better?'

She asked this with a strange eagerness, and laid her thin hand on Lucy's.

'Yes, dear, really better. He will soon be quite well. It is you who are the invalid now. You must make haste and get well, too.'

'Thank God!' said the feeble voice, and the thin hand relaxed its hold, and she fell back on the pillow. 'Someone told me he was wandering,' she said—'that he did not know anyone. But perhaps I am mistaken. It may be in me. I may have dreamed it.'

'Yes, dear,' Lucy said reassuringly, 'it is in you. You have certainly dreamed it.'

She left the old woman quite happy, but tears were dropping from her own eyes as she went slowly down the stairs of the lodge. She was not quite sure in this tender casuistry if she was not giving the Master's wife the sentence of death.

CHAPTER XVI.

THE OLD, OLD STORY.

What on earth possessed Lucy to go out into the lane again the next morning at that ridiculously early hour, before seven o'clock, she could never tell. She was not anxious about the Master. She had left him in good hands, sitting beside the window babbling about the lilac-bushes in the old garden.

Perhaps it was because it was such a lovely May morning that Lucy went out into the lane; it was a shame to stay indoors a minute longer.

A change had come over the scene since yesterday. The clouds had all passed away like magic, and the sun was shining, and the sky was blue above, and the earth was green beneath, and, oh, how the birds were singing! There was no excuse for Lucy being in bed. Most of the girls had been up working hours ago, and some had not been in bed since daybreak.

She didn't expect to meet anyone in the lane; she only went out, and looked round, quite by the way, and—and she saw Wyatt Edgell coming to her, up between the green hedgerows, where the hawthorn was in bloom, and beneath the blue sky, where a lark—where a dozen larks were singing, and she had never seen so delightful a picture before in her life.

Like the storm of yesterday, all traces of that midnight debauch had passed away. His face ought to have been pale and soddened, and his eyes dull and heavy, with great bags beneath them, but they were not the least changed. The fine intellectual beauty of the face was finer than ever, and the mere physical beauty, which no girl could look upon untouched, was seen to its best advantage on this sweet May morning.

Wyatt Edgell wore a straw hat with the ribbon of his college around it. He had just come from the river, fresh from his bath, and the sun had dried his hair as he had come along, and it curled all over his head in short crisp curls like a god. His face was glowing and his eyes were shining; he looked a picture of perfect health and manly beauty.

We have had so many studies of Venus rising fresh from her bath, but the artists have not been so keen on Adonis.

A sweet thing in oils, not 'The Bather,' but 'The Bathed,' would be a novelty on the walls of the Academy.

There are no baths at Newnham, only six feet of zinc to splash about in, and that one has to take in turn at the end of a lane of girls waiting in the passage. Lucy wouldn't have had her turn for another hour this morning, so she had dressed without it, and had come out into the lane to take a bath of sunshine instead.

She looked paler than if she had had her turn of splashing in eighteen inches of water, but her hair wasn't limp and wet and untidy.

Her heart couldn't help beating a little faster as Wyatt Edgell came towards her, and her face burnt hotly. She could feel that she was blushing like a milkmaid.

'Oh, you here!' she said in quite a tone of surprise. 'I didn't expect you this morning.'

He didn't believe her. He couldn't look down into her glowing face and believe she had put on all those blushes to meet the burning gaze of Apollo, unless, indeed, she expected Wattles.

'No?' he said with a smile, and he imprisoned her hand; 'but I couldn't keep away. I had something to tell you this morning.'

'About the Master?' she said, turning pale.

'No; it has nothing to do with the Master. I asked for him at the lodge as I came out, and they told me he had had a good night. Phyllis Brannan is with him, and she is a host in herself.'

Lucy tossed her head.

'Oh, you know Nurse Brannan?' she said coldly.

'Yes,' he said gravely; 'I have reason to know Phyllis, best and kindest of nurses. If ever there was a woman true as steel, it is Phyllis Brannan.'

Lucy sniffed impatiently. She hadn't come out without her bath at seven o'clock in the morning to hear the praises of Nurse Brannan. She was quite sure she would be quite as good a nurse after a reasonable probation, and she wouldn't keep her hair so untidy.

'What had you got to tell me?' she said shortly.

It was not exactly encouraging; but Edgell smiled and drew her away from the gate and up the lane, and then she discovered that he still held her hand.

She drew it away sharply and stopped. She really didn't care to walk any farther with him if he were only going to talk about Nurse Brannan. She had been fighting a dreadfully hard battle with herself all night, all the previous day—ever since that conversation with Eric—and she had worked herself up, like the martyrs of old, for a big sacrifice, for the stake, if need be; and now, after all that struggle, there wasn't going to be any stake at all.

Nurse Brannan was going to the stake, perhaps. She was ready at any time to do all sorts of disagreeable things without making any fuss about them.

'Would you mind walking this way?' he said, and he led Lucy unresisting up the lane into that narrow part, past the posts, between the high hedges, that shut them out from all curious eyes.

'I have come to ask you a question,' he said, speaking low, with a little catch in his voice, 'and I want an answer before I go back to work. The Tripos begins on Monday. Will it be worth while to go in for it?'

'What do you mean?' she said; but she knew very well what he meant.

'I think you know what I mean, Miss Rae—Lucy. I think you know more about me than any other woman. If you will tell me I have anything to work for, I will go back and work, and—and some day I will come to you again; but if—if there is nothing to work for, I shall go down to-day.'

'You would not throw up your chance?' she said. She was quite pale, and she was trembling all over.

'I should certainly throw it up. What would be the use of a degree to me with that before me? There is only one thing, Lucy, to stand between me and it. My sentence must come from your lips. Am I to go back and work?'

No one looking at him standing there in the sunshine, with that smile on his face, would have dreamed the issue that hung on the girl's lips. She couldn't realize it herself; she could only gasp and tremble. He had quite taken her breath away. She would have given the world to run away without giving that fateful answer, but the lane was narrow, and he stood before her.

'Well,' he said, watching with his eager, questioning eyes the changes on her face, 'am I to go back to work?'

What could she say? Her lips faltered, and the words would not come; again she tried, but his sentence lingered.

There was a merle singing in the elm-tree above, and a thrush was calling for its mate, and the wood-pigeons were cooing softly in the orchard over the hedge; everything was so glad and happy and full of life and love on this May morning; every voice in nature was pleading for him.

Her face was dreadfully pale, and her lips were quivering, and her heart was beating like a hammer. She looked up into his face with a strange white terror in her eyes, and she saw the scarf round his throat. It was the coloured striped scarf of his college, and he wore it twisted on that balmy morning round his throat. The sight of that scarf decided her.

'I think you must go back to work,' she said softly, with just a little wan smile.

He caught her in his arms, to his heart, and kissed her on the forehead.

'God bless you, Lucy!' he said—'God bless you, darling!'

The pressure of his arms, the strange, sweet pressure of his warm lips on her forehead, brought the blood back to her heart, to her cheeks, and she drew herself away, flushing scarlet.

A Newnham girl came in at one end of the lane, and a Selwyn man came in at the other, and they went back to their respective colleges and told the tale. It was all over Newnham at breakfast-time that Lucy had been seen kissing a man in broad daylight just outside the walls of the college.

The old, old story has been told a great many times, in a great many ways, but it had never been told at Newnham before or at Girton in such a barefaced way. It will be told in the public streets next, or perhaps in the Senate House.

CHAPTER XVII.

IN THE PICTURE-GALLERY.

The term wore on, and there was nothing talked of in Cambridge but examinations. How could one talk about anything else when it was the subject uppermost in everybody's mind? There were the boat-races, and the college balls, and the concerts, but exciting as these were to the sisters and cousins of the men, they were of secondary importance to the exams.

The nearer the day approaches for the dreaded trial the more dreadful seems the finality of the approaching result. Nobody questions the finality of the sentence at the time, and when it happens to be adverse men go away and hide their heads and think that all things are at an end for them. By-and-by the gates of Hope are opened afresh and things don't look quite so bad, and in nine cases out of ten nobody knows out of Cambridge whether a man has taken a high degree or not.

Perhaps it is different with women, the cases being more exceptional; a girl who has done well usually goes through life with an affix to her name, spoken with awe by her admiring friends—'Fifth Wrangler,' 'First Class Moral Science,' 'Senior Op,' and so on.

There would be a good many girls do well at Newnham this term. There would be several first-classes, and some good seconds, and a few, very few thirds. Women never take Poll degrees, so that all, every one, would go out in Honours.

There was a great fuss made with the girls who were going up for the exams. They were fed and petted and looked after just as if they were in training. There were special dishes for them at the High, and they were taken out for exercise, or driven out for airings, and put to bed at given hours. It was not the fault of the authorities if they did not reflect honour on their college.

The men were not the objects of such tender solicitude to their Tutors and Deans. They were left pretty much to themselves, and went to bed when they liked, and got up when they liked, and took their food or left it. Those who liked took exercise, and those who didn't sported their oak and worked until they were deaf and blind, and their brains were so addled that they could hardly find their way into the examination-room.

Wyatt Edgell sported his oak from morning till night during those few days preceding the Tripos examination, but he didn't addle his brains. They were not brains easy to addle by work. The men remarked that this close application, which would have made most men seedy and stale, seemed to agree with him. His eyes were brighter, and his step was lighter, and more assured than heretofore, and he held his head like a man who was going to win, and he hummed snatches of songs—love-songs mostly—as he crossed the courts or climbed his staircase, taking two and three steps at a time, as a man of his youth and strength should do.

A change had come over him since that morning when Lucy had told him to go back to work. He had not seen her in the lane since, though he had gone up to Newnham every morning, and stood staring at the gate until the bell rang for prayers, and then he had gone up the narrow little path between the hedges, and visited again the spot where he had taken her in his arms.

If she had been there when he made these matutinal pilgrimages to the spot, he would surely have taken her in his arms again, and great would have been the scandal at Newnham.

Lucy didn't go out in the lane again alone after that morning. She was quite frightened at what she had done. She couldn't very well have done otherwise. What woman would? She had saved him—at least, she told herself she had saved him. He would go back to his work now, and he would take his degree, probably a very good degree. She didn't dare to speculate any farther; she stopped at his degree. She never said a word about what she had done to Cousin Mary; she wouldn't have told her for the world. Mary had only pointed Wyatt Edgell out to her on the steps of the chapel a month ago. She didn't know him from Eric Gwatkin a month ago, and now she was engaged to marry him!

No wonder Lucy was frightened, and wouldn't have run the risk of meeting him alone for the world. She developed suddenly a violent affection for Miss Stubbs, and used to implore her with tears in her eyes to accompany her in her visits to the lodge. She was such a dreadful little coward, she didn't dare to go alone.

The Master was no worse; his memory had gone, and his physical powers were weakened, since his accident in the garden, but there was no immediate danger. He might go on babbling in his second childhood for weeks or months.

Lucy met the Senior Tutor at the lodge sometimes when she paid her afternoon visits, but she never went to his rooms again. She wouldn't have risked meeting Wyatt Edgell on the stairs for all the coaching in the world. She would rather have been ploughed.

The Tutor couldn't say any more to Lucy about Cousin Mary and the Master's wife making the lodge their home when he met her at these times, as Maria Stubbs was always with her. It seemed likely that the Master's wife would have a home elsewhere before long, and the arrangement would fall through.

Maria had fallen in love with the long gallery of the lodge, as everybody does who goes to St. Benedict's, and she used to wait for Lucy there while she paid her visits to the invalids. Miss Stubbs never did things by halves, and she made herself acquainted during these visits with all the old portraits on the walls. She knew every one of them, from the pale foundress in her sober pre-Raphaelitish dress, to the old Master in his scarlet gown. She had established quite a nodding acquaintance with all of them, and she had got up most of the facts of their history. She knew more about them than Lucy, though she had lived among them for months.

One day while she was poring over the old portraits in the gallery a man came in. He had come up the stairs two at a time, and he had looked eagerly round when he got into the gallery.

There was nobody there but a red-haired girl in spectacles, and the old dead and gone Masters. Yes, there was the foundress, but he didn't care a button for the foundress. He was looking for a real flesh-and-blood woman; his pulses were leaping, and his heart was thumping against his side, and his eyes were shining—he had just finished the first part of the exam.—and just at this moment the fairest creation of the finest master on canvas wouldn't have satisfied him.

He walked to the end of the gallery looking for Lucy—she might be hiding away in any of the little oriel windows—and Miss Stubbs watched him.

She was so glad to see his countenance fall when he couldn't find her. A woman would not have shown her disappointment in that transparent way. She would have made the best of it, and talked to the man who was there, but Edgell glared at Maria savagely, and didn't seem inclined to talk.

'Lucy Rae is with the Master,' she said sweetly; she knew instinctively that he was looking for Lucy. 'She will be here presently.'

Edgell tried to look as if it didn't matter, and he wasn't particular whether she came now or at midnight, but he didn't take Miss Stubbs in.

He fidgeted up and down the gallery, stopping every now and then before a picture, but never looking at it, or staring out into the court below from the old latticed oriel window. He was standing in the recess of the window idly tattooing on the pane when Lucy came in.

She didn't see him until she reached the window, and she came running down the gallery in that energetic way peculiar to the students of colleges for women.

'I'm afraid I've kept you a long time, M'ria; I hope you don't mind——' and then she paused, and Edgell came towards her with his hands outstretched.

He would have taken her in his arms, but there was that hateful Maria at the end of the gallery. He came to Lucy as a lover should come to his mistress, with the love-light in his eyes, and his whole being quivering with passion.

'My darling!' he said, and he took her hands.

Lucy had no idea of being kissed like a milkmaid with Miss Stubbs looking on, and she drew her hands quickly away.

'You here?' she said.

'Yes,' he answered, looking down upon her with that warm light in his eyes and his lips smiling; 'where else should I look for you? I have waited in the lane every morning in the week, and you have never come since—since that morning——'

'The Master is better,' she said, dropping her eyes; they were such sweet, shy eyes they could not meet the hot flame in his.

'And was it only to hear about the Master you came?' he said in a low voice that thrilled her and brought the colour into her cheeks.

'It was to tell me about him you came.' Her voice trembled in spite of herself, and her heart was beating tumultuously.

'It was because I loved you I came, Lucy—darling! I could not live without a sight of your dear face. I have lived a whole week without you, and it has seemed a year. You must not leave me alone again so long, darling!'

There was more in the tone than in his words, and Lucy looked up anxiously into his face.

He read the question in her eyes and he smiled gravely, almost sadly.

'No,' he said, 'thank God, not that!' and he stooped and kissed her forehead reverently between the bright brown ripples of her hair.

Her face grew warm under his touch, and she trembled and drew back. Suppose that girl in the gallery had seen him? It would be all over Newnham. And the servants might come in at any time, or Cousin Mary; and Mr. Colville might walk into the gallery unannounced, as he was accustomed to do. Oh, it would be dreadful to be caught kissing like a housemaid!

'And you have been working hard all this time?' she said, when she had got the little oak table that stood in the window well between them.

'Yes, I have been working pretty well. I shouldn't have done a stroke if you hadn't given me something to work for. I should have thrown it all up, and gone down.'

'Oh, it would never have done for you to have gone down—you who are expected to bring so much credit to the college! It would have disappointed everybody, and your own people most. What would your people have said?'

'They would have been disappointed—and—and I think my mother would have been sorry. She is such a tender, indulgent mother; she has never refused me anything. She has always stood between me and my father, and covered up all my shortcomings, but she couldn't have covered up this, and—and there would have been a row. Yes, I think it would have disappointed her.'

His eyes were tender and softened as he spoke of his mother, and Lucy thought as she stood there of that dreadful scene when she found Eric on his knees beside the couch, and she wondered how his mother would have covered up that.

She looked up at the warm, tender face of the man bending over her—he had got round the table—and with a sudden terror she saw the mark on his throat—he had not covered it; he wore no scarf to-day, and his collar was open, and the purple mark was visible on the white skin.

He saw her eyes travel to—not to his face; they stopped short at his throat, and a white look of terror came into them.

'Yes,' he said, reading her thoughts—her transparent thoughts—'she would have covered up this, but it would have broken her heart.'

He drew his collar up round his throat as he spoke and Lucy's eyes filled with tears.

'It is all over and past,' she said bravely; 'there will be no need to "break her heart" now. You will fulfil all her expectations; you will make her happy and proud—oh, so proud! If men who are tempted to do silly, selfish things would only pause and think of the people who love them!'

Edgell drew her nearer to him.

Maria Stubbs was not looking that way; she really was a most sensible girl, she was entirely absorbed in the pictures.

'I will think of you, then,' he said in a low voice that vibrated with passion, 'when—when I am tempted; but I must be sure of your love, Lucy, or it will be no good; there must be no mistake about it. It must be the real thing; a make-believe, a sham, would never save a man! Tell me if—if at such a time, darling, I may think of you?'

He put the question solemnly, though his lips were smiling, but his eyes were looking down into hers as if they would read her soul.

Lucy's face grew pale and troubled; she knew exactly what his question meant; she felt limp and frightened, dreadfully frightened. Anyone might come into the gallery at any moment, and he was holding her in a grasp of iron and reading her little transparent soul through and through. She could not escape from him.

She had no alternative.

'Yes,' she murmured almost inaudibly; 'you may think of me if—if it will help you.'

He took her in his arms for one brief moment—he forgot all about Maria Stubbs—and kissed her lips and her eyes.

'My darling!' he murmured—'my darling!'

Lovers have such a limited vocabulary, they are obliged to have recourse to unmeaning repetitions.

Miss Stubbs had behaved beautifully till now—no Newnham girl could have behaved better; but there is a limit to all human endurance, and the limit of Maria's endurance had been reached.

'I hope you are nearly ready,' she said in a most unpleasant voice; 'because if not I must go.'

'I am quite ready, dear,' said Lucy, nearly crying. 'I have been ready a long time.'

She could have blessed Miss Stubbs for taking her away. She was dreadfully frightened, but it was with a strange, delicious terror that stirred her pulses like a tumult of joy.

CHAPTER XVIII.

CAPABILITY STUBBS.

It was clearly Lucy's duty not to go back to Newnham, whatever Maria Stubbs' hurry might be, until she had told her Cousin Mary what had passed between her and Wyatt Edgell in the gallery.

It is not usual, even at Cambridge, where there have been so many social revolutions of late, for young women to receive the visits of gentlemen, and exchange the privileged amenities of engaged persons, without acquainting the elders of their household.

There was no one to acquaint at the lodge but Cousin Mary. It was no use telling the Master, he would confuse it with Dick's courtship that had been over sixty years ago, and he would be telling Nurse Brannan that Lucy's mother first met her lover in a dancing-booth at a fair. The Master's wife was almost past telling; she had been growing weaker day by day ever since that accident; the world had been slipping away from her ever since. She had ceased to take any interest in anything that was going on around her. She seldom spoke now; sight and strength and speech were all failing. When she did speak, she had only one question to ask: 'How is the Master?'

But Lucy would not admit that she had any engagement yet to tell anybody about. She had only told Wyatt Edgell that he might go back to work, and she had further told him that he might think of her at certain times.

This was all; no promise, no real engagement. Of course he ought not to have taken her into his arms until he was properly engaged. He had been premature, but Lucy had no one but herself to blame for it.

This is how Lucy reasoned as she walked back to Newnham with Miss Stubbs. She went straight back without seeing the Master's wife or Cousin Mary; she positively crept out of the lodge as if she had done some shameful thing, and was afraid of being found out. She was very nice to Maria on the way. She called her dear, which is quite an unheard-of thing among the Stoics of Newnham, but Miss Stubbs was not to be taken in.

'It's pretty far gone,' she observed with a sniff, when Lucy made a timid little allusion to Edgell's visit to the gallery.

'Oh dear no, not at all!' Lucy said sweetly.

Miss Stubbs raised her red eyebrows. It was those dreadful red eyebrows and red eyelashes that made her so—so unlovely.

'Oh,' she remarked in her unpleasant way, 'I thought I heard—ahem!—some—some kissing. I may have been mistaken; perhaps it was the wind.'

'The wind was very rough this afternoon, dear; it was rattling the shaky old lattice dreadfully.'

Miss Stubbs smiled scornfully. There hadn't been a breath of air all the day.

'I suppose it's a settled thing?' she said presently.

'Settled? Oh no; not at all!'

'Then it ought to be!' Maria said sharply. 'You've given him encouragement enough. He's been hanging about the lane every morning this week. It's known all over the place that he's waiting for you.'

'But I haven't met him!' Lucy said stoutly. She wasn't going to be sat upon by Maria.

'No; oh no! you haven't met him this week; we should all have known it if you had, because we've all been on the look-out since that day when you were caught kissing in the lane. I shouldn't have mentioned it—though it's not good form in a woman's college—if it hadn't occurred again to-day. It's all right, I suppose, if you are engaged.'

'But I am not engaged!' said Lucy impatiently.

She was not going to be lectured by Maria. Nobody would ever think of kissing Maria in the lane.

'Then I don't understand it,' Miss Stubbs said stiffly.

'Oh, you poor creature!' Lucy said with a weak attempt at a laugh, and her cheeks scarlet. 'I am only encouraging him for his own good. I have only told him he may work; he is sure to take a high place, but he would not do anything if I did not encourage him. Think: all his life depends upon it. You would do the same if you were in my place.'

Miss Stubbs did not say she wouldn't, but she blushed beneath her freckles, and her eyes softened beneath the red lashes. There were depths in her eyes that Lucy had never seen in them before, and she was looking at Maria sharply—unfathomed depths, for nobody had tested the depths and height of Maria's love. Perhaps a brave man, who does not look on the outward appearance, or who prefers red hair, may some day, and he will have no cause for regret.

'And what will happen when—when the work is done, and he has won the high place?' Maria asked softly.

She was thinking how she would love above all things to fire a man who loved her with ambitions. She would fill him with the noblest ambitions, and when he had climbed the ladder, when he had realized all his dreams, she would not cheat him of his reward.

'And what then?' she repeated, when she found Lucy did not answer.

'Oh, I don't know. I have not made up my mind. Whatever happened, it would be a great thing for him to have done the work—to have taken his degree, that could never be recalled. I am sure I have done right—in—in encouraging him, as you term it.'

'I think it would be base—and mean—and unworthy—an unwomanly thing to throw him over in the end!' Maria said, with a little catch in her voice. She couldn't find adjectives strong enough, and she had to pause between each.

Wyatt Edgell went back to his rooms across the court with great swinging strides, and he climbed the stairs three at a time. He met the Senior Tutor coming out of his rooms at the top of the stairs, and the little snatch of a love-song he was singing died on his lips. Still, his lips were smiling, and his eyes were shining, and his face was earnest and set. It was the face of a man who was going to do something—who was going to win.

'How have you done?' the Tutor asked, stopping him. He asked it with a smile; he hadn't any doubt about how he had done.

'Not so well as I could have wished, sir. I shall do better in the next part.'

There are two 'parts' in the Mathematical Tripos. If a man gets through Part I. he is allowed to proceed farther; he is allowed to go in for Honours. There could be no doubt about Wyatt Edgell being 'through' in the 'first part.' He was quite safe in going back to work for Honours. There is a week between the end of one examination and the beginning of another. There is time to pick one's self up and prepare afresh for the fight—the real fight this time.

Wyatt Edgell went back to his room and 'sported' his oak. It was open just for a minute after Hall, and Eric Gwatkin came in.

Eric had been working at his Special—he took theology, about as stiff a Special as a man can take—all the week, and he had just come to the end of his exam. There would be Hebrew on the Monday, about which he knew very little; if he should make a stray shot it would count, but the real work of the exam. was over. He was looking limp, and used up, and dejected. His eyes were dull, and his cheeks were flabby, and his hair, which he wore long, hung down in a spiritless way. He was the greatest possible contrast to Edgell.

'Well, Wattles,' he said, looking up when Eric came into the room—'well, have you floored the examiners?'

Eric didn't exactly turn green, but his flabby cheeks turned a shade paler.

'It's all over, dear fellow,' he said with a gulp—he hadn't got anything to swallow. He had just come in from Hall, but he gulped down something. 'The examiners have floored me. I'm ploughed, to a certainty.'

He sat down as he spoke on the couch where Edgell had lain on that day, and tried to look cheerful.

'Nonsense, old man! it isn't so bad as that. You are through, for certain.'

'No; I don't think I am through.'

'Well, suppose the worst, if it gives you much pleasure to anticipate it; you can come up again in October.'

'No; I shall not come up again. I shall go down and try something else. Remember, I have already tried two professions. I shall take it, if I fail, that—that the Church is closed to me. I have an offer of something in the City, and I should have to go abroad for a time, and then settle down to work. Perhaps it's the right thing for me, after all.'

'Nonsense, Wattles! What would you do stuck on a high stool in the City? You'd be getting off it half a dozen times a day to go on your knees. It's no use your choosing a profession that isn't very near the ground, where you could be on your knees all day long. That's the only profession you've got any chance in, Wattles.'

Eric smiled, and if Edgell hadn't been looking straight before him in that way he had of not seeing anything within a hundred miles he might have seen that his eyes were red, and that there was something very suspiciously like a tear in the corner of one of them.

'You are working in earnest,' he said presently, nodding towards the table where Edgell was seated, which was covered with books and papers.

'Ye—es,' said the other with a smile, still looking out of the window at the patch of sunset sky over the gray battlements of the college—'ye—es; I've got something to work for. I didn't do half well in the first part; I wasn't sure—quite sure—but it's all right now, and I shall go in and do my best. You have never seen me do my best, Wattles; you will see me do it now—for—for Lucy's sake.'

His face was very noble and tender. It was an ideal man's face—strong, and self-reliant, and masterful, and inexpressibly tender. It moved Eric watching him from that couch, and knowing so much about him.

'It is settled, then?' he said presently, again swallowing something unsatisfactory that seemed to stick.

'Yes; it is settled. She has given me an antidote, a charm, against that accursed thing. She has told me to think of her.'

He was thinking of her now as he lay back in his chair watching the sunlight steal along the roof, and up, up, up the spire of the college chapel. He was thinking of Lucy's sweet eyes, and her blushing cheeks, and the golden ripples of her hair, and he was telling himself that the thought of her would be a tower of strength to him in the future, that he would never, never fall again. When the old temptation came, let it take what form it would, he should be able to meet it. He would only have to think of Lucy.

Eric watched him as he sat on the couch opposite. He guessed what was passing in his mind. His own mind travelled over the ground with him, and presently he paused and sighed. He had come to a cul-de-sac.

'Well,' Edgell said, looking round like one aroused from a day-dream, 'what are you croaking at, Wattles?'

Eric made a feeble attempt to smile; it was a very poor attempt, and it only made his poor tired face look more ghastly.

'I only hope, dear fellow, it will answer,' he said huskily.

'Of course it will answer. It is the only thing in the world for me, and for such as me. There is nothing but the love of a woman that can hold a fellow back when—when he has gone so far as I have; there is nothing but a woman's love that could reach down, down—God only knows how deep—and pick a fellow up who has fallen into the pit, that can drag a man out, wounded and maimed, from under the very wheels of Juggernaut at the risk of her own life and reason. There is only one kind of love that can do this.'

Eric looked at him with a strange pity in his eyes.

'You think it is right to put her to such a test?' he said.

'I do not think anything about it. If she loves me, she will not think any trial too hard. Tush, man! you know nothing about love if you do not know that love delights in sacrifice. It must have its altar—the rites could not be celebrated without an altar—and it must have its offering—its free-will offering—its victim. It withholds not its dearest—how should it? Love has no self.'

Eric groaned. He knew nothing about a woman's love. He didn't believe that little Lucy could ever love a man like that.

'My dear fellow,' he said, 'you judge a woman's nature by your own. All women would not rise to such heights.'

'The woman that I loved would,' said the other confidently. 'You will have a chance of putting it to the test before long. If—if I am kept, it will be Lucy's love that will keep me; but if—if it happens again, it will be as you say—I shall have judged a woman's nature by my own.'

The smile had faded from his face, and his eyes were cold and hard, and his lips were pressed tight together. It was not the same face that had smiled upon Eric when he came into the room.

Eric was ashamed of himself, and hung his head. He ought not to have questioned Lucy's love. Nobody had ever loved him, nobody but Pamela, and she was always bullying him. He ought to have been silent until he had found out for himself what a woman will do for the man she loves.

'It must never happen again, dear old man,' he said, laying his hand affectionately on Edgell's shoulder. 'Remember, you have vowed——'

'I know all that,' Edgell interrupted impatiently. 'Do you think all the vows in the world would hold me back, when—when that accursed thing came upon me? You have never been tried yourself——'

'No, no, no, thank God!'

'You may well thank God. I tell you, if the breaking the oath I have sworn—the oaths I have sworn—I have sworn dozens—hundreds—would lose heaven itself, I should still break it—I should not be able to resist when the temptation came upon me.'

'You are right to mistrust yourself,' Eric said sadly. 'Oh, my dear fellow, if you would only trust Him who is the unfailing Strength of all them that put their trust in Him, and who would be a Strong Tower to you in the face of the enemy!'

'Dear old Wattles!' Edgell said good-humouredly. 'I knew you only wanted an excuse for going on your knees. I'm awfully busy now, old man. I'm going to work till daylight—and—and if the Enemy, as you are pleased to call him, should come—I'll think of Lucy!'

He looked past Gwatkin to the blue sky over the roof of the chapel. The sun had all but set, and the vane at the top of the spire had caught the last remnant of fleeting sunshine and rent it in twain.

CHAPTER XIX.

A STRONG TOWER.

'Weakness to be wroth with weakness.'

It was a dreadful time of heartburnings at Newnham through all the next week; not at Newnham only, but all over Cambridge. So many Triposes were on, and the week's interval between the first and second parts of the examination for the Mathematical Tripos was being made the most of by the coming Wranglers and Senior Ops.

There were half a dozen girls at Newnham going in for Honours in mathematics, but there was only one that was expected to take a high place—a very high place—among the Wranglers of the year. There would be several Senior and Junior Optimes, but there would be only one Wrangler this year.

The hopes of Newnham were set on Pamela Gwatkin, who was expected to do such great things, to win such honour for the women's college. A dark rumour had reached St. John's and Trinity—who like to divide the honours between them—that they were likely to be left behind in the race—far behind. They were uneasy and anxious, though they wouldn't have owned it for the world, for—

'At times the high gods, who o'er papers preside,
Send a lady from Newnham to chasten their pride.'

The rumour caused a great deal of midnight oil to be burnt in Cambridge during the first week in June. Wyatt Edgell never went to bed till daylight; not that the rumour disturbed him, he only laughed gaily when he heard that 'the lady from Newnham' was Wattles' sister. Perhaps, being twins, he measured them by the same standard.

He never saw Lucy all through that week, though he went every morning at the usual hour up the lane. He didn't linger at the gate now—he had no time for lingering at gates; but he looked up at her window. He had found out which was Lucy's window, and he paid his accustomed pilgrimage to that sacred spot in the narrowed lane between the hedgerows, that were all white with May now, and then he would hurry back to his work. He would take back with him from Newnham, as a memento of his visit, a bit of sweet-briar from the hedge, and he would lay it on his table before him, that something of the fragrance of his love might be about him while he worked.

He wrote to her during the week a little letter that would have set any other woman's pulses on fire, but it only frightened Lucy. She couldn't understand the vehemence of a man's love. She didn't answer it—she couldn't without compromising herself completely; but she sent him a message by Eric.

It was not often that Eric Gwatkin visited his sister at Newnham. She did not encourage his visits, and she was always too busy to talk to him. He came up one day in the middle of the week; his examination was over, and he had nothing particular to do, and he came up to see his sister. He had been slumming all the afternoon in that odorous district round Magdalen Bridge, and he had come up to Newnham to see if Pamela would give him some tea.

Pamela was not in her room, and Eric had leisure to look round and see how his sister amused herself. One can tell so much from a room in daily use what people's occupations are.

Pamela did not amuse herself much, unless she found recreation in the higher mathematics.

Her table—it was an eight-legged affair in old oak—groaned beneath the weight of the books on mathematics that were piled upon it. It was as much as the eight legs could do to support it.

Eric quite shivered when he saw those books and the problem papers that were scattered about; the ink was still wet on some of them. He couldn't have worked out one of those problems to have saved his life. Oh, Nature had made a great mistake! She ought to have made Pamela the man. What was the use of giving all that brain to a woman?

Perhaps Eric thought so; not for the first time, indeed; he may have got used to the thought as he moved uneasily about Pamela's books. There were shelves and shelves of books in this girl's room, and there were not a dozen in Eric's: a Bible and a few theological books, and some Church histories, and nothing more; no poetry, or travels, or philosophy, or fiction—oh no, no fiction!

There were books on Pamela's shelves that made his hair stand on end. He groaned as he read the titles, and he had cold shivers down his back.

To think they should be twins! Oh, Nature had made a great mistake!

He was still reading the titles on the backs of Pamela's naughty black books, and cold shivers were running down his spine, when the door opened and a girl came in.

He looked up, with mild reproof in his eyes, expecting to see Pamela; but it was not his sister, it was Lucy.

Lucy had not come into Pamela Gwatkin's room by choice. She had been sent with a message from one of the Dons, and she had come under protest.

She forgot all about the message when she saw Eric.

'You here?' she said.

There was no reason why he shouldn't be here, in his sister's room. She had just received that letter from Wyatt Edgell, and she was wondering how she should answer it, and the sight of Eric seemed to bring a feeling of relief to her mind.

'Oh, I have been wanting to see you so much!' she said eagerly; she was so afraid Pamela would come in and interrupt them. 'I want to know—how—how Mr. Edgell is going on—if—if anything has happened since——'

Eric understood what she meant, though she spoke incoherently; and he understood her agitation and reluctance.

'No,' he said slowly, looking at her with a strange pity in his eyes, 'nothing has happened in that way, thank God! He is working hard; I am afraid too hard.'

'Oh, I don't think work will hurt him!' she said scornfully. She remembered how the girls worked here. What the men called 'work' was only play to them. She wasn't at all afraid that her lover would work as hard as Pamela, for instance.

'I don't mean that,' he said; 'I'm not afraid of his breaking down. I'm only afraid that when the strain is over—he—he will feel it—he——'

He was a very awkward young man; he could only stand there stammering and stuttering, while the girl looked at him with dilating eyes.

'You mean,' she said with a shiver, 'that when the strain is over he will go back to his old way—that he will not be able to withstand——'

She could not finish the sentence; there was a strange sinking at her heart—a dreadful unutterable loathing and sickness that she could not overcome—and she sank down white and trembling in a chair and covered her face with her hands. The sight of Eric had brought back that awful scene, and she was thinking of that gap in his throat; she could never get it out of her mind.

'No, no, by heaven! not that!' he said almost fiercely. 'He will never, never fall away again in that way, please God; but it is you alone that can keep him. His salvation—heaven forgive me for saying it!—is in your hands.'

'My hands?' Lucy repeated feebly.

'Yes,' he said gravely, almost sternly, 'in your hands. Your love can hold him when nothing else can; it is to him a strong tower against the face of this enemy. You must not fail him in his need.'

'A strong tower!' Lucy moaned. 'Oh, you don't know what you say! I am such a poor little thing—you don't know how weak I am. Oh, why did he choose me?'

She sat with dilated eyes and white stricken face, moaning and wringing her hands. He was very sorry for the girl, but he couldn't spare her. He was thinking of that look on Edgell's face when he had said what a woman's love could do for him.

'Why do men choose women?' he said almost harshly; 'perhaps it is fate, who can say? He loved you, or he would not have chosen you. Oh, you don't know what it is to win the love of such a man!'

'No—o!' said Lucy meekly, with her little smile—her tiny white smile—'I'm afraid I don't. I'm such a little thing! I could not have a large soul like—like Pamela. Oh, why didn't he choose Pamela?'

'It is too late to ask that question now; he has chosen you. Are you going to be true, and loyal, and put yourself aside, as some women do, or are you going to fail him at the last moment?'

It was a hard question to answer; Lucy could not have answered it if she would. How could she tell—she who had never been tried—to what great occasion she might rise? She might be a heroine yet, though she didn't look like one, sitting there weeping and wringing her hands.

'You will not fail him now; remember his future is in your hands. He will do great things with a woman by his side to encourage him to noble aims, to fire him with noble ambitions. Oh, you do not know what your love will do for him! He will have a great future with you by his side.'

Still Lucy moaned and wrung her hands.

'I shall be always afraid,' she said; 'I shall never feel safe. I shall always be thinking day and night of—of what may happen.'

'It will be your own fault if it happens. It is only your love that will keep him; if that should fail, God help him!'

'I am such a poor little thing!' she moaned.

While she was sitting weeping there, Pamela came in, and Lucy jumped up and brushed the tears from her eyes, and puckered her little level brows, and tried to look as if she hadn't been crying. She forgot all about the message she had to give Pamela, and when the sister and brother were talking she slipped out of the room.

'What's she crying about?' Pamela asked him as Lucy closed the door behind her. 'Has anything happened to that—that Mr. Edgell? or is the Master worse?'

'The Master is no worse; but Mrs. Rae is ill, very ill,' Eric answered. He was not at all disposed to talk of Wyatt Edgell's love for Lucy to his agnostic sister.

'And Mr. Edgell, has he been having another attack? Has he been attempting suicide again?'

'Hush, Pamela!' Eric Gwatkin exclaimed almost harshly. He could not bear to hear his sister speak of Edgell in that way. 'You don't know what you are saying. That was an accident, and he had been ill. If you only knew Edgell, you would not say such things. He is the best and noblest fellow in the world, and he is the dearest friend I have.'

'They say he is to head the list this year; that he is to be Senior Wrangler,' Pamela said in her cool, contemptuous way.

'Yes, he is sure to head the list. There is no one to touch him in the 'Varsity.'

Pamela smiled.

Eric had forgotten what rumour was saying about her—that it would be a neck-and-neck race.

'He is working hard, then?' she said indifferently.

What could it matter to her if he were reading hard or raving on his couch with delirium tremens?

'Yes; he's working like a horse—like a giant, rather. He can do six days' work in one every day. No one can have any chance with him.'

Pamela didn't ask Eric to have any tea, and he went away as he came. She didn't even go to the front door with him. She said good-bye, and sat down to the eight-legged table among her books, and left him to find his way out by himself.

He knew his way pretty well. It was not the first time he had been there. When he was nearly at the end of the first passage a door opened and a girl came out and stopped him. It was Lucy.

'I have been thinking of what you said,' she whispered, with a little break in her voice, 'and I will do what I can. Tell him from me not to work too hard; to—to take care of himself—for my sake.'

Her voice broke down entirely, and she went into the room and shut the door.

He hadn't got to the end of the passage before another door opened, and another girl's head was put out—the head of a girl with red hair. It was Maria Stubbs. She watched him to the end of the passage, and then she sniffed in her unpleasant way and went into Lucy's room.

She went in without knocking, and found Lucy on her knees. She had flung herself on her knees beside her couch, and was wildly imploring Heaven to make her love strong enough and tender enough to keep this man safe who trusted in her.

She looked up when Maria came in, and stumbled up from her knees, pretending she had been looking for something under the couch, as she had been pretending just now she hadn't been crying; but she didn't take in Miss Stubbs.

'Who was that man you were talking to in the passage?' Maria said bluntly. 'It didn't look like Mr. Edgell.'

'No,' Lucy said meekly; 'it wasn't Mr. Edgell. It was Pamela's brother.'

'And he brought you a message from your lover? Of course he is your lover. I like to call things by their right names. I prefer to call a spade a spade.'

'No, he didn't bring me a message,' Lucy said, with some spirit.

She wasn't always going to be trampled upon by Maria.

'But you sent a message by him. I heard you give him a message. Oh, it's no use trying to deceive me!'

'I couldn't help it—indeed I couldn't help it!' Lucy moaned; and then she sat down upon the couch beside which she had been kneeling, and began to cry.

She was feeling so dreadfully in need of sympathy and advice that she was bound to tell somebody. She couldn't bear all the burden of this terrible secret on her little weak shoulders. The great terror that haunted her would not be so dreadful to face if she could share it with another.

She told Maria Stubbs the whole story from the beginning; she kept nothing back.

Maria listened in silence to the end. Once or twice she was surprised into an exclamation, and her face grew pale beneath the freckles, and if Lucy had been looking at her she would have seen the tears gather in her eyes and Maria furtively brush them aside with the back of her hand. She would not have let Lucy see that she was crying for the world.

'What would you do if it were you, dear?' Lucy said with a little sob, when she had finished her tale.

'Do?' said Maria, and then she paused, and recalled the face of the man who had been waiting for Lucy in the long gallery of the lodge.

She had seen a good deal of him in those few minutes. She had seen quite enough of him to make up her mind what she should do if he were her lover instead of Lucy's.

'Do, dear?' she repeated, and her eyes beneath their pale lashes grew inexpressibly warm and tender, and her whole face softened and changed. It was plain and freckled no longer; at least, the freckles were there, but one did not notice them in that new wonderful beauty and exaltation that had come into her plain face that was plain no longer. 'I would be a strong tower to him against the face of his enemy!' And she meant it.

CHAPTER XX.

NO FOLLOWERS ALLOWED.

Lucy neglected those dear old people at the lodge shamefully. She was afraid to go to St. Benedict's lest she should meet Wyatt Edgell in the courts, or in the cloisters, or even in the gallery of the lodge itself.

They were well looked after in spite of her neglect. They would have been very badly off indeed if they had been dependent upon her. There was Cousin Mary, who was a tower of strength to everyone who trusted in her. Not a showy, pretentious tower with a flagstaff on the top, but a plain solid structure, against whose granite girth the storm of time and disaster would beat in vain.

Cousin Mary was the presiding genius at the lodge through all this sad time. She ruled the household, received the visitors—and there are always a good many callers at a college lodge in May term—and went from one sick-room to the other all day long, and often all night.

Nurse Brannan was still in attendance on the Master; it had been hard work to get the authorities of Addenbroke's to give her up so long, but the 'Heads' have a special claim upon the hospital staff.

The Master was gradually growing weaker day by day—weaker and more childish. He had forgotten already, in this short time, all that store of learning that had taken him years to collect. He had disencumbered his mind of a useless load of lumber—dry, musty old languages, Hebrew and Sanscrit and Syriac—which would be of no use where he was going. It had taken him a lifetime, a longer lifetime than most men, to accumulate it, and now, in a moment, it had been shot out in a load like useless rubbish. It had answered its purpose—it had advanced him in the world, it had won him repute and distinction, and it had made some money; and now, when its end was served, when it was only an encumbrance, it had all been shot down.

Perhaps other minds would pick it up, would select from the heap the things that were best worth preserving, and so the lamp of learning would be handed on to another generation.

Lucy came upon the Master once in one of her rare visits to the lodge—it was during the hours set apart for the Tripos Examination, when Wyatt Edgell would be away—and found Nurse Brannan reading to him.

She had opened the door softly and come in unobserved, and the curtains of the big, old-fashioned four-post bedstead concealed her from view. Nurse Brannan was reading the Bible to him. She was reading a parable; the words and the imagery took hold of him more than precept and promise; he had been expounding them all his life, and they had dropped from him with those other things.

She was reading the parables of the Lost Piece of Silver and the Prodigal Son, and every now and then she would stop and explain. She had a good deal to say about them, and the old Master listened meekly.

It quite took Lucy's breath away to hear that little bit of a nurse explaining the parables to the Master of St. Benedict's. He had preached hundreds of sermons in the college chapel from that very chapter; it had always been a favourite subject with him. It had always had a fitting application to those fresh young minds in the benches beneath him that were perennially engaged in wasting their substance in riotous living. He had read it in every ancient tongue in which it had ever been written. And now a little nurse-girl, who couldn't even keep her hair tidy, was explaining it to him.

'Yes,' he was saying in his slow, quavering voice; it was weaker now than when Lucy last heard it faltering over those closing words in the Litany in the college chapel—'yes, I mind it quite well. I heard it when I was a boy standing at my mother's knee. She was a poor woman; she would have searched for it all night if she had lost a piece of silver, she would not have rested till she had found it. I was the youngest of all her sons, and when she read that chapter to me as a boy standing there, I used to think that I was the Prodigal, and that by-and-by, when I had wasted all my substance in a far country, I should come back like the Prodigal to my father's house, and ask to be taken in. I've been wanting to go back a long time, my dear; I'm getting tired and old, and I should like to go back. Do you think he would take me in?'

'We will see what the Prodigal's father did when he went back,' said the nurse; and then she read in her soft, slow, earnest voice the concluding words of the old, sweet story.

Nurse Brannan had a wonderful power in reading God's Word, giving by tone and accent a new bearing to the familiar words of Scripture. Lucy had heard the words hundreds of times before, and had hurried over them in her scrambling way of reading her morning portion; but to-day they seemed to convey a special message. She stood there, behind the curtain, while Nurse Brannan read and the old Master listened.

'It seems very clear,' he said, when she had finished. 'It seems just as my mother said. I will arise and go to my Father—I have nowhere else to go—I have changed a good deal in all these years, but—but He would not be likely to change——'

'No,' said Nurse Brannan; 'He has not changed!'

Lucy's tears were dropping fast; she could not trust herself to go in. She crept softly out of the room and shut the door, and went across the landing to Mrs. Rae's room.

The Master's wife was always glad to see Lucy; she gave her better accounts of the Master than anyone else in the household. She looked up when Lucy came in, and noted with her failing eyes, instinctively sharpened by love, that Lucy had been crying.

'Have you seen the Master?' she asked, with a little catch in her voice.

'Yes, oh yes! he is better to-day, and giving the nurse quite a discourse upon the parables. You remember what lovely sermons he used to preach upon the parables?'

The Master's wife smiled; she remembered every word of them. They were her comfort and stay now, those old sermons of the Master's; they made the way quite clear before her; they removed all the difficulties. She would have been shocked if she had known that that nurse from Addenbroke's had been so presumptuous as to attempt to explain the parables he knew so much about to the Master.

'You must get me a volume of his sermons, my dear—his first sermons; I may have forgotten some of them; and Mary shall read them. It will not be like hearing his voice, but—it—it will bring back something of the old time.'

Lucy stayed longer than she had intended at the lodge. She had only reckoned to look in and pay a short visit to each sick-room, and have a chat with Cousin Mary, and go away; but she had to go to the Master's library and fetch that volume of sermons before she went.

The Senior Tutor was sitting down in the Master's place at the Master's writing-table, answering the Master's letters, when Lucy went into the library. It would be his own place soon. He usually came over to the lodge for an hour in the afternoon now, and attended to whatever college business there might be to attend to, and look through the Master's college correspondence. He used to go through it with Mary once, when she opened the Master's letters; now he went through it alone.

He rose when Lucy came in, and made her sit down in her old seat by the window. He wanted her to talk about herself. He was sure she missed his help; she would never be able to pass the Little-go without some more lessons.

They taught beautifully at Newnham. They teach conscientiously at women's colleges: they don't believe in tips and short-cuts, and mere getting up of likely passages; they plod industriously through the dull, dreary round. The Senior Tutor didn't believe in Lucy's plodding; he would have liked to give her a tip or two.

Lucy declined to talk about herself; she was full of the dear old people upstairs, and the affecting scene she had witnessed in the Master's room.

'He is getting weaker every day, in body as well as mind,' the Tutor said thoughtfully. 'He has not had nearly such good nights lately.'

Unconsciously he was keeping a barometric measure of the Master's increasing weakness. It is not an ennobling thing to wait for dead men's shoes.

'No-o,' said Lucy, 'but I hope she will go first;' and then she burst into tears. 'Oh, I don't know how we shall tell her that he is gone!'

'Do you think at her age she would feel it so keenly? The separation could not be long.'

'Oh, you don't know what her love is. It seems only to have grown with the years.'

The Tutor sighed, and looked out of the window into the garden beneath, and his thoughts wandered away to a time long past, when such a love might have been his. Perhaps his fancy had gone back to a brown-haired girl, who had waited for him until her face had grown wan and her eyes sad with waiting, and who had not had Mrs. Rae's patience. Well, she would have been old and florid and stout now, and her sweet face—it was sweet once—would have been seamed and wrinkled with the cares of, oh, so many children!

Well, it was just as well as it was. The Tutor recalled his wandering thoughts, and looked at Lucy.

She was quite worth looking at as she sat in the window-seat. Her face was graver and sadder, and her eyes were steadier, and her lips were not so loose as they once were. It is astonishing how girls' lips tighten after six months in a women's college. Perhaps this is due to their difficulties with mathematics, and to the anxiety that ethics and Latin prose give them, to say nothing of modern languages and natural science.

She had certainly grown more womanly since she had been at Newnham: that added seriousness supplied just the charm that was lacking. Perhaps it was quite as well that brown-haired girl had not waited.

'Do you think you could love anyone so long, Lucy?' he said presently.

It was not the words, but the voice in which he said them, that made Lucy look up and her face grow warm beneath his eyes. She was dreadfully angry with herself for blushing. It was quite idiotic for a girl to turn as red as a poppy when a man old enough to be her father addressed her.

She shook her head.

'Not a man you loved very much, Lucy? Mrs. Rae must have loved the Master dearly for her love to have lasted so long. I'm afraid to say how many years she waited for him.' And again the Tutor sighed: that brown-haired girl had soon grown sick of waiting.

Again Lucy shook her head.

'I am not like the Master's wife,' she said.

She was thinking of Wyatt Edgell. Why would men make such large demands upon a woman? All women were not made on such large lines. Why would they not be content with a little reasonable love—the calm, steady flame that would burn very well if nothing happened to put it out? What more could they want?

'I think you would make quite as good a Master's wife,' he said, bending over her with that warm light in his eyes that had brought the poppy-colour to her cheeks; and he had taken her hand. 'I think your love will be quite as well worth winning. I hope yours will be as happy a life, dear Lucy, as hers, and that it will be crowned with a fuller and more perfect joy——'

There is no knowing what would have happened if Lucy had not at that moment suddenly remembered that Mrs. Rae was waiting for the book of sermons she had sent her to fetch. She snatched her hand away from the Senior Tutor's just in time, and made a hurried excuse that Mrs. Rae was waiting for her to read to her; and she took the first volume of the Master's sermons she found on the shelf, and ran out of the room.

She could hardly trust herself to read to Mrs. Rae. She made a dreadful mess of her favourite sermon. Whatever other talents she had developed at Newnham, she had not developed a talent for reading sermons. It brought the tears into the dear woman's eyes to hear her; she thought of the kind voice that was so sweet to her ears, that she had last heard breathing those well-remembered words, and she turned her worn white face to the pillow to hide her tears.

'You are sure the Master is no worse to-day?' she said to Lucy as she came away.

'Oh yes, quite sure. He was preaching quite a sermon to nurse on the Prodigal's return.'

Lucy was just in time as she hurried out of the college gate to meet the men coming in from the examination.

They were looking worn and tired, and some were looking glum, and others had assumed an air of cheerfulness that sat ill on their anxious faces. One or two had the examination papers in their hands, and were adding up with their friends the questions they had scored off. The process did not seem to give them unmixed satisfaction.

Lucy thought that her lover must already have passed through the court, as he was not among the crowd at the gate, and she was congratulating herself on having escaped him, when she saw him coming across the road.

She couldn't run away; she was obliged to stop in the face of all those men at the college gate and shake hands with him. She wasn't at all sure he would not take her in his arms before them all. There was no saying what he would do. He never did anything like other men; he did not measure the world and its customs with the impulse of the moment. Was not the world made for him?

Wyatt Edgell didn't take her in his arms, and he didn't kiss her in the face of all the men assembled at the college gate, but he walked back by her side to Newnham.

'Well,' she said eagerly, 'and how have you done?'

He was glad to see she was flushed and eager; he didn't know it was the fear of what he was going to do that had moved her and heightened her colour.

'I have been thinking about you every day,' he said. 'If I have not done well it will be your fault, not mine.'

She would much rather he had been thinking about his work, but she did not say so.

'It is nearly over,' she said, with a little catch in her voice; 'only one day more. What will you do when it is over, when you have nothing more to work for?'

'I shall come to you for my reward.' His eyes were blazing down upon her with a sudden heat of passion that made her tremble. 'I shall come to-morrow night, after the exam. is finished. I shall come to the old place in the lane.'

He did not tell her that he had been there every morning of the week.

'It is so hard to get out of nights,' she said. 'We are not expected to go out after Hall.'

He stopped in the middle of the path and laughed.

'Ah!' he said. 'No lovers allowed, and all that sort of thing; no whispering beneath the moon. Never mind, my dear; if they won't let you whisper beneath the moon, I've no objection to lamplight. If you must not meet me in the lane, Lucy, I shall come up to the front-door.'

'Oh, I'm sure that will never do!' she said, almost tearfully; she was dreadfully afraid he would keep his word. 'They wouldn't let you come in, I'm sure. You are not a brother—or—or a cousin——'

'No, my dear, thank God! I am neither of these undesirable things. I am a lover—my darling's own true lover!'

'Then I'm quite sure they won't admit you!' Lucy said very decidedly. 'Lovers are not even mentioned in the rules.'

'Well,' he said, shrugging his shoulders. They were such handsome, manly shoulders. They didn't stoop, or droop, they were not round or misshapen, or one an inch higher than the other, like so many scholars' shoulders. They were broad, and square, and manly, and they had the strength of a giant. He rowed five in his college boat, and was the best 'forward' in the 'Varsity football team. 'Well,' he said, looking down at the girl's dainty profile, and the curve of her soft cheek, and the dimple in her chin—he had looked at them afar off across the benches in the college chapel every Sunday since Lucy had first come up—'well, my dear, if they won't admit me at the front-door, I must find some other way. "Love laughs at locksmiths."'

He was still looking down at her profile—it was not very far off now, it was very near his shoulder—and he had possessed himself of her hand, when three girls came slowly up to the gate where they were standing.

Lucy saw Pamela's face a long way off, and her heart sank within her. She remembered suddenly that she was late for tea, and she snatched her hand away, and ran hurriedly down the path, and left him standing there to meet Pamela, and Maria Stubbs, and one of the younger Dons who had a deeply-rooted prejudice against lovers.

CHAPTER XXI.

A BLOW TO NEWNHAM.

Lucy saw no more of Pamela until after Hall. She thought she had escaped—quite escaped. After all, Pamela had not seen much; she had only seen Wyatt Edgell talking to her at the gate. Other girls talked to men at the gate—brothers, cousins, even coaches sometimes—when they had anything particular to say that couldn't wait for the proper opportunity, but lovers never.

It had gone so far that Lucy was obliged to admit that he was a lover. She admitted with a sigh what other girls—what Pamela Gwatkin, what Maria Stubbs—would have given anything—everything, even renounced the higher culture—to have been able to admit.

Capability Stubbs was walking with Pamela when they came across the lovers at the gate of Newnham. Capability took in the whole scene in a moment: perhaps she took in rather more. She coloured it with her own vivid imagination; she surrounded it with an atmosphere entirely her own. There was not a detail in the picture that was not brought out distinctly by this mental process and stamped upon her memory.

She was thinking about it all the time she was at Hall. She had no appetite for her dinner. She couldn't get the picture of the lovers parting at the gate out of her eyes. She sat staring across the soup, and the entrée, and the gooseberry-tart, at the white wall opposite. Perhaps it was all photographed there: the manly figure with the great square shoulders; they were stooping now, and the head was bent—it was almost touching Lucy's hair—and his eyes were looking into hers, and his lips were smiling——Pah! what is the use of describing the lips of another girl's lover?

Miss Stubbs broke off abruptly, and began to press the gooseberry-tart upon her neighbour. She had quite forgotten until now that it was her duty to look after Pamela. All the girls who go in for a Tripos are under special surveillance during the time of their examination, and a keeper is deputed to watch over them and see that they take their food properly and go to bed at ten o'clock. It was Maria Stubbs' duty to look after Pamela. The soup had gone by and the meat, and she had never once thought about her charge. Perhaps she hadn't eaten a morsel. She was looking white and hollow-eyed, and had that starved appearance peculiar to scholars whose brains absorb all the material intended for the body. She did not look as if she had eaten a good dinner, as if she had gone conscientiously through the menu. In point of fact,

Pamela had only trifled with her plate, and finding that her keeper was not watching, had not eaten a morsel, and now there was only the gooseberry-pie left.

Maria Stubbs pressed the pie upon her with tears in her eyes. She entreated her, if she valued her place in the Tripos, if the honour of Newnham was dear to her, to partake of that pie; but Pamela was not to be persuaded.

Conscience-stricken, Maria got up from the table and retired to her room. Half an hour later she emerged from it with a tray, and hurried down the corridor to Pamela's door. She didn't find her working as she expected—it was the very last night for work; to-morrow the examination would be over. She found her sitting at the window looking out at the sunset.

Pamela was not generally fond of sunsets, and she never sat at the window like other girls. She had no time to spare for sunsets, and she preferred the Windsor chair at her writing-table to any other chair in the room. It was empty now, and her books were closed, and her papers were all put tidily away. She had quite done with them, and she was looking out of the window.

Maria put down the cup of cocoa and the cake she had brought on a little table by Pamela's side, and watched her while she took it. She took it obediently. It was less trouble to take it than refuse it, but she didn't put any heart in it.

'It will all be over soon, dear,' Maria said by way of encouragement.

'Yes,' Pamela said wearily, and she looked out at the white gate which someone had left open. Perhaps she was thinking that she would soon pass through it, and her life here would be ended.

Maria looked in the same direction; but the gate brought something else to her mind, and she forgot all about Pamela and the cocoa.

'Oh, the pity of it!' she murmured; and her eyes lingered on the spot where Wyatt Edgell had last stood.

'The pity of what?' Pamela said impatiently. She was nervous, irritable, over-strung, and everything jarred upon her.

'Nothing, dear, nothing,' Maria said soothingly. 'I was only thinking of the man that girl is fooling. Oh, what idiots men are! Fancy a man—a real man, not a fool—throwing himself away upon that pink-and-white baby!'

Pamela was listening with an abstracted air, but the colour crept up under her skin, and her lip curled.

'You mean the St. Benedict's man?' she said, smiling with a sort of contempt.

'Yes; the man that was talking to her at the gate. Oh, Pamela, did you see his face?'

'Ye—e—s; I saw his face. I have often seen him before. He is Eric's friend. I have known him ever since he has been up.'

'He has known you—you, Pamela—for years, and yet he has chosen her?'

'There is no accounting for taste—at least, for men's taste,' Pamela said scornfully; but she did not look at the girl she was speaking to; she looked out at the sunset.

'I tell you what it is,' Miss Stubbs said with an air of conviction. 'He has been dreaming all his life about the ideal woman, and what his fancy has painted her; and with this myth, this creation of his own heated imagination in his mind, he has met this—this baby, and he has invested her with all the attributes of his ideal. It isn't Lucy Rae he's in love with; it's the ideal woman that he has been all his life imagining.'

Pamela smiled in a dreary way, but she still watched the sunset.

'Perhaps the circumstances—the very unusual circumstances—under which he first met her had something to do with it,' Maria went on in a lower voice. She was thinking of that scene in St. Benedict's that Lucy had described to her. 'Oh, you don't know what a meeting it was, Pam!'

'Yes,' said Pamela, with a little break in her voice, 'I know what it must have been to her; but no one can tell what it was to him.'

'You have heard, then! How did you hear?' Maria asked breathlessly.

'She told me. She told me the first night; she could not sleep, and I found her wandering about the corridor in a panic of fear.'

'Did she tell you all—quite all?'

'She told me everything,' Pamela said; and again her lips quivered.

'Has she told you she has promised to marry him?'

'No, she has not told me that,' Pamela said with that rising tell-tale colour in her cheeks, and a hard steely light in her gray-blue eyes, which were no longer watching the sunset; 'but I don't think she will marry him.'

'I am sure she will not marry him,' said Maria hotly; 'she will fool him and ruin his life. She is too great a coward to marry him!'

'She would be a brave woman to marry him, knowing what she knows,' Pamela said with the hot blood in her face again; 'but I don't think she will spoil his life.'

'Oh, you don't know! How should you know, you who are made on such large lines? He has placed the keeping of his life—think of it: of his life, body and soul!—in her hands. He believes that nothing but the love of a woman can save him; and he has implored her—that poor thing—to be a tower of strength to him.'

'Her!' Pamela murmured with her scornful lips, and the rising colour in her face.

'Yes, dear, he has asked her. He has made the mistake that men always do make: he has asked the wrong woman. He ought to have asked you or me. I don't think we should have failed him, Pam. We should not stop at the tower; we should have gone down—down into the mud and the mire. There is no depth so deep where our love would not have followed him, and we should have lifted him up. I am quite sure we should have lifted him up; we should have dragged him out of the very jaws of death and hell itself, if we had perished in doing it. Oh, I am sure that our love would have saved him! We should not have stopped at the tower.'

Maria stopped, not at the tower, but for want of breath. The red sunset light had quite faded out of the sky, and the gray night was closing in, and already the shadows were filling the silent room.

Pamela drew back from the window into the shadow.

'No,' she said hoarsely, 'we should not have stopped at the tower.'

The next day was the last, the very last, day of the examination for the Mathematical Tripos. It was the last, the very last, opportunity of making up for all the failures and mistakes of the past week. The front place of the year was to be won or lost on that last day. Its result would be final, quite final.

No wonder Maria Stubbs' conscience smote her when she remembered how she had neglected Pamela at Hall the previous day. She tried to make up for it at breakfast. She plied her with eggs and ham and porridge, but Pamela had no appetite for these dainties; she implored her with tears in her eyes to consume at least a spoonful of porridge, but Pamela was not to be moved. She went fasting to the exam., and Maria went with her so far as the door. She went quite early—girls always do go earlier than the men; they are always in their places, calm and collected, five minutes before the time, when the men generally arrive breathless at the door just as the hour is striking.

As Pamela walked up King's Parade in the sweet June sunshine, Wyatt Edgell passed her on the way from St. Benedict's to the Senate House. He was swinging along at a great pace, with the bearing of a man who was assured of an easy victory. His eyes were shining and his lips were smiling as they had smiled at Lucy. He had no eyes for any other woman; he passed the Newnham girls without seeing them.

His mind was full of the ideal woman who had promised to meet him in the lane when the exam. was over.

Maria Stubbs remembered the tower, and flushed scarlet; but Pamela shivered. She was looking dreadfully pale when Maria left her at the door. She would have liked to have gone in with her and sat by her side and held her pens, or picked up the blotting-paper, or collected her papers; but the examiners were inexorable, and Maria came sadly away.

Pamela pulled off her gloves and glanced over her paper; it was about as nice a paper as the last day's paper of the Mathematical Tripos usually is. There were several questions that Pamela had got at her fingers' ends; they would have puzzled the men, doubtless, but to a Newnham girl, who had worked for her Tripos as conscientiously as Pamela had worked, they were a mere bagatelle. She pulled off her gloves and glanced over her paper, and began work in the quiet, methodical way in which the students of women's colleges take their examinations. There was no heat, no excitement, no hurry whatever, nothing to disturb or bewilder.

She ought to have done uncommonly well with those nicely fitting questions; but instead of working she sat staring at her paper. The examiner, walking up and down the room, between the tables, noticed her abstraction. Once he paused and asked her if she was not feeling well; and then suddenly it dawned upon her that the time was going on, and that she had not yet begun. She had never felt it so hard to begin before; she had never felt that strange reluctance, like a clog upon her memory, that made the wheels of that fine bit of machinery drag heavily.

The reluctance—it was nothing more—grew and grew upon her. The questions were quite easy; she could have answered them with the smallest effort, but her mind refused to grapple with them.

It was like bringing a horse to the water; the water was cool and delightful, and it had only to stoop and drink; but it would not stoop. Pamela could do nothing as she sat there with the time slipping by but think of the man she had met in King's Parade, and wonder how he was getting on at the Senate House over the way with the paper that lay before her. She followed his progress question by question, and when she had come to the end of the paper she gave a sigh of relief—a big sigh, for the examiner who was at the other end of the room heard it, and the girls sitting opposite heard it and looked up.

They saw a very common sight in an examination-room—a girl with a gray dead face slipping off a chair to the floor. Pamela had fainted.

They brought her to, somehow, though everybody was begrudging the time she spent upon her; and then somebody took her back in a fly to Newnham.

It was an awful blow to Newnham. Everybody reproached Maria Stubbs. She hadn't half looked after her. Nothing that anybody said hurt poor Maria like the prickings of her own conscience. She was guilty in the matter of that last Hall. She had forgotten all about her charge until the gooseberry-pie!

She nursed Pamela tenderly all through that wretched day. She did what she could to atone for her past neglect. She brought her little messes of Liebig and arrowroot every hour; she watched beside her with the patient fidelity of a dog, while Pamela would have given worlds to be left alone in her darkened room. She locked the door against her officious nurse once, when she had gone out to fetch the everlasting beef-tea, and Maria made such a ridiculous noise outside, that threatened to bring all the Dons upon her, that she was obliged to get up and open it again. There was nothing to be done but to turn her face to the wall, and let the faithful creature potter about her to her heart's content.

CHAPTER XXII.

READING THE LISTS.

It was the oddest state of things that can be imagined at Newnham all through that next week. The order of everything was reversed. It had been all work—real, desperate work—now it was all play.

It was hard work enough to get through the days. The exams. were all over. There was nothing for the girls to do but to wait with what patience Heaven had given them for the lists to be out. Some of them were already quite indifferent to the lists, and when the strain was over had gone to bed, like Pamela, and turned their faces to the wall. Others had locked their doors and gone through their papers over and over again, and had made up their minds exactly where they should be placed when the lists came out. Some, more wise than the rest, had put their papers in the fire, and relieved their overburdened minds with large doses of fiction.

There was not a book opened in Newnham through all that week but yellow-backs. Annabel Crewe declared that she had read eleven before the week was half out, and a Natural Science girl had discovered that an infallible method for distracting one's thoughts from 'ologies' was to keep three sensational novels going at once.

One by one the Tripos lists came out, and the girls who had gone to bed for good thought better of it, and got up again, and came down to be congratulated, and admired, and made much of. The foolish virgins who had burnt their papers, and behaved with corresponding frivolity through all their University career, received the due reward of their folly, and were snubbed and condoled with in the most approved fashion. If one is down one must expect to be sat upon, or what would be the advantage of success?

The women's colleges had nothing to complain of. They had more than one first-class in every Tripos. They had beaten the men on their own ground; they had not only kept their place, but they were coming more and more to the front every year. They will win their degrees soon. Already the opinion of the Senate is equally divided; very soon the balance will be in their favour, and then all things will be possible.

The list of the Mathematical Tripos is read out last of all. It is not read until May Week has well begun, when the boat-races are half over, and the college concerts are in full swing, and picnics on the river and luncheons in college rooms are the order of the day.

The list is read out inside the Senate House, as befits the dignity of the occasion; but this particular year it was rumoured that the lists would be read out from the steps. Some distinguished visitors were expected at noon, and the Senate, in their zeal for the encouragement of learning and other virtues, were about to confer upon them Degrees of Honour, and the Senate House was full of carpenters preparing for the auspicious occasion.

Half an hour before the appointed time for reading the list the girls of Girton and Newnham and the men from every college in Cambridge assembled on the clean-shaven lawn before the south door of the Senate House. It was a glorious June morning, and the crowd could afford to wait. Having waited so long, they could wait a few minutes longer. To some those few minutes were a boon; the delay enabled them to pull themselves together, and bear with what courage and resignation they could call to their aid the fateful verdict they would presently hear read out.

The girls were more impatient than the men. They had reached the spot a quarter of an hour earlier, and had secured all the front places. They crowded the steps of the Senate House to the very doors, and they filled the broad path beneath the windows. A cool, compact, delightful crowd—a bevy, one might almost say—a bit of bright refreshing colour amid the rusty gowns and limp, disreputable caps of the undergraduates.

But the lists were not read out from the steps, and the girls crowded round the Senate House doors in vain. When it wanted a few minutes to the hour a window was opened just above the heads of the girls on the path, and a man looked out. He wore an M.A. hood, and there was a Proctor hiding away behind him in a white tie. The men sent up a shout and a howl—a shout for the examiner and a howl for the Proctor, who happened to be unpopular. The faces of the girls who had crowded up the steps and round the doors fell. They had expected to be in the very best place, and they were quite out of it. They could look on the eager faces of the men below them and the girls in the crowd, if this was any compensation. They could see how vainly the men strove to hide their anxiety beneath a veil of indifference or careless hilarity, and how the girls made no pretence at all of concealing their feelings, but looked as if they would like to tear that bland little examiner at the window limb from limb.

Among the girls who thirsted for his blood was Maria Stubbs. She had come quite early—one of the first—and she had settled herself on the top step just outside the Senate House door, and she awaited with devouring anxiety the reading of the list. It was not her list; it was Pamela Gwatkin's list. She had left her at Newnham in bed, with the curtains drawn to keep out the daylight, and she had taken away her watch, that the dreaded hour should not disturb her, and she had gone in at the last moment, and found her broad awake, with her weary eyes watching the door. She need not have troubled herself to take away the watch. Pamela knew the time to a second. She had been counting the hours all the night, and now she was counting the minutes.

'You are going to the Senate House?' she said, looking up. 'You needn't hurry back. I know exactly where I am.'

'We all know where you ought to be,' Maria said, hanging her head. 'The men would have been nowhere if it hadn't been for my wicked neglect!'

She was so angry with Lucy for being the innocent cause of her preoccupation that she wouldn't let her walk with her to the Senate House. She would hardly let her stand on the steps beside her, but Lucy wasn't to be pushed aside. She had as much interest in the list that was about to be read as Miss Stubbs.

There were a great many mothers and fathers and sisters and cousins there of the men whose names would presently be read out, and there might have been some sweethearts present; but there was not a single girl in all that crowd of sweet young English womanhood that did not envy Lucy.

'Time, sir, time!' the men shouted, and the examiner smiled benignly down on the crowd beneath.

'Time! time!'

How eager the men were! They couldn't all be Senior Wranglers!

Perhaps there were not many expectant Senior Wranglers there. It is not often that a man whose name is on every lip has the courage to face the ordeal. There is always a chance of disappointment. Wyatt Edgell was not among the crowd. Lucy must have seen him from her elevated place on the steps as she looked down at the upturned faces of the men, had he been there. Eric Gwatkin was close beneath the window among a crowd of St. Benedict's men, but Edgell was not among them.

'Time! time!' the men shouted, but the examiner only smiled and looked at his watch.

The minute-hand of the clock of great St. Mary's had travelled round to within a few seconds of the hour. A Proctor who was standing near the examiner, with the list in his hand, looked down at the crowd of undergraduates beneath with an eye to business, and took down the names of the men who were making a row.

It was the unpopular Proctor, and at the sight of his unwelcome face at the window the crowd beneath set up a groan, and in the midst of the groan the clock of the University church struck nine.

'Time!'

It was time indeed. The examiner opened the list, and held up his hand for silence. The men were still groaning as he read out the first name on the list:

'Senior Wrangler—Wyatt Edgell, St. Benedict's.'

The St. Benedict's men set up a great shout, and Eric Gwatkin waved his cap in a ridiculous manner. Lucy would have liked to wave her hat, too, she was so absurdly elated. She hadn't thought what a great thing it was to be Senior Wrangler until she saw how the crowd applauded. She quite flushed with triumph; it was her victory—hers! If it had not been for her, her lover would not have thought the prize worth winning. He had won it for her sake!

She was so proud and happy she did not hear another name in the list. What did the disappointment of others matter to her? Her cheeks were flushed, and her eyes were dancing with triumph. Oh, it was a proud thing to have a lover a Senior Wrangler!

Pamela Gwatkin was only equal to fifth—fifth Wrangler—and when Maria Stubbs went down the steps of the Senate House Lucy saw she had tears in her eyes. Of course, she was crying for Pamela's defeat. As if Pamela could have had any chance against her lover!

Lucy ran nearly all the way back to St. Benedict's. She wanted to be the first to congratulate her lover. Fast as she ran, Eric Gwatkin was there before her.

There was a strange hush in the outer court as she entered the college gate. There was no shouting like she had heard in the street and in the Senate House yard. There was a strange, ominous silence. The men were standing about the court in knots, and the porter was talking to a little group of men at the gate.

Lucy's heart sank within her. Had anything happened to the Master or Mrs. Rae? She thought the men looked at her with a strange kind of pity as she passed through the court, and they took off their caps as she passed. It was quite an ovation. Her lover was Senior Wrangler. She was quite in a flutter of pride and expectation; still, her heart sank within her.

Eric Gwatkin met her in the cloister; he was hurrying across to the lodge. She thought he was coming to tell her. What else should he come to the lodge for? The Master was past telling.

'Oh!' she cried, running to meet him, 'how does he bear it? You have told him——'

She paused, and her voice faltered with the question on her lips. Eric's face was white and anxious, and he was not smiling. He was not the least like the man who was waving his cap under the window of the Senate House.

'You have not heard——' he said.

'Heard what?' she cried impatiently. 'Is the Master——'

'No—no,' he interrupted; 'it is not that—it is not the Master.'

'It is Mrs. Rae?' she said, with a chill feeling at her heart. She was sure something had happened.

'No, it is not Mrs. Rae. Oh, Miss Lucy! how can I tell you?'

'It is he!' she said in a stricken voice, and with that dreadful feeling at her heart. 'Oh! what has he done?'

She was standing wringing her hands in the middle of the cloisters, and the men were passing through, and everyone could see her.

'Hush!' Eric said almost harshly; 'he has not done anything—at least, he has only done what others do at this time. There was a bump supper last night, and—and Wyatt was there; and when Mr. Colville went in this morning to tell him of his great success, he was on the floor in one of his old attacks. It is all over the college, and everybody is dreadfully shocked—that is all!'

'All!' Lucy said bitterly. 'You speak as if the shame and exposure were nothing. Oh, I shall never be able to face it!' She only thought of herself.

Eric Gwatkin was very sorry for her. He would have spared her if he could. It was better for her to hear it from his lips than from others.

'He has done great things,' he said. 'It was enough to turn anybody's head. He will go down in a day or two, and the temptation will not occur again. You do not know—how should you?—how great the temptation is—what a supreme moment this is in a man's life!'

'No,' Lucy said, with a shiver, 'I do not know.'

They had reached the door of the lodge while they were talking together, and Eric had rung the bell.

'Why do you ring?' she said sharply.

He hung his head.

'I came over to see if Nurse Brannan can be spared for a few minutes,' he said guiltily.

'Is he so bad as that?' Lucy asked; but she did not offer to go to him.

'Ye—es; he is very bad. Mr. Colville is with him, and he thought that the nurse ought to be with him until the doctor comes.'

'You have sent for a doctor?'

'Yes; the Tutor has sent for a doctor, and—and he has noticed that scar.'

'And you have told him?'

'Yes; I have told him. How could I help it?'

Lucy went into the lodge covered with shame and humiliation. She was so proud and happy when she entered the college gate. She had made up her mind to tell Cousin Mary all about her engagement. She was going to her to be congratulated—to be envied and congratulated by everybody in Cambridge. Now she wouldn't have owned it for the world. How lucky she hadn't told Mary!

CHAPTER XXIII.

'GOING DOWN.'

It was rather hard to spare Nurse Brannan on this particular morning; harder than usual. The Master had passed a bad night; he had not slept at all, and he was decidedly weaker. He had been wandering all through the night, and he was still wandering feebly when Lucy came into his room in the morning. He had been going over the old scenes of his youth; he had been travelling back to the sweet green fields and the hills and valleys of his earliest recollections.

When Lucy came into the room he was propped up in bed, babbling about the old scenes and the old places. The blind was drawn up, and the June sunshine poured into the room. Nurse Brannan never denied her patients sunshine. 'Let them have it while they may,' she used to say; 'they will have no need of it by-and-by.' The sun was shining into the room now, and on to the bed, and on to the face of the old Master.

Lucy had not seen him for several days; she had been busy with her examinations, and she was struck with the change in him—an indefinable change that sharpened his rugged features as if a chisel had been passed over them. They were rugged still, but with an added nobleness, and there was a light upon them that Lucy had not seen there before. His dim blue eyes were looking up at the window, and he did not see her come in the room. They were looking with that shining light in them above the gray battlements of the old court to the bright bit of blue sky beyond.

'I think he can be safely left,' Lucy said; 'he is very quiet. I will stay with him till you come back. You must not be long; I have an examination at ten o'clock. You must not stay more than half an hour.'

Nurse Brannan promised to come back within the half-hour, and Lucy took her place beside the bed. She had a dim idea that she ought to have gone herself to Wyatt Edgell in his humiliation, not have sent a hired nurse, but she put the thought away from her. It was not a real engagement, she told herself. She had only consented to it to give him a motive for work. He could not hold her to it now; no one could expect her to be bound by a promise given under such conditions. How lucky it was that no one at St. Benedict's knew of her engagement!

The Master would not let her thoughts wander long. His hands were feebly groping about the coverlet of the bed, and Lucy saw that he was making an effort to get up.

'No, dear Master,' she said; 'no, I wouldn't get up yet. I would wait till nurse comes back; she will be here soon.'

'I was going to meet her, my dear,' he said; 'I have been travelling all night. I came by the coach to the cross-roads; it is a long journey from Cambridge, and I am very tired. I thought it would never end, and the morning was slow in breaking. It broke at last; I never saw a finer sunrise, a higher dawn. The coach put me down at the cross-roads; I had nothing to carry—I had left everything behind—and I have been walking over the hills since daybreak. It's wonderful how little they have changed: I knew every field and hedge on the way; and the old trees and the mile-stones in the road, I knew them every one; and the broken cross in the churchyard, and the old gray tower. The tower looks taller now than it used to, and the vane was shining in the sunlight as I came along; I could see it a long way off, gleaming like gold, and pointing the way.'

The old Master paused for want of breath; he had worn himself quite out. He lay back on the pillow, with the sunshine streaming on his worn face. Lucy could not help noticing how shining it was—shining like the old vane.

'Strange,' he went on presently, talking to himself in a lower tone—'strange! the cross was there, and the church, and the tower, and the old elms in the yard, and the rooks cawing in the branches—I knew the cawing of those old rooks again—but I could not find the Vicarage gate.'

Lucy was beginning to get impatient. Nurse Brannan ought to be back by this time. Her examination would begin in a quarter of an hour. She didn't care anything about that Vicarage gate; there was nobody waiting for her at the gate.

The Senior Tutor came in while she was fuming and fretting about the time.

'I thought you would want to get away,' he said to Lucy, 'so I came over to sit with the Master. We can't spare Nurse Brannan just yet.'

Cousin Mary came in, too, just after him; she generally came into the room a minute or two after the Senior Tutor. She had not been able to come in before, she was in such close attendance on the Master's wife. Mrs. Rae had had a restless night, but had just fallen asleep, so Mary had stolen away.

'This is a dreadful thing about Mr. Edgell,' she said. 'The college was so proud of him; it will be a terrible blow.'

'Yes,' said the Tutor; 'it will be a great blow. It is unfortunate it should have happened just now; it will get so talked about.'

He was thinking of the credit of the college, not of Wyatt Edgell.

'What will he do?'

'Oh, he will go down with his friends. I have telegraphed for them; they will be here by noon; and when he can be moved they will take him away. It appears this is not the first time. He attempted suicide the other day; I saw the mark on his throat——'

Lucy did not wait to hear any more. She ran away as fast as she could, and left Cousin Mary and the Tutor talking by the Master's bedside.

They took no notice of her. They did not even look at her. Oh, if they had only known!

Wyatt Edgell's people came at noon. Lucy saw them crossing the old court when she came back from her examination—an elderly man with a striking resemblance to her lover, and a tall stately woman with a pale beautiful patrician face.

They ought to have been proud and happy people. This should have been a red-letter day in their lives—a day of thankfulness and congratulations and unutterable joy; a day when the tears come with the smiles, and the glad words falter on the lip, and there is a strange catch in the voice, and a dimness before the eyes, when the most eloquent speech begins and ends with a 'God bless you, my boy!' uttered in a very shaky voice.

There were no congratulations to-day and no smiles. If there were tears no one saw them—only a hard break in the voice when Wyatt Edgell's mother thanked the Tutor for his interest in her son. She didn't even look at Lucy as she passed. Something in the rustle of her rich trailing skirts as they swept over the stones of the court brought to the mind of the Master's niece those old stories the Master was so fond of telling—of the stall in the butter-market, and the meeting of her grandfather with her high-spirited ancestress in the dancing-booth at the fair.

It was quite as well that nobody knew about that engagement.

Lucy had another examination in the afternoon—her last. She hastily swallowed some cold luncheon that was laid for her at the end of the long dining-table at the lodge. There was no one present but herself. Mrs. Rae was not so well, and Cousin Mary had a tray carried up into her room, and Nurse Brannan could not leave the Master.

Lucy had no appetite for the solitary meal. Something was choking in her throat all the time she sat at the table, and she could not swallow anything.

She looked in at the Master's room before she went off to her exam. He was still searching for the Vicarage gate. Mrs. Rae was asleep or dozing; she did not appear to notice her when Lucy opened the door of her room. Cousin Mary was still with her—she seldom left her now—and she was looking tired and worn out for want of rest. It did not occur to Lucy to offer to take her place; besides, she had to go to her exam.

'I can "go down" to-night, dear, if you like,' she said to Mary, before she went away, 'if I can be of any use here. A lot of the girls have "gone down" to-day. Term is quite over. I can either come home to-day or Monday, which you think best.'

'Nurse Brannan has not been to bed for a week,' Cousin Mary said wearily, 'and—and I'm afraid I am getting worn out; but you must do as you like.'

Lucy went off to her exam.; but for all the good she did she might just as well have stayed away. She was very sorry for those old people at the lodge, but what else could be expected at their age? She was more distressed about her lover. Nurse Brannan had stayed with him until the paroxysm had abated, and he had sunk into a deep sleep.

He would probably awake from it, the doctor who had been called in said, not very much the worse for the carouse, and unconscious—quite unconscious—of what had happened.

What would he do when he awoke? Lucy was pondering this question in her mind all the time she was in for her exam., when she ought to have been occupied with the questions on the paper before her. She hadn't answered it when she got back to Newnham. She had only gone back to pick up some things she needed and to get her exeat, or go through the ceremony that takes the place of an exeat at a college for women.

She had to say good-bye to two or three of the girls who were going down; some were going down altogether, and their paths were never likely to cross again. Among these last was Pamela Gwatkin. She was going down, broken in health and spirit, and she had no present intention of coming up to Newnham again.

She was up and dressed when Lucy went into her room to say good-bye. She was sitting at her old place at the table, tearing up some papers. She had torn up a lot already, and they were lying in a heap by her side, and Maria Stubbs was on the floor packing her books.

Pamela looked up when Lucy came into the room.

'Well?' she said, with a large look of scorn in her eyes that made Lucy's cowardly little heart sink into her shoes. 'Well?'

It wasn't very much to say, but a great deal can be got into a word of such varied meaning. Lucy saw in a moment that Pamela knew all.

'I don't know what you mean,' Lucy said with some spirit.

'No,' said Pamela scornfully; 'I suppose not. You have not seen him then?'

'Seen him?' Lucy exclaimed, flushing scarlet, and her eyes smarting with tears of anger and humiliation. 'I never intend to see him again! His own people are here.'

'What has that got to do with it?' said Maria, sitting down on the floor in the middle of a heap of books.

'Everything. He doesn't want me if he has got his people.'

Lucy was thinking of Wyatt Edgell's mother. She had been haunted by her pale patrician face all through the exam.

'I don't see that,' Maria said hotly. 'He will want you more. You ought to stand between him and them, and see they are not too hard upon him. I think you ought to have gone to his mother at once, and told her everything.'

'I?' Lucy gasped—'I?'

'Yes, you. Who else should take his part at a time like this? Oh, you are a poor coward! You are not half good enough for him!'

The tears were in her eyes as she spoke; she had to put up her hand and dash them off her hideous pale lashes. She looked as if she would have liked to have taken Lucy in her strong arms and shaken her.

'I'm afraid I am a coward,' Lucy said humbly; and then she began to cry.

She wasn't content with crying, she began to sob hysterically. She had gone through a great deal that day, and her nerves were shaken. Maria got up from the floor and came over to her. She put her on the couch, and took off her hat, and stroked her hair back, and soothed her, but Pamela took no notice of her; she only sat tearing up her papers.

'You would do the same if you were in my place,' Lucy sobbed; 'you would be afraid to venture. What girl in her senses wouldn't?'

Miss Stubbs smiled.

'I know some girls who wouldn't,' she said.

She was very angry with Lucy—angry and impatient; but that did not account for the hard break in her voice.

'Hush!' Pamela exclaimed harshly; 'it is not her fault she has so small a soul.'

'I am sure you would not do otherwise,' Lucy sobbed, not heeding the interruption. 'You would be afraid to—to marry him. Oh! who could marry him?'

Maria's eyes were shining, and the hand that was stroking Lucy's hair trembled; but Pamela's face was hard and stony as she sat tearing up her papers, and her thin lips were pressed tight together.

'You would never be safe,' Lucy went on, defending herself. 'You would never know what he would do. He might break out at any time—he might kill himself, he might kill you!' The picture was too appalling, and Lucy subsided into a fresh passion of tears. 'Oh, I could never run the risk!' she said with a shiver; 'I should never be safe!'

'Not if you loved him?'

Pamela asked the question in a low voice—low and vibrating with passion. She had not intended to give a voice to her thoughts. She would have given the world to have recalled the words after she had spoken.

'No,' Lucy exclaimed passionately; 'not even if I loved him!'

'Oh, you poor thing!' said Maria Stubbs, with her eyes flashing, and her freckled face all aglow with a strange fire.

'Let her alone,' Pamela said wearily—'let her alone. How should she do otherwise? It is not her fault that she has not a large soul. Let the poor little thing alone. She can only act according to her lights. Let her alone.'

They let her alone—at least, they said good-bye to her in a strained, unemotional way. They didn't shed a single tear in that parting. Maria Stubbs kissed her on both cheeks, and told her to write to her and say how the Master of St. Benedict's was. She didn't say a word about her lover. Pamela kissed her on one cheek—at least, she made a peck at her, and said some cold, formal words of farewell, and went wearily back to tearing up her papers.

When the good-byes were said, the poor thing with a small soul crept humbly down the stairs. Everybody cannot be made on such large lines as Pamela Gwatkin.

CHAPTER XXIV.

THE VICARAGE GATE.

The old Master of St. Benedict's had not found the Vicarage gate when Lucy got back to the lodge. He had been searching for it all through the long June day, and he had not found it yet. He was lying back propped up with pillows when Lucy went into his room, and the sunset light was falling on his face. All the hard lines had been smoothed out of it; the furrows that years of work and thought had stamped upon it were all smoothed out, and it was like the face of a little child.

His eyes were open, and Lucy thought he was watching the sunset. It had already slipped off the grass in the court below, and it had climbed the chapel wall and reached the gray battlements at the top, where the bits of blue sky could be seen between. She went to the window and drew up the blind that he could follow it still higher, and he watched it with a strange wistfulness as it slid off the chapel roof, and lingered for a few moments on the spire.

Everything had slipped out of his life like the sunset light, and now that, too, was fast slipping away. He watched it until it had faded quite away, and then he closed his eyes with a sigh. Lucy watched beside him through the early part of the night; she was to call Nurse Brannan at daylight. He lay very quiet, wanting no watching, until past midnight, and Lucy thought he was sleeping. She was conscious of no overwhelming sorrow. Perhaps she could not feel things deeply like some people. He had lived his life—his useful, honourable life—and now he would pass away full of days and honour.

She wondered vaguely as she sat beside the bed in the silent room—so silent that she could hear the ticking of the Master's watch on the dressing-table—what would become of her. Things might have been different—so different; but she did not dare to think of that now. It was unreasonable of Pamela Gwatkin and Maria to blame her. No one in their senses would blame her.

Lucy could not help repeating to herself, as she sat there thinking over the events of the miserable day, Pamela's question, 'Not if you had loved him?' 'No,' she told herself impatiently, 'she would not be justified in making such a sacrifice, however much she loved him. Nothing could justify it. Girls were not expected to make such sacrifices for their lovers. No girl in her senses would think of it.'

Lucy's meditation was disturbed by the Master's rambling monologue. He had been dozing through all the early part of the night, and about midnight he awoke and began talking to himself in low, disconnected sentences, his mind wandering off in strange fancies and old recollections, which escaped from his lips in broken sentences. He had forgotten the Vicarage gate now, where Rachel used to wait for him in those far-off days when he came back term after term from college. He had gone back in memory to an earlier time. He was a boy again in his father's fields; the old faces of his infancy and childhood were about him. He was a boy again in the old humble home, among the old humble folk.

He babbled in his rambling, disconnected way about things and people that Lucy had never heard of, only now and then she caught a familiar name that his memory had gone far back to seek. She didn't shrink now from the mention of her humble progenitors: the dear old rustic with a hayband round his legs, the dairywoman who kept the stall in the butter-market. At this solemn time these distinctions seemed but a small matter. The years had rolled back, and the rustic in his furrow and the Master of St. Benedict's were again boys together in their father's field. There were no distinctions now to separate them; there would be no distinctions ever again. They had all slipped away with the labour and the learning of the intervening years; with the well-earned honours—the scarlet gown and the doctor's hood; they were all among the things that had been. There was nothing left but love and tender trust—the heart of a little child.

The hours dragged wearily on; it seemed to Lucy as if the sweet June night would never end. There was not a light in a single window in the college court, and there were no stars in the sky, only the clouds hurrying on their noiseless way. The silence of the darkened room seemed to the frightened watcher to grow more oppressive as the night wore on. She could hear the rapid tick, tick of the Master's watch on the dressing-table; it could not beat the moments out fast enough. Oh, it was dreadful to hear it hurrying on, and to know that it was ticking off at every beat the few remaining moments of a human life!

Lucy listened to it until she could bear it no longer. Should she call Cousin Mary, who was with the Master's wife in the room across the passage? She had got as far as the door to call her, and then she recollected that Mrs. Rae was always listening for any sound from the Master's room, and that she would be disturbed.

The thought of the watchfulness of the Master's wife, and the love—the faithful love that had stood the shocks of more than sixty years, and had only grown truer, and deeper, and tenderer with the years—smote upon Lucy like a blow. Oh, she had never known what love was, if this was a woman's love!

She asked herself, as she sat beside the Master's bed watching the feeble, groping hand straying over the coverlet, as if it were searching for something, what the Master's wife would have done if she had been in her place. Would her love have stood the test? It had been all fair sailing with her—a long, long sequence of success, distinction, and honour. There had never been a cloud upon the horizon of her love; there had been no harder test than the test of years of patient waiting, and the happy fulfilment of all her dearest hopes. There had not been a single disappointment. Her love had never been tried like Lucy's.

Oh, it was too cruel that this blow should have fallen upon her! Lucy was quite sure that if her lines had fallen in such fair, still places as Mrs. Rae's, she would have made quite as devoted a wife. She would have been the tenderest and most loving wife to a successful man—to a man without any moral or mental taint, to a man of stainless reputation; but to a poor, miserable wretch, who had no control over himself, who wanted to be watched, and guarded, and restrained, who might at any moment do some dreadful thing——Oh, no, no, no!

Lucy couldn't finish the picture, it was too terrible. She could only throw herself sobbing on the floor beside the Master's bed and grovel on the ground with her face in her hands in a paroxysm of humiliation and despair too deep for words.

Oh, why had she such a small soul? 'I am made on such small lines,' she moaned in her self-abasement. 'I am such a mean, pitiful creature. I want to be happy, and safe, and prosperous, and everything to go smooth. I cannot rise to great occasions like other women. I cannot make sacrifices that other women would love to make. I am not Pamela—I am not even Maria Stubbs!'

Nurse Brannan came in while Lucy was on the floor beside the bed. She pretended that she was kneeling—Lucy was always pretending things. There was quite sufficient reason to account for her tears and for her kneeling beside the Master's bed. All who loved him in life should have been there, where Lucy was, kneeling and weeping. There was no one else left to kneel and weep but Cousin Mary, and Nurse Brannan fetched her presently, when she saw how near the end was.

They watched beside him until the dawn, and then the nurse drew the curtain up and let in the faint gray light of the new day. Lucy sat sobbing miserably beside the bed, and Cousin Mary held the feeble hand in hers—it was too feeble to grope any more; and the rapid beat of the Master's watch on the table beat out like a swift shuttle the solemn closing moments of the Master's life.

The sky above the chapel roof turned from gray to rose, and rose to gold. The vane on the spire caught the first gleam of the rising sun, and at the same moment the Master opened his eyes. He looked round on the group by the bedside with a glad, dazed expectation in them that had caught the brightness of another morning. He was looking round for someone; perhaps if she who he was looking for had been there he would not have seen her. His lips were moving, and Lucy bent down to hear what he was saying.

'I shall meet her at the gate,' he said. 'She is sure to be waiting at the gate.'

The sweet June morning broke, and the sun rose over the gray battlements of the old court and the roof of the college chapel; but to the old Master there was a newer day and another morning.

When Lucy came in to see the Master's wife later in the day she found her still dozing. She had not taken notice of anything or anyone all through the night. She had not missed Mary from her side; but when she heard Lucy's voice in the room—she was only speaking in a whisper—she opened her eyes, and Lucy thought she knew her.

'It is I, dear,' she said in a shaky voice. She could not keep her voice steady or the tears out of her eyes. 'It is Dick's little daughter.'

The patient face on the pillow smiled, and she moved her hand towards her—a little thin, shadowy hand, that was feebly groping about the coverlet, oh, so like the Master! Lucy took it in hers, and smoothed it between her own soft, warm palms.

Her lips were moving, and the girl bent over her to catch the words. It was the old question; she had never anything else to ask.

'How is the Master?'

Lucy ought to have been prepared for it; but she wasn't. She was so broken down and unstrung and worn out with that night of watching that she was not prepared for anything.

'Oh, you poor dear!' she said. 'Don't you know that the Master is well? He is quite—quite well!'

'Quite well?'

'Yes, quite well.'

Then Lucy began to cry. She could not keep her tears back any longer, and Cousin Mary turned her out of the sick-room. Nurse Brannan found her sobbing in the window-seat, and ordered her to bed, where she soon cried herself to sleep.

With the unimpaired appetite of youth for sleep, Lucy slept through all the long June day. She slept until the sunset light again touched the roof of the college chapel.

It would be slipping off it presently, like it had slipped off the day before, when the Master was here to watch it.

Perhaps he was watching it now.

Lucy would not have awakened even then, if Nurse Brannan had not aroused her.

'Come,' she said, shaking her; 'get up at once. Mrs. Rae is asking for you. Come at once, or you will be too late!'

Lucy did not stay to dress. She hurried across the passage with her hair falling over her shoulders and her dressing-gown, which she did not stay to put on properly, trailing on the ground behind her. Her nerves were so over-strung that it seemed to her that its rustle on the floor sent a whisper after her the whole length of the passage. It was like the Master's voice.

The face on the pillow had changed since she had seen it last. It was sharper and grayer, and the breath came shorter and at longer intervals.

The shadows were already closing around her when Lucy came into the room. She no longer opened her eyes when the girl spoke to her—she would never open them again here—but her lips were moving.

Lucy bent over her with her ear to the failing lips, but she could not catch the faint, broken words.

'I cannot hear you, dear,' she said, while her tears fell on the meekly folded hands that were groping no longer. 'I cannot catch what you say. Is it about the Master?'

She had touched the right chord—the only chord that stretched across the gulf—and the feeble lips moved. They only framed a single word:

'Where?'

'Where is the Master?' Lucy said eagerly. 'Oh, he is waiting for you at the gate. His last—last message was: "I shall see her at the gate!"'

The face on the pillow changed. It changed as Lucy bent over it.

The great, solemn change! Over all the weakness and the weariness came, not a shadow, but a light—the wondrous light of the full fruition of her changeless love.

CHAPTER XXV.

THE STALL IN THE BUTTER-MARKET.

The Senior Tutor took all the trouble of the funeral—or the funerals, rather—off the Master's nieces. He came over directly he heard that the Master was dead, and arranged everything. He knew his last wishes, expressed long ago when he was in health and the end seemed a long way off.

His wishes had been so clearly expressed that there could be no doubt about them. He had provided for every contingency. He was to lie beside his wife. If she preceded him, he was to be laid by her side wherever she was laid. If he should happen to die before her, he was to be carried back to the old place, to the old churchyard where all his humble forefathers lay, to go back to where he had started, and find his last resting-place where his life had begun. In no case was he to be buried in the college chapel. They might put up a brass for him on the old walls, among the carven tombs and tablets of the old Masters and Fellows, but the dust of his bones should not mix with theirs.

The Senior Tutor carried out his wishes faithfully. He arranged everything. There was nothing for the Master's nieces to do but to see to their own humble mourning. He came over directly he heard of the Master's death, and he was coming backwards and forwards to the lodge all the day. He wanted to get a sight of Lucy; he only wanted to see her for a few minutes; he would have preferred to see her alone. He had arranged exactly what he should say, and the time had come for saying it.

Whatever it was he had to say he had to put it off, for Lucy did not make her appearance all through that sad day.

She was so nervous and overwrought when all was over that Nurse Brannan had to put her to bed; and when she came in in the night, finding that the girl was awake and weeping, she came into her bed and lay down beside her.

Lucy could not go to sleep until she had poured out all her trouble into her sympathetic ear. She wouldn't have told Cousin Mary for the world.

Perhaps Nurse Brannan knew all about it without being told. She knew more about Lucy's lover than Lucy herself knew.

'Do you think I could do otherwise?' Lucy asked, weeping, when she had told her all her sad little story.

'Not unless you loved him very much,' Nurse Brannan said promptly. She could understand a girl doing a great deal for a man she loved.

'No—o—o,' Lucy said hesitatingly. 'I don't think I ought to marry him even then. One never knows what he may do. I should never feel safe.'

If the room had not been quite dark, Lucy would have seen that Nurse Brannan was smiling with a contemptuous sort of pity; but, whatever she felt, she only soothed and petted the weeping girl as if she had been a little child.

'You are quite right, dear,' she said; 'one never knows what such a man will do when there is no influence strong enough to restrain him. I don't think you would be strong enough to hold him back. He ought to marry a woman with a large nature, who loved him devotedly—and I think he would tax her devotion to the uttermost.'

Lucy turned to her pillow with a sigh.

'Ah!' she murmured, 'it is the old story. I am a poor thing with a small soul!' Still, she was helped and comforted.

Eric Gwatkin came over to the lodge the next morning and asked for Lucy. He was charged with a message of condolence from her lover. She saw him in the long gallery among the pictures of the old Masters. It was such a grave and stately place, there was no room for sentiment here. She knew the trial had come, but Nurse Brannan had helped her to meet it.

She looked such a white, weeping little Lucy as she came down the long gallery to meet him. She seemed to have grown so small, to have shrunk into herself with this sorrow that had fallen upon her, that Eric Gwatkin hesitated to deliver the message that had been committed to him. She had been so sorely tried within the last two days, how could he add to her pain? He would much rather have taken her in his arms and comforted her, and offered her their safe, sure shelter from all the storms of life. He would have given the world to have the right to take her in his arms, but he had to deliver his message.

Perhaps Lucy would have preferred it if he had. She wanted to be loved and comforted, and, above all things, to be safe.

But Eric Gwatkin had not come courting on his own account. He was only the bearer of a message of sympathy from her lover. It sounded cold and formal as it fell from Eric's faltering lips. If he had come himself and taken her in his arms, if she had felt the warmth of their strong pressure and his breath upon her cheek, it might have been different—it might have been quite different.

After all, it is the occasion that makes the heroine.

Eric delivered his message of sympathy, and Lucy stood white and downcast, with wet eyelashes and trembling lips, waiting for that other message that she knew was coming. He looked at her standing there—he was only a man—and he hadn't the heart to deliver it. He was so sorry for her. He was conscious of another feeling besides which he would not have owned for the world, but he couldn't keep it out of his eyes.

His eyes were full of tenderness, but his lips were faltering in a most absurd way while Lucy waited.

'You have another message for me,' she said presently, seeing he faltered and hesitated to speak.

'Yes,' he said, 'I have another message.' But he didn't attempt to deliver it.

If he had had no tenderness for the girl he would still have hesitated. How could he, looking at the white, shrinking little figure, lay this heavy load upon her?

'What has Mr. Edgell asked you to say to me?' she said in a thin, reedy little voice that she couldn't keep from shaking.

'You have heard,' he said huskily, and with a voice low and ashamed in his throat; 'everybody has heard what has happened. Knowing this, he has sent me to ask you if you will give him another trial. It is never likely to happen again—God helping him, it will never happen again—but, knowing this, and what has gone before, he has bid me to ask you if you will give him another chance.'

He paused and looked above Lucy's head; he could not look her in the face.

'His fate is in your hands,' he went on, without looking at her. 'It depends upon you whether a happy and useful life is before him. If you are true to him he will have the strongest motive to lead an honourable and honoured life that a man can have; but if you refuse to give him a chance, he will abandon all hope—he will have no inducement to make a stand.'

He said nothing about risking her happiness. It might not have occurred to him that he was asking her to risk the ruin of her young life on the chance of saving his friend. Still, he did not look her in the face.

'How can I answer him?' Lucy said, wringing her hands.

'You can only answer him as your heart dictates,' he said huskily. 'Remember, in refusing him this last chance, you are snatching away a rope from the grasp of a drowning man.'

Oh, what a coward he was: he could not look the girl in the face!

'Oh, this is horrible!' Lucy said, with a moan, and then she sat down on one of the high-backed chairs against the wall and began to cry. Her nerves were so shaken that tears came readily now.

If there was one thing more than another that Eric Gwatkin hated, it was to see a woman cry. Pamela never cried. Perhaps these foolish tears showed him more than anything else the girl's weakness. He was dreadfully sorry for her; he was sorry and ashamed of his errand. How could he press this sacrifice upon such a little weak creature?

'I am such a poor thing!' Lucy moaned, wringing her hands. 'I should never be able to influence him. Oh, you don't know how weak I am!'

Eric smiled sadly, and sighed. He knew exactly how weak she was; he would not have had a woman stronger.

'I am not like Pamela,' Lucy went on, with her little feeble moan.

'No,' he interrupted her hastily, 'thank God! You are not like Pamela.'

Lucy looked at him with wonder, through her tears, not unmixed with reproof.

'If I were Pamela,' she said, with some dignity—'if I had a great soul, and were made on larger lines, like Pamela, I should give you a different answer.'

'I must tell you,' he said hastily, interrupting her—'I must tell you, before you give your answer—your final answer—that Edgell releases you from your engagement; that he reproaches himself for having ever asked you to risk your happiness in his keeping. He begs me to say that if you have any fears or misgivings, if you have no confidence in his resolution—if you doubt him or yourself—it would be better for you to give him up.'

Lucy sighed.

'But if you can be so generous as to give him another chance, he will never, never, God helping him, betray your trust!'

Lucy looked at him with a break in the dull misery in her face. Why hadn't he delivered this part of his message first? Why had he talked about snatching away a rope from a drowning man?

'I am very grateful to him,' Lucy said, in a small shaky voice; 'tell him I am very grateful to him. I do not deserve so much love. Ask him to forgive me if he can; I am such a poor thing. I have no courage—I cannot even be generous!'

She broke quite down. She could not trust herself to say any more. She took her lover at his word. Eric Gwatkin gave her one more chance before he went away.

'Remember,' he said, 'it is his last hope of reform.'

But Lucy only moaned, 'I am such a poor thing—I have no courage!'

He went away, and left her weeping in the gallery, under the picture of the Old Master. Surely he would have approved her decision.

It was a dreadful time at St. Benedict's all through that sad week. The boat that was going to do such great things—that was going to make a bump every night of the races—did not row during the three succeeding nights.

Perhaps it was quite as well that it did not; the bumps might not have come off, and, at any rate, it had the credit of them. Most of the crew had gone down; there was nothing to stay up for. All the men, indeed, who were not staying for their degrees, or who had not people up, went down at once. There was nothing to keep them here: the college concert had been put off, and the boat ball, and the supper that was to celebrate the bumps. There was not a single festivity to celebrate; there was nothing but a funeral to stay up for.

A few men stayed up for it, and all the Tutors and Fellows. There was quite a large muster in the college chapel at the early service, when the coffins of the old Master and his wife were brought in and placed in the clear space in the body of the chapel, between the long rows of benches. There were no flowers to hide the dreary outline of the coffins—nothing to cover up their nakedness; there were no flowers heaped up in the Master's empty stall beneath the organ-loft, but someone had laid on the seat of the adjoining stall, which was draped with black, like the Master's, a wreath of immortelles. Someone—no one seemed to know who—placed the little solitary wreath on the coffin of the Master's wife, and it travelled with her down to its last resting-place.

Not a few of the Fellows of other colleges, and all the 'Heads,' followed the little sad procession to the railway-station. There were but two mourners to follow: Cousin Mary and Dick's little daughter. There were no other relatives left. The Old Master had outlived all his kin.

The Senior Tutor went down with the women to Northwold. He had made all the preparations. And as the sun was sinking at the close of the sweet June day he stood bareheaded beside the open grave, where the Master of St. Benedict's and his wife lay side by side.

They buried him in the old churchyard where his humble forefathers slept. Their stones, aslant now, and overgrown with moss and lichens, were all around him. Lucy could not help reading their rudely-carven names and homely epitaphs, as she stood listening to the solemn words that were being read over the Master's grave.

There was a Richard Rae among them who had 'died in sure and certain hope of a joyful resurrection.' What could he have done more if he had been Master of a college?

She lingered among the graves with the Tutor, and read the simple records of her humble race. She could trace her family back to the seventh generation; it was quite a long line of descent: Davids and Nathaniels and Marthas and Marys, but there was only one Lucy, the high-spirited ancestress who had kept the stall in the butter-market, and met her lover at a dancing-booth at the fair.

They left the old Master sleeping among his kinsfolk, in the old churchyard that his memory had gone back to, close to the Vicarage gate. The setting sun was shining on the church tower and on the old vane that had lingered so long in his memory, and the rooks were cawing in the old elm-trees overhead, as they turned away and left him to his rest. He would sleep more peacefully here under the daisies and beneath the dewy heavens than amid the scenes of his learned labours, under the stones of his college chapel.

The mourners returned to Cambridge the next day; there was nothing to keep them here. Before they went Lucy asked the Tutor to take her to the butter-market. Everything had changed, but the old market still stood where it had stood for centuries, with the quaint stalls and the old brown awnings, and the rude boards spread on trestles where the country folk displayed their homely wares.

There was an old woman sitting behind that corner stall now, lean and brown and wrinkled as an autumn pear. Lucy bought some flowers of her before she went away; it might have been her namesake.

It was among these homely surroundings, in this morning walk, that the Senior Tutor asked Lucy to be his wife. He knew all about her birth, and those old stories of the Master's—he had heard them dozens of times—and he had just taken her to the stall which that other Lucy Rae had once kept.

He couldn't have chosen a happier moment to press his suit. Lucy's heart had quite failed her. It had been failing her ever since that morning when she met Eric

Gwatkin in the cloisters, and at the sight of that stall in the butter-market it was at its lowest ebb. She had no spirit left in her; she had no one to cling to. She wanted to be loved and comforted and petted, and Cousin Mary was not good at petting. The Senior Tutor's offer came at the right moment; he couldn't have chosen a more auspicious time.

Lucy didn't exactly jump at him. She was too bewildered and broken down and upset generally to jump, but she asked him to give her time—to give her a week to think about it.

When a girl asks a man to give her time, he generally knows beforehand what her answer will be.

CHAPTER XXVI.

COUSIN MARY.

Lucy couldn't do things like other girls. She couldn't go straight to Cousin Mary and tell her that the Senior Tutor, the new Master of St. Benedict's, had asked her to be his wife. There was no reason why she shouldn't have told Cousin Mary. She had no one else to tell. She wouldn't have dared to have told Pamela Gwatkin or Maria Stubbs.

They had gone down now; everybody had gone down. Wyatt Edgell had gone down the day that Lucy sent back that answer to his message. He had gone without taking his degree.

Everybody was crying out at his folly, and a great many people—wise people—thought they knew the reason why, but no one guessed the real cause of his hasty departure from Cambridge.

Lucy was not sorry that he was gone. She could not have met him again in the court in the cloisters. She would not have been sure that he would not have taken her in his arms, and that all her fine resolutions would not have melted away. But he was gone down. She had nothing more to fear from him. She had an ugly dream about him the night he left Cambridge, a dream that haunted her still.

She dreamt that Wyatt Edgell was falling over the edge of a precipice, and that he held out his arms to her, but she would not reach out a hand to save him.

There was a great deal to be done in these lonely days of the Long Vacation. There was a good deal to be done, and now it could be done quietly, with no lynx-eyed undergraduates looking on.

Of course, they would have to turn out of the lodge—at least, so Cousin Mary said, when they were talking things over a few days after the Master's funeral.

The Master had behaved very generously to his niece; he had left her all the furniture of the lodge and what little money he died possessed of. He had made no mention whatever in his will of his nephew Dick's little daughter. The will had been made years ago, when Lucy's father was living, and she was not dependent on his bounty.

It was really very lucky for Lucy that the Senior Tutor had made her an offer at such a time.

'We shall continue to live together, of course, dear, if you have no other plans,' Mary said, and she paused to see if Lucy had any plans about her future, but Lucy was silent.

'I suppose you will give up Newnham now?' she continued presently, and Lucy thought there was just a shade of derision in her voice; but this was only fancy.

She might be excused for fancying it, for she had been plucked in both her examinations. She had failed in both parts of the Little-go. There was quite reason enough to account for her failing at such a time that she need not have fancied that Cousin Mary underrated her powers.

'No, I shall certainly not give up Newnham,' Lucy said with some spirit. 'I shall go in for the examination again in October. I shall continue at Newnham until—until——'

She couldn't finish the sentence, but stopped short in the middle, and blushed delightfully.

'Until what?' Cousin Mary said bluntly. She hated to see girls blushing; she never blushed herself.

'Until I am married,' Lucy said softly, and her eyes fell and her colour rose.

It was a great pity that the new Master of St. Benedict's was not there to see her.

'Married?' Mary repeated, with a little break in her voice. 'Whoever are you going to marry, child?'

She had a vision of Eric Gwatkin; she had often seen him looking at Lucy in the college chapel, and she remembered that he had called to see her several times lately. Why hadn't Lucy told her of it before?

'Mr. Colville has asked me to marry him,' Lucy said humbly.

The room didn't turn exactly upside down; if it had, all the books would have tumbled out of the shelves, and the old Worcester vases on the mantelpiece would have been broken to pieces, which would have been a thousand pities, and the furniture of the room would have been generally disarranged.

Something happened—Mary Rae never exactly knew what; she was only conscious of a band tightening round her heart, and that when she tried to speak her voice sounded a long way off.

'Mr. Colville?' she repeated in her distant, faint voice.

'Yes,' Lucy said bashfully, as if it were the first time any man had asked her to marry him; 'but I have not given him an answer yet. What answer do you think I ought to give him?'

Cousin Mary was not going to advise Lucy on this point. She knew what answer she had been prepared to give him the last twenty years.

The Master of St. Benedict's came over to the lodge for his answer the next day. He hadn't been formally elected Master yet, but the matter was practically settled. He and Mary had been doing the Master's work together for years past.

But it was not to see Mary he came to the lodge now; he asked to see Lucy, and she came to him in the gallery.

Lucy knew exactly what he had come for, and she had his answer ready for him—quite ready. It had cost her something to make up her mind. She couldn't marry a man with gray hair—only iron-gray as yet—and with a bald spot on the crown, and with a big red throat, and bushy eyebrows, and a crop of wrinkles round his eyes, without a pang. She was only twenty—sweet and twenty—and her life was before her. Yes, it cost her a pang to accept the Senior Tutor.

Perhaps it would have cost her more to reject him. He had a good deal to offer. Lucy did not lose sight of that in making up her mind. If she refused him she would have to toil through life as a governess—possibly a nursery governess. One cannot teach what one doesn't know, and a term's residence at Newnham had taught Lucy one thing: that she knew very little, and that that little was not worth much.

Perhaps if she had passed her examinations with honour—had come out in the first class—she might have given the Senior Tutor a different answer. Immense possibilities would have opened before her. She might be Senior Wrangler, Senior

Classic, Senior Theologian—oh no, women are never theologians; she might have been a first class in any Tripos, and by-and-by, when the way was made clear, she might take a high degree, and wear a scarlet hood, and—there will be such things—she might be a female Vice-Chancellor!

Now all these dreams were over. That Little-go examination had nipped her hopes in the bud. There was no other way of enjoying the highest dignity the University has to bestow than by marrying the Master of St. Benedict's. He would be Vice-Chancellor some day, and she would rule by proxy.

Lucy lay awake all one night thinking over these things. She would have preferred to marry Wyatt Edgell, all things being equal, and she shed a few small tears at giving him up. In fact, her pillow was quite wet in the morning.

She accepted the Senior Tutor the next day. She told herself that she had no more love to give away to any man: that her heart was dead within her, and that the tender dream of her youth was over, and that henceforth her life would be a dreary round of duties—perhaps dignities—but there would be no pleasure in it.

Nevertheless, when she had accepted Mr. Colville, and he had kissed her in a paternal way, and she had gone through the gallery with him, and the big drawing-room—that had been so little used during the life of the late Master—and had discussed the alterations and improvements he was going to make, she felt quite interested in life—interested, if not animated. There is nothing like furnishing for giving one an interest in life.

Mary came upon the lovers while they were discussing these details. Lucy's eyes were shining, and there were two pink spots on her cheeks which Mary had not seen there for many days, when she came across them in the big drawing-room. Mary quite understood the girl being moved, she would have been moved herself; but she did not know that the burning question that had moved Lucy so deeply was the upholstery of the drawing-room.

The new Master of the lodge had set his heart on yellow—yellow satin and dark oak. He had seen a yellow room somewhere. Lucy loved pinks and blues, and delicate creamy tints that would match her complexion; she would not have had a yellow drawing-room for the world.

Mary came upon them when they were discussing this burning question. And then Mary had to be told.

The new Master told her in as few words as he could, and about as awkwardly as a man dealing with a new subject and addressing an unsympathetic audience. He got over it as quickly as he could. He was sure Mary would have no sympathy with him. He was sure that she despised him for his ridiculous infatuation for this little bit of a girl. He was rather ashamed of himself.

'I hope you will continue to make the lodge your home,' he said to Mary, with an awkwardness that was quite new to him; 'there is no reason why you should leave it. There is plenty of room in it for all. You will keep your old room'—'and your old place,' he was going to say; but he checked himself in time, and said: 'I am sure your advice will be everything to Lucy.'

Mary Rae smiled; not scornfully, not even proudly, but with a sort of pity in her eyes, and her face was grave, and her voice was steady.

'No,' she said coldly; 'I could not continue to make my home here. My plans are all settled—quite settled. Lucy will stay with me—until—until she marries'—she could not help a little break in her voice—'and then I am leaving Cambridge altogether. I am going back to my old place, to my own people.'

The Senior Tutor had heard nothing about Mary Rae's people until that day; he never knew she had any people; he had forgotten all about her mother's relatives.

Cousin Mary began to make her preparations for leaving the lodge at once. She was only taking with her to the little house she had engaged at Newnham a few necessary things. She was leaving a great deal of the old furniture behind. It had been at the lodge for over a century. It was heavy and clumsy, and some of it was worm-eaten; it was ill suited for a modern residence. It had been taken off by one Master after another, and now, unless the new Master turned it out into the court, or threw it out of the windows into the Cam, it would remain where it had so long stood.

Lucy consented to its staying almost unwillingly. She had no idea how valuable those precious old relics of carved oak, and Chippendale, and old Sheraton furniture would have been in the eyes of a connoisseur.

She didn't mind the old blue Worcester vases remaining on the mantelpiece, where they had stood so many years; but she would have preferred some modern gimcrackery for the drawing-room. Her heart yearned for little satiny chairs with gilt backs, and plush five o'clock tea-tables, and all the latest abominations of the modern upholsterer.

It was very sad work turning out all the old Master's papers, going through all his drawers and turning out all the private records of his life.

Mary never knew until she went through his papers how generous he had been to all those poor relations she had left sleeping beside him in the churchyard at Northwold. Some of these old letters she turned out from their hiding-places, yellow with age, written by hands long folded, touched her deeply. Some were from her own kin, and some, most of all, from Lucy's father, grandfather, great-grandfather, three generations, all telling the same story of benefits received, of the unfailing liberality of that generous hand.

Mary did not know what to do with the papers. The Master had left little else—an old scholar's wardrobe, a rusty gown and hood, an old-fashioned silver watch; no rings or jewellery or knick-knacks; nothing but books and papers, everlasting papers.

Lucy would have burnt them all unread—nothing would have given her greater pleasure than to have put all the musty old lumber in the flames; but Mary would not destroy a single line.

She gathered the old family letters together and took them away with her to the little house at Newnham; but she left all the old scholar's papers, his Semitic manuscripts and pamphlets in crabbed characters that she could not understand a line of, behind her. The labours of his long useful life she left behind to the college that had enabled him to pursue these studies. Perhaps a younger scholar coming by some day may look over the heap, and pick out from it what is worth preserving.

Mary was in a great hurry to get out of the lodge. She need not have got out until the end of the Long Vacation, but she chose to clear out at once. Lucy was a little angry at all this haste. She would much rather have stayed at the lodge than have gone into a small, uncomfortable little house at Newnham.

She wrote bewailing her lot to Maria Stubbs, but she didn't say a word about her engagement to the Senior Tutor.

Maria answered her letter by the next post. She was staying up in town in a small lodging in Bloomsbury, in order to be near the reading-room of the British Museum, and she wrote and begged Lucy to come up and share her poor rooms. Her letter touched Lucy, and brought the tears to her eyes. She remembered how she used to hate Maria, and wouldn't notice her in the street. Her letter contained some information that interested Lucy, and may have had something to do with her tears.

Pamela's brother had gone abroad with Wyatt Edgell; he had been engaged by his family to travel with him and look after him. Pamela had only heard from Eric once since he had been away, and he had not written hopefully of his charge; but Maria did not give any particulars.

Lucy would have given the world to have seen that letter of Pamela's. She remembered what Eric had said about taking away a rope from a drowning man, and she recollected that dreadful dream.

Oh, if she could only have seen that letter! Perhaps even now it might not be too late.

The Master—he was really Master now—came in while her eyes were yet wet with tears. He had brought with him some patterns that had just arrived for the hangings of the new rooms. It was really a serious question. The effect of everything would depend upon the colour of the hangings. In deciding this important point Lucy forgot all about Pamela's letter.

CHAPTER XXVII.

OCTOBER TERM.

October had come, and term had begun again, and Cambridge was full of new faces—fresh young faces that would soon lose their smoothness and roundness, and that delightful ingenuousness that distinguishes successive generations of Cambridge freshmen.

There were a great many girl freshers at Newnham this term, and several of the old familiar faces were no longer seen. Pamela Gwatkin had come up for another year. A scholarship, the Grace-Hardy Scholarship, which is only given to girls in their fourth year, who have done well in a Tripos, had been awarded her to enable her to proceed to the second part of the Mathematical Tripos. When women year after year stand first on the list of the Smith's prizemen, it will be necessary to create a third part, when probably the majority of the candidates will be women.

Pamela Gwatkin had been working hard all through the Long Vacation, and she had come back pale and hollow-eyed, and oh! so lean. She will be like a deal board by the end of the year, and her beautiful, serious eyes will have nothing but mathematics in them.

Lucy had come back to work, too, but there were no mathematics in her eyes. She had just been plucked again in that horrid Part II. of the 'Previous,' which takes in Mathematics and Paley; but she had passed the classical part. She had only come up for one term. She was to be married in the spring, and she was quite, quite determined to get through the Little-go before she took her place as the wife of a Master of a college. She wouldn't be pointed at by everybody in Cambridge as a Failure!

She had got her old room next to Maria Stubbs, and she told Maria all about her engagement the first night after Hall.

Maria didn't bully her as she expected she would, perhaps she would have done the same thing herself had she been in her place.

She thought Lucy a very lucky girl; nobody had ever fallen in love with her, and asked her to preside over a college lodge, though she was twice—a dozen times, at least—as clever as Lucy. She couldn't, for her part, think what men saw in Lucy. Cousin Mary often—indeed, she had always—wondered what the Master of St. Benedict's saw in Lucy. Mary had quite given up the lodge long ago. The shabby, old-fashioned bits of furniture that she had taken away with her had all been carried over the college bridge to the little house at Newnham. She had only taken the oldest and the shabbiest things away; she had left everything that was worth leaving at the lodge.

People who had known her well remarked when they came up in October how much she had aged during the Long Vacation. She was not only looking, but she was feeling old and changed. Something had gone out of her life.

The Master of St. Benedict's noticed the change with a little twinge of conscience, but his hands were too full just now to think very much about any other woman than the woman he was going to marry.

The lodge was full of workpeople; the old place was being turned upside down. The plaster and the paint and the whitewash had been scraped off the old oak, and, oh, what a lot of beeswaxing it took to make it brown and mellow with that delightful old dull polish upon it that antiquaries love! There were all sorts of discoveries made during this pulling down and building up of old panelling. Rooms were unearthed, and musty old cupboards and passages laid open, and no end of old windows that had been blocked up for centuries brought to light. Lucy had to come over to see all these discoveries, but Mary never came to the lodge again after the day she left it. That chapter of her life was closed.

Not many people congratulated Lucy on her engagement. Very few people in Cambridge knew of it. Everyone had been expecting the Senior Tutor for years to marry the Master's niece; and when, after the Long Vacation, the engagement was spoken of, nobody ever dreamed it was Lucy.

Mary had very properly gone away from the lodge until she could return as its mistress; and Lucy—well, Lucy had gone back to Newnham to fit herself for her work as a governess. Under these circumstances she got very few congratulations.

Everybody would congratulate her fast enough when the time came. She was not doing a thing that there was no precedent for. Nearly all the heads of the Colleges in Cambridge had married young wives. It was quite the fashion.

It was not so long ago that Fellows of colleges could not marry at all, but now the order had been reversed, and the first use the dear old things made of their new liberty was to marry wives out of the nursery. As the Poet of the University touchingly put it:

'It hath been decreede, that ye Fellowes may wed,
And settle in College walls;
And wake ye echoes of cloistered life,
With their lyttel chyldren's squalls.'

There had been no children's 'squalls' heard in the lodge of St. Benedict's within the memory of the oldest Fellow in the college; no pattering footsteps on the stairs, no children's voices in the long dim galleries, had disturbed its monastic quietness. The Fellows who in their turn had been Masters of St. Benedict's had been old, old Fellows when their turn came, and one only of all their number that anyone living could remember had taken to him a wife.

Perhaps other women were not so patient and faithful as the old Master's wife.

Lucy would not have been so patient; she was getting impatient already, now the novelty had worn off. She was not sure that she was doing the best, the very best thing she could with her life; that she was making the most of it, that she was 'arranging' it aright, as they put it at Newnham.

Her heart misgave her as she pictured her future, her prosperous future, as the wife of the Master of St. Benedict's. The quiet, stately life of a college lodge oppressed her. She was sure she should soon weary of its stateliness and its loneliness. She pictured herself sometimes standing at the old oriel window and looking down at the lusty young life in the court below and longing to be in the midst of it. She was longing already. The sight of young lovers in the college Backs filled her heart with a strange tumult, and the sound of a fiddle coming from the open window of a man's room as she passed through the court set her feet twinkling. There is a great deal in heredity.

The Master met her at the lodge one day when she was in this mood. She had been working at mathematics all the morning, and she was nervous and overwrought; she had been feeling a strange depression for several days, and had come over to see the alterations at the lodge in order to shake it off.

The Master took her out into the Fellows' garden to see the new greenhouse. It had been rebuilt, and, late as it was in the season, it was ablaze with Lucy's favourite geraniums. He had considered her taste entirely, and filled it with the flowers of her choice. She ought to have been grateful, at the least, and expressed her gratitude in any of the little pleasant ways that engaged people are wont to express their feelings.

She ought to have gone round sniffing the flowers, and picked the choicest red geranium and stuck it in the Master's coat; but she did nothing of the kind. She sat down on a bench and began to cry. She couldn't keep the tears back.

Perhaps the sight of the new greenhouse had brought to her mind that scene when the old Master had fallen in the garden, and Wyatt Edgell had carried him back to the house.

Lucy couldn't account for her tears. She said it was the air of the greenhouse had made her faint, and her lover walked back with her to Newnham.

'You are sure there is nothing the matter?' the Master said before he left her; he didn't leave her at the gate, he went straight up to the door of Newe Hall with her. 'You are sure that the faintness is quite gone?'

'Yes,' she said, 'it is quite gone. It was only the heat and the smell of those horrid geraniums.'

This was rather hard on the Master, as he had gathered them together for her benefit.

There were still traces of tears on her cheeks when she got back to Newnham, and her eyes were red, and everybody could see she had been crying. Maria Stubbs saw her coming up the path with the Master, and she saw in a moment, directly she came into the hall, that there was something amiss. Nothing escaped Maria.

She followed Lucy into her room and shut the door behind her.

'You have heard, then?' she said.

Lucy noticed that she spoke in a more subdued tone than was usual to her, and there was a catch in her voice that jarred upon her ear.

'Heard what?' she said wearily. 'I have only just come back from the lodge. I have heard nothing.'

She was not very anxious to hear Maria's news. She thought it was one of the old things that was always happening: someone had passed an exam., or someone had been plucked, or someone had broken down. She was so used to these things that she did not care a straw which it was, and she began drawing off her gloves, and threw her hat down on a chair. When she had done this she became aware that Maria was looking at her with a strange pity in her eyes.

'And you have not heard?' she said with a little hard break in her voice.

'I have heard nothing,' Lucy said impatiently.

'Oh, you poor dear! How can I tell you?'

Lucy looked at her startled and amazed, with a sudden terror in her eyes.

'It is about—about——'

Her lips grew suddenly white, and refused to pronounce the name of the man who for so short a time had been her lover.

'Yes,' Maria said softly, 'it is about Wyatt Edgell.'

'He—he—oh, don't say he is dead!'

Lucy fell on her knees beside the couch and clutched Maria's gown. She was white as a sheet, and her lips were quivering.

Maria Stubbs threw her arms around her, she thought she would have fallen, but Lucy pushed her aside.

'Oh, don't tell me he is dead!' she moaned. 'Don't tell me I have killed him!'

'Hush!' Maria said almost fiercely, but her own eyes were full of tears, and her voice faltered as she spoke. 'It isn't your fault that he is dead. He would have died just the same whether you had given him up or not.'

She spoke to unheeding ears, for Lucy had fallen with a little cry to the floor.

She tried in vain to rouse her. Her face was perfectly colourless, and her lips were white, and she lay like a log where she had fallen.

Maria undid her dress and loosened the things about her throat, and threw some water over her face and hands, and then, finding she didn't revive at all, she got frightened and ran to get assistance. Pamela Gwatkin was the only girl who was in her room at that hour, and Maria implored her to come at once.

Pamela was sitting with her hands clasped before her and an open letter in her lap. She looked up when Maria came in with a bewildered look in her eyes, which were heavy with weeping.

'You must not ask me,' she said harshly; 'I would not put my hand out to save her. You must ask someone else. I can never, never forgive her!'

If Pamela could not find it in her heart to forgive the girl who had ruined Wyatt Edgell's life, it was harder for Lucy to forgive herself.

As she lay tossing with fever in her little darkened room for weeks after that miserable day, she reproached herself a thousand times for having murdered her lover. The shock of Wyatt Edgell's death had told on her already overwrought nervous system, and it had given way, and she had been struck down with brain-fever.

It was not an unusual thing in a women's college.

No one but Pamela Gwatkin and Maria knew the real cause; everyone else, doctors and all, put it down to overwork—to the mathematics she was getting up for the Little-go.

Nobody attached any meaning to her wandering, not even when in her delirium she called herself a murderess; she didn't mince matters, she shocked Cousin Mary by declaring that she was a murderess. She was for ever raving about that dreadful scene, when she had found Eric Gwatkin on his knees beside the couch, and in her dreams she was ever helping him to sew up that awful wound. She couldn't get that gaping wound out of her eyes.

Nurse Brannan came over from Addenbroke's to Newnham to nurse Lucy. Perhaps she could have thrown some light on the girl's wanderings, but she was silent. She nursed her back to life, and soothed her and comforted her in the first wild abandonment of her grief and remorse, as she had comforted the old Master. She had only one kind of medicine for all the diseases of the mind. She had only one set of old-fashioned remedies. She read Lucy in those first weak days of convalescence the same, the self-same, words from the same old Book that she had come upon her reading to the Master at the lodge. She had only one story to tell to all her patients—an old, old story. It seemed quite new to Lucy as she sat listening to it in those weak tired days; it seemed to her that she had never heard it before.

When she was well enough to talk about anything, Lucy insisted upon talking about the subject that was uppermost in her mind. Nurse Brannan let her have her way; she could not have stopped her if she would.

'You have nothing to reproach yourself with, my dear,' she said to her when she found there was nothing to be gained by silence; 'it would have happened in any case. With that tendency and that awful heritage, you could not have prevented it.'

Then Lucy learned, what she had only surmised before, that Wyatt Edgell had died by his own hand.

'You must tell me how it happened,' she said, 'and who was with him; you must not conceal anything.'

'There is very little to tell, dear. Eric Gwatkin was with him. He could not have had a truer or more devoted friend.'

'No,' said Lucy with a sigh; 'he loved him more than I loved him; he would have laid down his life for him.'

'Yes, I think he would. They were away alone together in Scotland, on some shootings that Mr. Edgell had taken, when it happened. He had been moody and out of sorts for several days, and had stayed indoors wrestling with his disease. Eric did not leave him day or night during this dreadful time, and on the fourth day the temptation seemed to have passed, and he went out on the moors. Eric was with him alone when it happened; there was no keeper near. It was all over, and—and he was quite dead when the keeper came up. There was only Eric to witness that it was not an accident. Oh, he behaved splendidly! He did everything. He brought the dear fellow back to his people; he covered up all the dreadful part of the story; and no one—no one belonging to him—will ever know that it was not an accident. It would have broken his mother's heart; it would have killed his old father, who was so proud of him; it would have been a crushing blow. Oh, Eric was quite justified—

it must have cost him a great deal to cover it up, but he was quite justified; he behaved splendidly!'

When Lucy got well enough to see anyone, the first person she saw was the Master of St. Benedict's. He had inquired for her every day during her illness, and he had sent daily messages by Mary. He reproached himself for letting her walk back on that last day he had seen her. He ought to have known that she had broken down when she fainted in the greenhouse.

He was not at all prepared for the change in her. She had not only grown thin and white, but her eyes had changed; they were graver and steadier, and something that used to be there, he didn't know what, had gone out of them.

'The lodge is quite finished,' the Master said cheerfully, as he took his seat by her side; 'your home is quite ready for you, my dear.'

Then Lucy had to say to him what she had sent for him to say. It was rather difficult to say, and she said it in her little weak, faltering voice.

'I have found out,' she said, 'while I have been lying here, that I have made a mistake. It is not the first mistake I have made—and—and thank God I have found it out in time!'

Her voice broke, and her lips quivered, and a faint flush of colour came into her cheeks.

'We have all made mistakes, my darling,' the Master said, stroking her little thin hand that lay on the coverlet. 'Don't let this little mistake you have made, or fancy you have made, trouble you; you have all your life to set it right. You have only to get well as fast as you can; your new home is ready, quite ready, for you.'

Lucy shivered.

'That is it,' she said eagerly; 'I want you to help me to set it right. I have ruined one man's life; I will not ruin another. I—I want you to give me up.'

She did not tell him she was not worthy, she knew that would be of no avail; she only asked him to give her up.

'You do not love me, Lucy?' he said reproachfully, when he found that all other arguments failed to move her.

'No,' she said sadly, 'I do not love you enough. I never, never could love you enough to marry you for yourself. I should have married you for—for the sake of your position—it is a great thing to be mistress of a college lodge—and, and I wanted a home, and to be taken care of—and loved—and I had nothing to give in return.'

It took a long time to convince the Master of St. Benedict's that Lucy hadn't accepted him for himself. He hadn't looked in the glass lately, or his eyes had grown dim—he hadn't seen that the brown locks of his youth were turning gray, and that he was getting bald, and fat, and florid. There were plenty of women in the world who would have loved him for himself still; there was a dear woman in the adjoining room who had loved him for twenty years, and who would go on loving him in spite of his baldness—who rather preferred it, indeed.

The Master couldn't conceal from himself that the girl really desired to be free. Her words, her eyes, her manner, all showed him that she desired to break off her engagement. He had no alternative but to give her the release she sought.

CHAPTER XXVIII.

A COLLEGE 'PERPENDICULAR.'

A whole year had passed. There was quite time enough in a year for things to straighten themselves—for things that had gone wrong to get right again.

One thing that had once threatened to go wrong—very wrong—had righted itself. The new mistress of the lodge of St. Benedict's was in her right place.

The lodge had taken months to restore and refurnish, and the work had been carried out quite regardless of expense. It only wanted one thing when it was finished—a mistress to preside over its stately hospitality.

The Master had not far to go to find one. He did not go so far as Newnham College; he found what he sought at an unpretentious little house in the village, furnished with very shabby old furniture.

He ought to have been ashamed of himself to have gone back to Mary. No doubt he was ashamed, dreadfully ashamed; but he went back, nevertheless. He did what is always the wisest and the noblest thing to do; he went back and confessed his folly, and asked to be forgiven. He did not ask in vain.

Mary is now the most popular mistress of a college lodge in Cambridge, and the handsomest. She has grown quite young again; the ordeal she has passed through has only added a tender, pathetic nobleness to her beautiful grave face. The hope of her youth, of her mature womanhood, is fulfilled. She cannot help looking prosperous and handsome.

And Lucy? Well, Lucy went back to Newnham when she was well enough—when she had quite recovered—and passed the Little-go with distinction. She worked at her Tripos all through the next year, and Pamela Gwatkin was her coach.

She was about as unhappy as a girl with a 'small soul,' as she still described herself, would be, after what she had gone through; but her mathematics diverted her thoughts, and the prospect of her coming Tripos sustained her.

At the end of the year an event happened which affected Lucy's views on the subject of her Tripos; that cut short, in a not wholly unprecedented way, her University career.

At the close of the October term, the Master of St. Benedict's gave what is known in undergraduate parlance as a 'Perpendicular.'

At this particular 'Perpendicular' all the Dons and Donesses in Cambridge were present to do honour to the new mistress of the lodge, and the whole suite of reception-rooms, that had been the subject of such heartburnings to Lucy, were thrown open.

It was the first time that she had ever seen them lit up and filled with such a goodly company. She was there with Maria Stubbs and Pamela Gwatkin, as her cousin's guests. She had not altered much during the year; only her eyes were steadier, and she did not blush so readily.

She ought to have been blushing now, for she had just met an old friend who had taken her hand when they met and had forgotten to give it up again.

It was Pamela Gwatkin's brother.

He was in Orders now; he had been ordained nearly a year, and held a curacy in a village in the West-country, with the magnificent stipend of one hundred and fifty pounds a year.

He had gone through all the familiar rooms of the old lodge with Lucy, but he had hardly recognised them again. Only in the long gallery the faces of the old Masters looked down on him as of old, with a stately welcome in their grave eyes.

He had no idea that the dark, musty old place could have been so changed. He passed through room after room, with Lucy's arm in his; and presently, when she was tired, he sat down in the deep-recessed window of the oak-panelled saloon, where the Masters hold their annual feasts and eat their state dinners.

Full-length portraits of old Masters and Fellows hung on the walls, and above their massive gilded frames—they had been regilt lately—a rich carved frieze of oak went round the room; and above the great open fireplace was a quaint carven mantelpiece that was a sight to see. It was a room to delight the soul of an antiquary.

Lucy watched Pamela's brother as his eyes travelled round the room and took in all these things. He was such a simple, transparent fellow that she could not help reading his thoughts.

'What are you thinking of, Eric?' she asked him presently. She called him Eric.

'I—I?' he said, with a blush. 'I was wondering why you gave up this—how you could give up this!'

'Did you wonder?' she said softly, and her eyes, he saw, were very sweet and tender. He thought she lingered on the 'you,' and he looked at her with a strange trouble in his eyes.

'Yes,' he said with a sigh, 'I don't think many women would have—have given this up lightly. You must have had a reason?'

'Yes,' she said in her low voice, with a quiver in it, and that droop of her pretty mouth that he remembered so well; 'I had a reason.'

Something in her manner more than in her voice struck him, and the trouble in his eyes deepened.

'May I know—will you tell me the reason, Lucy?' he said hoarsely.

'I could tell anyone but you,' she said passionately, and then she turned away her face from him, but not before he had seen that her eyes were full of tears.

Then a strange light came suddenly into his eyes as he looked at her as she sat there in her soft white clinging gown, with her bosom heaving, and the rich colour sweeping over her neck and face.

'You do not mean——Oh, Lucy!' he said, and his voice shook, and the trouble in his eyes gave place to the light of a sudden wild hope.

Whatever she meant, it was whispered so low that it reached no other ear than his.

Before Lucy went back to Newnham that night with her friends she had a little interview with her beautiful hostess. Cousin Mary looked like a queen with her gleaming jewels and her rich dress.

It was not a dress intended to be crushed; it was intended to be put away carefully, and to be worn at no end of grand University receptions and dinner-parties; but Lucy threw herself upon it in the most unfeeling way, and let her foolish tears—they always flowed very copiously—stream down the beautiful satin bosom and over the lovely real lace.

'Oh Mary, congratulate me,' she murmured; 'I am going to marry Eric Gwatkin!'

She was going to marry a curate with one hundred and fifty pounds a year. She had thrown over the Master of a college, and she was asking Cousin Mary to congratulate her!

What can be expected of the children of such a union? They will neither be beautiful nor clever. Probably in a generation or two they will go back to the low estate from which they sprang, and another Lucy may keep the old family stall in the butter-market. Heredity has so many vagaries it is not safe to predict.

The success of the old Master may repeat itself in the male line, and another Anthony—Lucy's boy is called Anthony—may occupy with equal distinction as a Church dignitary another stall elsewhere.

Who can tell?

Meanwhile Lucy is famous for her poultry, and, like her distant progenitor, prides herself on the excellence of her dairy.

THE END.

Printed in Great Britain
by Amazon

79912818R00099